# The Sounds of Spectators at Football

# The Sounds of Spectators at Football

Nicolai Jørgensgaard Graakjær

BLOOMSBURY ACADEMIC
NEW YORK • LONDON • OXFORD • NEW DELHI • SYDNEY

BLOOMSBURY ACADEMIC
Bloomsbury Publishing Inc
1385 Broadway, New York, NY 10018, USA
50 Bedford Square, London, WC1B 3DP, UK
29 Earlsfort Terrace, Dublin 2, Ireland

BLOOMSBURY, BLOOMSBURY ACADEMIC and the Diana logo are trademarks of Bloomsbury Publishing Plc

First published in the United States of America 2023
Paperback edition published 2024

Copyright © Nicolai Jørgensgaard Graakjær, 2023

For legal purposes the Acknowledgements on p. viii constitute an extension of this copyright page.

Cover design: Louise Dugdale
Cover photo (c) Sascha Steinbach/Bundesliga Collection via Getty Images

All rights reserved. No part of this publication may be reproduced or transmitted in any form or by any means, electronic or mechanical, including photocopying, recording, or any information storage or retrieval system, without prior permission in writing from the publishers.

Bloomsbury Publishing Inc does not have any control over, or responsibility for, any third-party websites referred to or in this book. All internet addresses given in this book were correct at the time of going to press. The author and publisher regret any inconvenience caused if addresses have changed or sites have ceased to exist, but can accept no responsibility for any such changes.

Library of Congress Cataloging-in-Publication Data
Names: Graakjær, Nicolai, author.
Title: The sounds of spectators at football / Nicolai Jorgensgaard Graakjær.
Description: [1st.] | New York : Bloomsbury Academic, 2023. | Includes bibliographical references and index. | Summary: "Discusses how, when and why football spectators produce sound, and it examines the structures, meanings and functions of these sounds and their relationship to the football match as an experience"– Provided by publisher.
Identifiers: LCCN 2022019513 (print) | LCCN 2022019514 (ebook) | ISBN 9781501363740 (hardback) | ISBN 9781501363733 (paperback) | ISBN 9781501363757 (epub) | ISBN 9781501363764 (pdf) | ISBN 9781501363771
Subjects: LCSH: Music and sports. | Music–Social aspects. | Music–Psychological aspects. | Sounds–Social aspects. | Soccer–Songs and music–History and criticism. | Soccer fans–Social aspects. | Television broadcasting of sports–Social aspects.
Classification: LCC ML3916 .G693 2023 (print) | LCC ML3916 (ebook) | DDC 780/.0796–dc23/eng/20220506
LC record available at https://lccn.loc.gov/2022019513
LC ebook record available at https://lccn.loc.gov/2022019514

ISBN: HB: 978-1-5013-6374-0
PB: 978-1-5013-6373-3
ePDF: 978-1-5013-6376-4
eBook: 978-1-5013-6375-7

Typeset by Newgen KnowledgeWorks Pvt. Ltd., Chennai, India

To find out more about our authors and books visit www.bloomsbury.com and sign up for our newsletters.

*I dedicate this book to my son Bertram*

# Contents

| | | |
|---|---|---|
| Acknowledgements | | viii |
| 1 | Introductions | 1 |
| | 1.1 Motivation and purpose | 1 |
| | 1.2 Subject matter, approach and materials | 5 |
| 2 | Overview of existing contributions | 17 |
| | 2.1 Contributions on sounds of spectators in the stadium setting | 18 |
| | 2.2 Contributions on sounds of spectators in the televised broadcast | 29 |
| 3 | The stadium setting | 35 |
| | 3.1 What? | 35 |
| | 3.2 Where and when? | 54 |
| | 3.3 Why? | 68 |
| 4 | The setting of the televised broadcast | 81 |
| | 4.1 What? | 81 |
| | 4.2 Where and when? | 87 |
| | 4.3 Why? | 99 |
| | 4.4 Football matches with no spectators in the stadium setting | 108 |
| 5 | Conclusions | 117 |
| Appendix | | 129 |
| References | | 145 |
| Index | | 165 |

# Acknowledgements

I thank:

Michael Bull for his help in developing and pitching the idea of the book to Bloomsbury.

Leah Babb-Rosenfeld, Rachel Moore, Elizabeth Kellingley, and the rest of the staff at Bloomsbury for orderly and efficient support.

My colleagues in the research group MÆRKK at Aalborg University for constructive comments to earlier drafts.

Anja and Bertram – my wife and my son – for everything.

# 1

# Introductions

This chapter introduces the book's motivation and purpose (see Section 1.1) as well as its subject matter, approach and materials (see Section 1.2).

## 1.1 Motivation and purpose

The sounds of spectators are pervasive at contemporary elite football. Normally, the sounds will appear frequently (week in and week out), unremittingly (over the total period of a match), powerfully (produced by thousands of people in close physical proximity) and extensively (listened to by millions of people through broadcast media). Spectators might not represent the largest direct source of revenue for football clubs, as match day revenues are currently surpassed by both broadcasting and commercial revenues for most elite football clubs (Statista, 2022). However, in addition to direct influences (e.g. ticket and merchandise acquisitions), the sounds of spectators arguably influence revenues indirectly by contributing to the coveted atmosphere of the game pursued by both broadcasters and advertisers; for example, the then Premier League chief executive argued, 'The whole economic model only works when the grounds are pretty full' (Scudamore in Robinson & Clegg, 2019, p. 301) – simply put: 'If the atmosphere goes, the TV will go, and if the TV goes, the money goes' (Marshall, 2014, p. 159).

An indication of the importance of the sounds of spectators for the televised broadcast can be observed when spectators are denied access to matches. Incidentally, as most football leagues around the world took precautionary measures to help prevent the spread of the Covid-19 virus during 2020 and 2021, numerous elite football matches were played in – and broadcasted from – stadiums without spectators; until then, such situations had materialized only rarely as when a home team was penalized for inappropriate spectator activities at a previous match. In these settings, spectator sounds became conspicuous by their absence – arguably illustrating that you 'tend to notice things and put them into the focus of your scrutiny and contemplation only when they vanish, go bust, start to behave oddly or otherwise let you down' (Baumann, 2004, p. 17). While a simple operation can help indicate the significance of the sounds of a televised match – for example, 'Try simply watching a soccer game or the news without sound: and notice what is missing' (Scannell, 2019, p. 3) – the live broadcasts of matches with no spectators offered pertinent manifestations of the significance of (the absence of) specifically the sounds of spectators. Tellingly, broadcasters soon began to implement recorded sounds of spectators to try to make up for what was indeed 'missing'. Conversely, indications of the significance of the sounds of spectators can also be seen from the perspective of 'missing visuals'. For example, observations have been made of a 'blind man who is regularly conducted to the football field, and works himself up into as hot a state of eagerness as his neighbours' (Edwardes, 1892, p. 627), and a blind fan who appreciate and 'love the atmosphere' of attending a match (Back, 2003, p. 311).

Generally, the importance of spectator sounds has been acknowledged in scholarly contributions. Predominantly, reference has been made to the sounds' appearance in the stadium setting, and, for example, the following suggestions have been offered:

- 'The scenes within the ground, the crowds and their banners, the singing and the chanting, played out against the backdrop of the stadium or its surrounding cityscape really are often the most spectacular parts of the event' (Bale, 1993, p. 10).
- 'The "atmosphere" of the stadium experience is heightened by the collective noise generated' (Gaffney & Bale, 2004, p. 30).
- 'Football creates soundscapes, and the embodied experiences of sounds, and of hearing and listening are central to the experience of football' (Woodward & Goldblatt, 2011, p. 3).
- 'The ostensible attraction of the stadium is, of course, the match on the field, but the spectacle that occurs at the stadium is so rich and so layered that it is a performance worthy of analysis itself' (Guschwan, 2016, p. 290).
- 'Spectators provide the "atmosphere" and that atmosphere is primarily auditory rather than visual' (Powis & Carter, 2019, p. 394).

Additionally, indications of the importance of spectator sounds for the experience of football in the stadium setting can be found in empirical studies based on spectators' evaluations and attitudes (e.g. Asakura & Ishikawa, 2020; Charleston, 2008; Cummins & Gong, 2017; Nishio et al., 2016; Uhrich & Benkenstein, 2010; see also Edenson, 2015).

As regards the televised broadcast of football, examples of scholarly interests are significantly fewer. However, at least the following observations can be found:

- 'In the televised presentation of sport, the crowd's roars, chants and cheers are crucial to the experience and atmosphere of the game' (Lury, 2005, p. 82).
- 'Much of the atmosphere of televised sport, and a lot of its affective appeal, is conveyed through sound' (Kennedy & Hills, 2009, p. 58).
- 'Their [sports events'] auditory qualities impact much on the texture, depth, and meaning of the experience of spectatorship' (Keys, 2013, p. 22).
- 'Mediated spectator response in the form of crowd noise yields enhanced perceptions of the exciting nature of broadcast sport' (Cummins et al., 2019, p. 111).

Additionally, from the perspective of production, the sounds of spectators have been said to indicate 'the excitement and intensity of a sell-out crowd' so that 'the viewer can instantly sense by audio alone the importance of any event' (Deninger, 2012, p. 111). Correspondingly, there exists extensive know-how relating to the production and broadcast of spectator sounds (see, e.g. Andrews, 2012; Gupta, 2020; Owens, 2021; Wittek, 2013).

These preliminary examples from the literature on the sounds of spectators at football illustrate a commonly held belief *that* spectator sounds are important to the experience of football spectatorship. However, it is not obvious from the available research *what* characterizes spectator sounds and *why*, *how* and *which* (aspects of) spectator sounds might be important. Consequently, the well-developed 'know-how' of organizers and broadcasters does not seem to be paralleled by a well-developed, research-based 'know-what' and 'know-why' when it comes to examining the structure, distribution and significance of the sounds of spectators. Indeed, several sources have observed a scarcity of scholarly contributions. For example:

- 'Indeed the ways in different people within the stadium both generate and experience sound as well as the ways in which sound affects individual experience of the stadium could be the focus of extended research' (Gaffney & Bale, 2004, p. 30).

- 'Little consideration has been given to the sonic dimensions of televised sport' (Durrant & Kennedy, 2007, p. 184).
- 'Despite the manifest importance of sound to football … there is little investigation of this aspect of play in those discourse areas that like to comment on what's important in culture: critical, cultural, and art theory; sports scholarship; journalism; even art itself' (Trail, 2010, p. 69).
- 'Considering the current interest in fan culture, singing among football supporters seems to have received remarkably little scholarly attention for an activity that is so fundamentally a part of their engagement with the game, and for a practise so widely spread, geographically speaking, across such broad populations' (Power, 2011, p. 97).
- 'The places where football is experienced, whether at the ground or at a distance, are often defined by sound, and sound is one of the often under theorized dimensions of sensory experience in sport, with the visual and visibility often carrying more weight' (Woodward & Goldblatt, 2011, p. 3).
- 'Few scholars of sport have attended, except in passing, to the sounds of sport' (Keys, 2013, p. 22).
- 'Perhaps the only specific scholarly article on singing is Jeff Hill's contribution on "Abide with me" and its association with the FA Cup final' (Nannestad, 2015, p. 320).
- 'Football songs and chants have been largely overlooked in the study of popular culture … studies focusing on the specificity of football songs and chants, and the soundscapes they produce, are still a rarity' (Ricatti, 2016, p. 36).
- 'For millions of people across the world, singing at soccer matches is the pinnacle of musical participation. Yet these songs have attracted little scholarly attention' (Lee, 2018, p. 367).

Based on these premises, the book draws together in a coherent form the most significant insights and themes from existing contributions. These insights are further developed by assessing them against a unique selection of case materials, which leads to replies to the questions: *What* are the structures of the sounds of spectators? *Where* and *when* are the sounds distributed at football? *Why* do the sounds of spectators emerge at football? The book thus aims to introduce, synthesize and refine insights on the sounds of spectators for the benefit of students and researchers within sound studies, musicology, media and communication studies as well as sports studies.

## 1.2 Subject matter, approach and materials

The subject matter of this book is the sounds of spectators as they emerge during the two halves of a contemporary elite football match where normally large numbers (i.e. tens of thousands) of spectators have gathered in the stadium. The book's primary focus on 'sounds' is illustrated in Figure 1.1 by the highlighted (white and foregrounded) egg-shaped circle named 'Sounds of'.

The focus on sounds is dual in the sense that it includes a focus on the sounds of spectators as they emerge (1) at football in the stadium setting and (2) at football in the televised broadcast. 'Context' refers to the outside world which 'surrounds' and embodies the broader circumstances of the settings of the examined sounds. The fact that the circle 'Sounds of' transcends the box of 'Settings (the stadium and the televised broadcast)' and overlaps into 'Context' is meant to indicate that only a few chosen aspects of the wider circumstances for the setting of the sounds of spectators at football will be included.

The figure indicates that 'sounds' are merely a part of what constitutes 'spectators' at football, and the 'sounds of spectators' are merely an aspect of what constitutes or goes on 'at football' – for example, the book does not include a focus on the aesthetics (see, e.g. Müller, 2008) or the tactics (see, e.g.

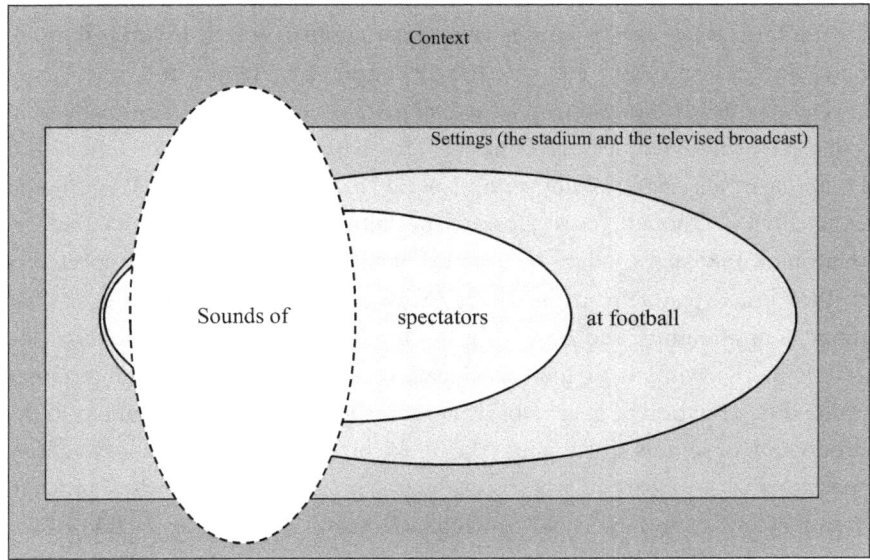

**Figure 1.1** Illustration of the book's focus.

Wilson, 2018) of a/the game of football. The dotted lines of the circle 'Sounds of' are meant to indicate that although the book does not include a systematic (let alone exhaustive) examination of either 'spectators' or 'at football', the book will include perspectives on how the sounds of spectators relate to, for example, the location and visual appearance of spectators and the sounds originating from other participants at football than spectators (e.g. the sounds of performers in the stadium setting and the commentators in the televised broadcast).

As regards 'spectators', the focus is generally inspired by the specification of the sports spectator as 'anyone who views a sports event' (Guttman, 1986, p. 5). Although Guttman's (1986) historical examination of sports spectatorship does not focus on the implications of the sounds of the sports event, obviously, this book relies on spectators' ability to (also) produce sounds and to 'listen to a sports event'. The relevant 'sounds of spectators' are thus the sounds produced by people at the match in the stadium, and the book focuses on the structure, distribution and significance of these sounds as they appear (1) in the stadium setting and (2) in the televised broadcast. The focus does thus not include the sounds which are possibly produced by spectators or audiences to the televised broadcast whether, for example, in the setting of private homes (see, e.g. Gerhardt, 2014), in bars (see, e.g. Weed, 2007) or at open air screenings and fan parks (see, e.g. Rowe & Baker, 2012).

The term 'spectator' is chosen over, for example, 'fan' to indicate that the book does not include a focus on the demographics, identity and practices of spectators outside the setting of a football match (such issues have already been extensively examined; see, e.g. Bonz et al., 2010; Brown, 1998, 2017; Dunn, 2014; Dunning et al., 2014; Jakubowska et al., 2020; Toffoletti, 2017; Waddington et al., 1998). Although, 'most fans are spectators and most spectators are fans' (Guttman, 1986, p. 6), a 'fan' – a term originally designating baseball spectators in the United States from the 1890s (Brown, 2017, p. 10) – usually implies more than attending and observing the football match (see, e.g. Giulianotti, 2002). In the book, a further specification of 'spectators' relies on a rather crude differentiation of observable differences in spectator's engagement in the production of sounds. Throughout the book, 'supporters' are thus used to define spectators who are particularly engaged in the production of sounds; significant examples of 'supporters' usually include spectators in the away section of the stadium as well as a particular group of home team supporters in another, designated section of the stadium (for examples of alternative and more refined differentiations of spectator identities, see Fuller, 2016; Giulianotti, 2002; Jack, 2021; Morris, 1981; Stewart et al., 2003).

In approaching the sounds of spectators from the perspective of spectatorship, I do not mean to imply that other possible perspectives are generally irrelevant. For example, the sounds' significance has often been highlighted from the perspective of performers: 'The noise of the crowd, the singing and chanting, is the oxygen we players breath' (Blanchflower in Back, 2003, p. 311; see further examples in Lawn, 2020, pp. 59–62). There also exits a widespread common-sense understanding that 'fans can act as a "12th man" in influencing the outcome of the match' (Edensor, 2015, p. 85; see also Guschwan, 2016; Hagood and Vogan, 2016; Jirat, 2007), and, actually, a few studies seem to support this common-sense understanding: Unkelbach and Memmert (2010) indicate that crowd density and noise can influence referee decisions leading to a home team advantage, whereas Sors et al.'s (2021) comprehensive study of the results of 841 matches played without spectators (due to the Covid-19 pandemic) documents a reduced home advantage and no referee bias. Furthermore, the sounds could also be considered from the perspective of football stadium neighbouring inhabitants who are unintentionally 'overhearing' (Goffman, 1981b, p. 132) the sounds and can 'guess what is happening in the game through sound' and 'complain of the ruckus that assaults their streets' (Marra, 2021, p. 41); in a similar vein, 'nuisances of football' have been observed to include the 'shouting and cheering of the crowd' (Bale, 1993, p. 118; for a study on the sounds' effects on dogs, see Carrieri-Rocha et al., 2020).

The latter examples also reveal that the sounds of spectators are not necessarily and unambiguously positive and desirable – in fact, even performers have highlighted the potential undesirable effects of the sounds: 'I didn't like the crowd making a noise. You have to be able to listen' (Muhren in Winner, 2010, p. 136; see also Otte et al., 2020). Although existing contributions' suggestions of the importance of the sounds (see the aforementioned quotes in Section 1.1) seem to gravitate towards positive dimensions and implications, it is not the purpose of this book to evaluate the sounds of spectators in terms of their desirability. Moreover, no matter how interesting alternative perspectives on the sounds of spectators might appear, the focus of the book is restricted to the structure, distribution and significance of the sounds from the perspective of the experience of spectatorship.

Generally, the book approaches the sounds of spectators qualitatively in the broad sense that it is concerned with questions of 'what' (related to the structure), 'where and when' (related to the distribution) and 'why' (related to the significance) rather than, for example, 'how many' and 'how much'. Furthermore, the book aims to provide an 'analysis which is open to emergent concepts and ideas and which may produce a detailed description and classification, identify patterns of association, or develop typologies and explanations' (Snape & Spencer, 2003, p. 5). Following the convention to differentiate between 'the institutional and organizational context', 'the structure and content of the text' and 'the audience' (Gruneau et al., 1988, p. 267; see also Wenner, 1998), the book approaches the sounds of spectators from a textual perspective. Accordingly, the book does not include systematic empirically based examinations of the reception of the sounds from the perspective of actual spectators and audiences. Consequently, whereas the book offers a qualitative, textual examination of the *potentials* and *actualizations* of the sounds' significance, the *realization* of the significance of the sounds in terms of their actual effects is not explored – for example, the book does not include empirical explorations of spectator's responses in the form of qualitative interviews (see, e.g. Kopiez & Brink, 1999; Marsh et al., 1978; Poulton & Durell, 2016; Serrano-Durá et al., 2019), questionnaires (see, e.g. Asakura & Ishikawa, 2020; Bensimon & Bodner, 2011) and physiological measurements (see, e.g. Bonetti & Hunziker, 2006; Swanepoel & Hall, 2010). Also, the book does not include an examination of processes of production of the sounds apart from what can be observed and deduced from the sounds' appearance in the stadium setting and the televised broadcast. Compared, for example, to the production-oriented interest for 'who produces television sport, why it is produced the way it is and what the consequences might be' (Milne, 2016, p. 2), the book focuses solely on what the 'consequences might be' in terms of the sounds' structure, distribution and significance in the end product of the televised broadcast. Accordingly, if 'what is missing is an account of wider influences that trickle down and shape how television sports programmes are made, who makes them and what they finally look and sound like' (Milne, 2016, p. 3), this book focuses on what televised football matches 'finally sound like'.

The book's approach is basically inspired by soundscape analysis as it approaches the stadium and the televised broadcast as 'acoustic environments' or representatives of an 'acoustic field of study' that can be defined and examined: 'We can isolate an acoustic environment as a field of study just as we can study the characteristics of a given landscape' (Schafer, 1977, p. 7; see also

Bonz, 2015). Specifically, the approach is inspired by the suggestion made by R. Murray Schafer regarding soundscape analysis that 'some system or systems of generic classification will have to be devised' and that typologies can help 'to discover the significant features of the soundscape' (Schafer, 1977, p. 9). While it is beyond the scope of the book to introduce more generally to sound(scape) studies (for general introductions, see, e.g. Bull, 2019; Pinch & Bijsterveld, 2012), the book approaches various types of sounds – and hereunder various types of the sounds of spectators – from the perspective of textual analysis, as already hinted at.

The text analytical perspective implicates different levels of examination including text, cotext and transtext (as an aspect of context). Examination of 'text' indicates a focus on the formal properties and aesthetics of various types of sounds of spectators. Given that the term 'cotext' can refer to 'that portion of text which (more or less immediately) surrounds it' (Mey, 1993, p. 184), the term is here used to designate a focus on how the sounds of spectators ('it') relate to a range of other textual elements ('that portion of text') that exist in the same immediate setting ('surrounds'). The examination thus seeks to specify the specific place and time – or the specific 'where and when' – of the emergence of the sounds of spectators (i.e. the 'texts'), and the term cotext denotes a focus on the relationship between the various types of sounds of spectators and other, coexisting 'texts' in the form of other sounds as well as non-auditory stimuli, behaviours and incidents. Whereas the perspectives of 'text' and 'cotext' refer to the immediate presence ('here and now') of the (co)texts at the match, the transtextual perspective here includes an examination of texts, circumstances and conditions which (have) exist(ed) beyond (outside and prior to) the particular match. Transtexuality designates an interest for 'the ensemble of any type of relation, explicit or not, that may link a text with others' (Lacasse, 2000, p. 36). The term literally indicates the transformation (indicated by the prefix 'trans') of (an excerpt of) a particular sound event (the 'text') from one structure to another.

Moreover, the book's approach is informed by semiotic perspectives on sound and music (for general introductions, see Middleton, 1990; Tagg, 2013, 2014). From these perspectives, the 'structure' of the sounds refers to the textual organization or the auditory 'building blocks' and the relations among them whereas 'significance' refers to both 'something that is conveyed as a meaning' and 'the quality of being important' (Merriam-Webster, 2022). The former can be viewed as a subdimension of the latter in the sense that the importance of the sounds of spectators includes – but is not limited to – the potential meanings that the sounds can be considered to convey. The textual examination specifically aims to account for a *'variability* of pertinence', which 'applies on two dimensions' relevant for the structure, distribution and significance of the sounds, respectively: '*what* is pertinent (that is, in the text); and, *to what, for whom* and *in what way* is it pertinent (the contexts, needs and place of the listening subject)' (Middleton, 1990, p. 240, italics in original).

As regards the setting of the televised match, the book focuses on 'the broadcast practices through which meaning is produced in televising of sport' and offers examinations of how the sounds are part of 'the content and structure of specific programmes' (Gruneau et al., 1988, p. 270). Accordingly, the book seeks to 'engage closely' with the sounds of televised football to 'explicate' their 'value ... and to cultivate a sense of it in others' (Zborowski, 2016, p. 21). In the stadium setting, the empirical observations of the sounds of spectators are based on my own attendance. The approach aspires to the idea(l) of the 'earwitness', who has been commended as an author who is 'trustworthy only when writing about sounds directly experienced and intimately known' (Schafer, 1977, p. 6). Accordingly, the approach can be described as participant observation which has also emerged as the preferred and recommended approach throughout previous studies on the sounds of spectators in the stadium setting. For example, it has been stated that the researcher needs to 'enter the swarming' (Trail, 2010, p. 75), and, similarly, that 'an involvement ... in the action is a basic requirement' to be able to 'share in the excitement and emotions which, for soccer fans, constitute the "electric" atmosphere' (Marsh et al., 1978, p. 119). However, evidently, there are limits to the level of engagement; for example, one observer is careful to emphasize that he is 'not participating in the racial chanting and abuse' (Holland, 1997, p. 266).

The present participant observations are qualitatively oriented and not supplemented by quantitative measurements (for examples of measurements of aspects of the sounds of spectators as data put into numbers, see Asakura & Ishikawa, 2020; Navvab et al., 2009). Specifically, the position I adopt resembles the 'minimally participating observer' which Bryman (2016, p. 433) defines as one type among a sixfold typology of different degrees of involvement in relation to the observed social setting and its members. This position corresponds to my physical location in the stadium settings. At all matches I was positioned in one of the home team sections (although not in the sections including the most engaged 'supporters', as defined previously) from where I would cheer alongside the spectators in the given section (e.g. when a home goal is scored); however, I would not join in on (let alone participate in activating) specific songs and chants. I have thereby been 'participating minimally' in the group's 'activities' (Bryman, 2016, p. 436).

Now that the subject matter and the approach have been presented, it is time to introduce the book's materials. In line with the predominant case materials of previous contributions (for notable exceptions, see Ashmore, 2017; Connell, 2017), the book's case materials are drawn from contemporary elite football. Specifically, the selection includes cases from the English Premier League (EPL) and matches involving Tottenham Hotspur. English football and the EPL seem well-suited for an exploration of the sounds of spectators at football.

Historically, football was first to develop into a professional mass spectator sport in England (Kennedy, 2009, p. 156), and, arguably, 'sport audiences have been vocal for as long as they have followed sport' (Gantz & Lewis, 2017, p. 244). It might not be entirely accurate to suggest that 'sport fans from the start were encouraged to display emotions, approbation and partisanship in an open and free-playing manner' (Kennedy, 2009, p. 156) – for example, 'early applause was directed at the visiting team in order to accord with the ethics of fair play' (Bale, 2003b, p. 86), and in a match day programme at Sheffield United from 1907, the organizers attempted to tone down the sounds of spectators during the match by a list of 'don'ts' including 'Don't think … you have the right to shout instructions', 'Don't boo at the referee' and 'Don't make yourself a nuisance to those around you by continual bellowing at the top of our voice, it gets on people's nerves and takes away a lot of the enjoyment of the game' (Mason, 1981, p. 232). However, although the 'source material covering the culture of the early soccer crowd is both sparse and fragmentary in its nature' (Nannestad, 2015, p. 320), it seems fair to suggest that partisan sounds of spectators soon became a regular accompaniment to football matches in England – as indicated in an essay on the late-nineteenth-century burgeoning 'new football mania' (Edwardes, 1892) including observations of 'language not to be found in grammars for the use of schools' and 'a number of empathetic and even mysterious expletives … remarkably unpleasant and not fit for a lady's ear' (Edwardes, 1892, pp. 622, 627; for further historical examples, see Dutta, 2015; Hill, 2009; Lawn, 2020; Mason, 1981; Nannestad, 2015; Pendleton, 2018; Russel, 1997, 2008; Webbie, 2020).

Moreover, there seems to be a consensus that in England 'the mid-1960s football became characterized by more assertive singing and chanting' (Bale,

1993, p. 22). The purported growth in chants and singing activities in the 1960s was stimulated by several factors including (according to Morris, 1981, pp. 304–5) the community singing movement and the performance of hymns (see also Russell, 2008), inspirations from increased travels to and broadcasts from international football contests and the wide(r) variety and availability of popular music. Morris pinpoints the 'sloping terraces of Liverpool's famous Spion Kop' as the place where 'a new ritual was born' (Morris, 1981, p. 305) during the mid-1960s, and Morris furthermore suggests:

> Some form of chanting occurs at matches all over the world, but nowhere does it reach the complexity or intensity of the performance at British clubs, where the ritual of singing of the tightly packed supporters has reached the level of something approaching a local art form. (Morris, 1981, p. 304)

Notwithstanding the issue of the exact origin of this particular practice of sound production by spectators, the singing and chanting by English (and British) spectators have reportedly influenced the production of sounds in other settings – possibly propelled by the early broadcasting of matches in England. English football would thus soon feature prominently both on national radio and television (Haynes, 1998) – BBC inaugurated live commentary broadcasts in 1927 whereas television coverage began in the late 1930s (Goldblatt, 2007, pp. 185, 401–2). While thousands of spectators would attend matches at the stadium, an audience of millions would follow matches through the broadcasts. For example, as early as 1950, the FA cup final would attract a television audience of over a million (Goldblatt, 2007, p. 334). Subsequently, BBC were among the 'key innovators in football coverage in the 1960s' (ibid., p. 402), and in 1964 the station introduced the long-lasting programme *Match of the Day* including weekly football broadcasts (Constable, 2014).

Also, international broadcasts emerged at an early stage. For example, in Denmark (as well as in Sweden and Norway), live broadcasts from the English First Division were introduced in 1969 (Dahlén 2008, p. 225; Hognestad, 2006), and during the 1970s and 1980s the live broadcasts obtained a prominent position through designated weekly programmes on the national, monopolized public service station Danmarks Radio (the Danish Broadcasting Corporation). Until 1988, when the Danish channel TV 2 ended the monopoly exercised by the Danish Broadcasting Corporation, the channel was the only national television provider of live international league football in Denmark, and the football was from England. Actually, as the result of a collapse of parts of the negotiations for television rights, for a period of time during the 1985/6 season, Scandinavia represented 'the one place on planet earth where it was still possible to watch live English football every weekend' (Robinson & Clegg, 2019, p. 28). The early distribution of televised matches in Scandinavia and other settings might help explain why the sounds of spectators at English matches have often been highlighted as an influential benchmark for the production of sounds in other settings (see, e.g. Fuller, 2016, p. 6; Irak, 2021, p. 41).

Currently, the EPL ranks high among the world's most followed and best-known football (and sports) leagues in the world. For example, before the temporary suspension of spectator attendance at the end of the season 2019/20, the average game attendance for matches in EPL was 39.315 and the average utilization of the stadium capacity was 96.8 per cent – by comparison, the average attendance for matches in the German Bundesliga was 40.867 and the average utilization of stadium capacity was 92.2 per cent (Transfermarkt, 2022). Furthermore, football's development into a global media phenomenon is exemplified markedly by the EPL which was founded in 1992 when 'television and Sky in particular became the financial underwriter and funder' which became 'the blueprint for the way that television would finance football as a form of "media content" and aggressively market this "television product" into international markets' (Boyle, 2019, p. 181). Presently, 'English Premier League matches and associated content are now broadcast in 212 territories, combining for near to five billion cumulative views every season' (Elliott, 2017, p. 5).

The selection of matches involving Tottenham Hotspur is partly motivated by convenience. I have long followed (and at one point obtained a membership of) Tottenham Hotspur, and the matches have been reasonably accessible. Also, this type of motivation for case selection is in line with many previous contributions; for example, contributors have often identified themselves as a 'fan' (see, e.g. Robson, 2000, p. 11; Gumbrecht, 2021, p. xiii). An important additional motivation to focus on matches involving Tottenham Hotspur is the rather unique circumstance of the club having played home league matches in three different stadiums within a short period of time – a circumstance which has facilitated, for example, the inclusion of empirically based perspectives on the influence of the build environment on the structure, distribution and significance of the examined sounds. Moreover, as I observe the sounds from three different locations as regards the physical distance to the pitch as well as the home team supporters and the away team supporters, the case material allows for an inclusion of empirically based perspectives on the significance of location within the build environment. Specifically, I have selected the following three matches:

- Tottenham Hotspur versus Leicester City at White Hart Lane (29 October 2016), where I observe the sounds from the seat 23, row 5, block 10 (a position close to the pitch, at the end of the side stand close to the section including the away team supporters). Attendance: 31.868.
- Tottenham Hotspur versus Liverpool at Wembley Stadium (22 October 2017), where I observe the sounds from the seat 360, row 24, area 551 (a position high up and close to the middle of one of the side stands; almost farthest away from the away team supporters and far away from the home team supporters). Attendance: 80.827.
- Tottenham Hotspur versus Chelsea at Tottenham Hotspur Stadium (22 December 2019), where I observe the sounds from the seat 16, row 18, area 501 (a position high up and close to the curve near the home team supporters; almost farthest away from the away team supporters). Attendance: 61.104.

In addition to the selection of home matches played in three different (and all practically filled) stadiums, the case materials include televised versions of the same three matches which were broadcast live on Discovery Networks Denmark's channel *6'eren* (the Tottenham-Leicester and Tottenham-Liverpool matches) and YouSee's channel *Xee* (the Tottenham–Chelsea match). In addition to facilitate an examination of the sounds of spectators in televised football, this selection allows for a comparison of the structure, distribution and significance of the ('same') sounds, as they emerge in the physical setting of the stadium and in the mediated setting of the televised broadcast. Furthermore, to refine the insights of the structure, distribution and significance of the sounds of spectators in the televised broadcast, the case material is supplemented by the inclusion of a televised match – that is, Tottenham versus Liverpool, played at Tottenham Hotspur stadium (28 January 2021), and broadcast on the channel *YouSee* – from the period when no spectators attended the matches and the broadcaster added recorded sounds of spectators.

It should be stressed that the case materials are not selected with the intent to provide a case analysis of – and hence to provide comprehensive and exclusive insights into – the sounds of spectators in England or at Tottenham Hotspur. It might be so that the sounds of spectators at football in England are somehow extraordinary. For example, the following suggestions have been offered:

- 'Nowhere is there the extraordinary richness and variety to be heard emanating from the crowded British terraces' (Morris, 1981, p. 315).
- 'Contrary to many other countries, English chants are oftentimes taken from real pre-existing songs, hymns or rhymes with lyrics and content modified to their needs' (Dutta, 2015).
- 'Perhaps the answer to English soccer's popularity lies beyond the database. Perhaps the key is in the aesthetics … the English fans' vocal energies and fanatical loyalties to their clubs' (Curley & Roeder, 2016, p. 81).
- 'Humour, like identity and rivalry, is a key ingredient of football chanting, particularly in Britain' (Lawn, 2020, p. 145).

Also, it might be the case that the sounds of spectators at Tottenham Hotspur are somehow extraordinary. At least, as regards other clubs, observers have suggested that significant differences exist between supporters as, for example, a 'high frequency of racism' from sections of Millwall supporters has been compared to an 'almost non existent' racial abuse by Crystal Palace supporters (Back et al., 2001, p. 43). Furthermore, it is not uncommon for (fan) observers to pedestalize and rank the production of sounds of spectators and supporters of certain clubs. For example, 'a lot of fans that support certain teams are thick, and are not very quick at picking up a response … Manchester City fans are certainly very alert and enjoy nothing more than developing routines during a match' (Redhead, 1997, p. 79). Additionally, attempts have been made to evaluate and hierarchize club chants based on, for example, their tunefulness (Howard, 2004), forcefulness (Kytö, 2011) and further quantitative and qualitative dimensions (see, e.g. the *Chantions League* table on the website www.fanchants.com).

However, there hardly exist objective, indisputably relevant criteria for the evaluation of spectators' production of sounds and chants. In any case, it is well beyond the interest and scope of this book to examine the issue of the possible extraordinariness of the sounds of spectators from the perspective of nationality and club affiliation. For example, although the examination of the case materials will necessarily lead to the identification of distinctive sounds – for example, the (lyrics and specific style of performance of the) chant *Oh, When the Spurs Go Marchin' In* only emerges at matches involving Tottenham Hotspur – what is of relevance to this book is the case's capacity to embody distinctive and illustrative qualities of the particular *type of* sound produced and experienced by spectators at contemporary elite football matches. Accordingly, the case material is proposed as an interesting and appropriate lens (inspired by Elliott, 2017, p. 6) through which to explore the phenomenon of the sounds of spectators at football more broadly. The examination of the cases thus aims for analytical generalization in the sense that the book will use the cases to assess available insights and theoretical concepts and develop new ones where relevant 'at a conceptual level higher than that of the specific case' (Yin, 2014, p. 41).

The following chapters address the structure, distribution and significance of the sounds of spectators, firstly (in Chapter 3) from the perspective of their appearance in the stadium setting and secondly (in Chapter 4) from the perspective of their appearance in the setting of the televised broadcast. Both chapters discuss the distinctive qualities and typicality of the sounds by drawing on observations from the examination of the case material as well as by assessing them against findings of existing contributions. Chapter 5, 'Conclusions', summarizes the findings and indicates how the insights might be of use to students and researchers within the disciplines of sound studies, musicology, media and communication studies and sports studies. Also, the chapter offers perspectives on how to further explore the sounds of spectators at football as well as related sounds. However, before moving on to an exploration of the structure, distribution and significance of the sounds of spectators at football, Chapter 2 introduces to a selection of the existing scholarly contributions on the subject matter.

2

# Overview of existing contributions

This chapter provides an overview of a selection of existing contributions on the structure, distribution and significance of the sounds of spectators at football. The chapter thus presents an initial reply to the suggestions (as indicated in Section 1.1) that not much research exists on the sounds of spectators at football. The overview can be considered to represent a self-contained contribution of the book, but the overview also serves to inspire and profile the following chapters' more elaborate and coherent exploration.

Although the chapter offers the hitherto most comprehensive overview of existing contributions, the overview does not pretend to be all encompassing, let alone definitive. For example, the overview is limited to publications in the English, German and Scandinavian languages. Furthermore, because the contributions are scattered across rather diverse fields of research that do not routinely interact with one another, the section offers a sort of 'narrative review' (Petticrew & Robert, 2006, p. 39) by synthesizing, presenting an overview of and offering a qualitive summery of a broad range of individual contributions. The overview focuses primarily on publications including a qualitative, text-oriented perspective (in line with the book's approach as presented in Section 1.2) on various aspects of the sounds of spectators at football produced within an academic context (excluding examination works and publications produced for solely didactical purposes). The overview begins by presenting contributions on the sounds of spectators in the stadium setting – representing most of the contributions – after which perspectives on the sounds in the setting of the televised broadcast will be presented.

## 2.1 Contributions on sounds of spectators in the stadium setting

When searching for contributions on the sounds of spectators in the stadium setting, it soon becomes apparent that a substantial body of contributions exists. Although the focus is here on scholarly contributions, this section will also include a short introduction to some of the most significant non-scholarly contributions some of which have been used by scholarly contributions.

In addition to embody a text-oriented examination within an academic context, the scholarly contributions considered in this section are characterized by a systematic and theoretically informed examination of (some aspect of) empirically specified sounds of spectators in the stadium setting. The overview includes contributions that focus specifically and principally on the sounds of spectators as well as contributions which offer substantial insights into the sounds, although these insights appear as part of a broader examination – the overview excludes contributions which largely reproduce insights from empirical materials examined in previous sources. When applying these criteria for inclusion, a total number of fifty-one contributions can be specified. The appendix of this book presents a table including a list of these contributions in chronological order (from top to bottom), and each contribution is profiled (see the columns) from a selection of perspectives relevant for the present purposes. Obviously, just as the table is not likely to present an exhaustive list of contributions, so does it not provide detailed insights into each of the contributions. However, the table offers an indication of the volume, variety and trends of the existing contributions, and further aspects of some of the individual contributions will be included as part of the examination in Chapter 3.

From this overview, several trends can be observed. Firstly, from the perspective of the time of publication, the overview indicates that contributions begin to emerge in great(er) numbers from around the turn of the millennium. Although the sounds of spectators at football have existed long before that (as mentioned in Section 1.2), before 2000 only a few contributions are available. There seems to be no one obvious explanation for this rather late arrival and increase of contributions, but contributing factors might conceivably include the circumstance that the subject matter has had no obvious disciplinary 'home' and that the subject matter (related thereto) has not generally been characterized by scholarly legitimacy. Moreover, the general awareness of the sounds of spectators was furthered particularly from the late 1960s as the international broadcasting of league football began to emerge pervasively (as indicated in Section 1.2).

Remarkably, among the earliest contributions are two of the most comprehensive yet frequently overlooked contributions, that is, Morris (1981) and Kopiez and Brink (1999). Morris (1981) exemplifies a contribution in which the examination of the sounds of spectators at football is part of a broader, book-length focus on football. Nevertheless, the examination is still unsurpassed when it comes to the empirical scope – for example, the study includes an examination and categorization of the lyrics of 251 distinctive so-called tribal chants (out of a total of 2,179 identified chants). Kopiez and Brink (1999) represent what I have found to be the only book-length scholarly contribution devoted exclusively to an examination of the sounds of spectators at football. While this contribution also includes a significant number of songs and chants, the comprehensiveness of the study is primarily represented by an unsurpassed variety of analytical perspectives.

However, the impact of Morris (1981) and Kopiez and Brink (1999) on subsequent contributions does not seem to measure up to their comprehensiveness. Arguably, although Morris positions himself as an 'anthropologist making an unbiased field-study' of football – approached as 'one of the strangest patterns of human behaviour to be seen in the whole world of modern society' (Morris, 1981, p. 8) – his mainly zoologically informed, sociobiological approach does not correspond with the theoretical background and interests of subsequent studies. As regards Kopiez and Brink (1999), the adopted approach of musicology might help explain why also this contribution has been often overlooked – although an additional and perhaps more critical reason seems to be the existence of a language barrier. Illustratively, whereas the contribution features notably in contributions written in the German language, the contribution is almost entirely ignored in contributions written in the English language. Therefore, it seems appropriate to consider the contribution as the 'standard work cited by everyone' (Lavric, 2019, p. 4; translated by the author) only when the modification is made that 'everyone' refers to contributors writing in the German language. Incidentally, possibly as the result of Kopiez and Brink's (1999) explicit acknowledgement of the input offered by Morris (1981) – which represented one of the very few available contributions at the time of production – Morris (1981) is referred to more extensively in contributions written in the German language than in contributions written in the English language.

Secondly, from the perspective of the fields of research – identified and listed in the table in the appendix based on the self-identification of the author(s) and/or the publication outlet and the adopted theoretical approach – the contributions represent a wide range of disciplines. Generally, contributions from within the disciplines of sociology, anthropology, ethnography and linguistics predominate, whereas, for example, sounds studies and musicology obtain a more marginalized position. The list of fields of research indicates that, as already hinted at, the sociobiological variant of anthropology represented by Morris (1981) has not been followed up upon, whereas the musicological approach of Kopiez and Brink (1999) has only been adopted by a few subsequent contributions. Actually, musicology is oftentimes explicitly opted out; for example: 'It should also be mentioned that we are only concerned with the lyrics and not the music' (Lavric, 2019, p. 7; translated by the author), and 'the analysis in the present study focuses on the words of the chants with no reference to the music' (Tamir, 2021, p. 225). In terms of their impact on subsequent approaches, the anthropological, ethnographic and cultural studies-oriented contributions by Armstrong and Young (1999), Robson (2000) and Back et al. (2001) should be considered seminal; illustratively, these contributions are referred to more commonly than Morris (1981) and Kopiez and Brink (1999).

Thirdly, from the perspective of the empirical method for sourcing and accessing the sounds, the contributions can be grouped in two based on whether or not the sounds have been sourced from their unmediated distribution at a match in a stadium setting. When sourced from the stadium setting, the adopted method is mostly some form of participant observation (although the method is occasionally merely implied). The observations are often supplemented by recordings, and in a few cases, the recordings act as the absent observer's 'extended ear'; for example, Morris (1981) notes that he 'arranged for recordings to be made at a number of matches in England during the 1978–9 season' (p. 306). Moreover, Marra and Trotta (2019) exemplify an attempt to provide an all-encompassing observation of sounds based on a distinctive and unique recording procedure, that is: 'Matches were recorded using three pairs of stereo microphones set in three different sections of stadium terraces' and subsequently 'the recordings were synchronized between themselves and with the radio broadcast' (Marra & Trotta, 2019, p. 75).

Another group of contributions relies on an examination of sounds sourced from various kinds of mediated settings – except for a few contributions' reliance not on actual sounds but on (non-auditory) transcripts and historical documents (see Hill, 2009; Khodadadi & Gründel; 2006; Nannestad, 2015). Whereas the observers (occasionally based on planned recordings) in the stadium setting adopt what could perhaps be coined an 'own-' or 'first-ear' (or 'extended-ear', with respect to recordings) approach, the contributions in this group rely on 'other-' or 'second-ear' sourcing of the sounds. Sound sources include a variety of mediated curations of sounds, most notably the websites www.fanchants.com (see Daiber, 2015; Fantoni et al. 2020; Lavric, 2019) and www.fangesaenge.de (see Beljutin, 2015; Brunner, 2009; Wilter, 2011).

It is characteristic of both groups of contributions that the exact location from where the sounds have been observed and/or recorded is left undisclosed. While this is a basic condition of the reliance on 'second-ear' recordings – for example, the curations do not specify from where inside the stadium setting, the sounds have been recorded – it illustrates a disinterest in studies reliant on 'first-' or 'extended-ear' observations. The existing contributions thus share a lack of attention to the fact that the sounds of spectators in the stadium setting will inevitably reach each and every spectator from different, fluctuating directions and at varying volumes – actually, a significant proportion of the sounds of spectators expectedly never reaches the observer – and this situation illustrates that the observer (or recordings based on a single microphone) necessarily captures the sounds from a specific point of audition (POA).

By not specifying and considering the implications of the observer's (or recording's) POA, the contribution's observations are often presented as if they are derived from 'omni-listening' – a term here suggested for the (implied) ability of the observer to identify and document sound events from a privileged, all-encompassing POA. Incidentally, the above-mentioned multimicrophone recording of Totta and Morra (2019) might seem to embody 'all the sounds that were there'. However, it is (at least) doubtful whether recordings (in any form) will have the capacity to capture 'all sounds'; for example, 'no matter how football is defined, microphones will have trouble capturing its sounding' and, specifically, 'even if we managed to make a sound record of IT ALL, we would eliminate particular sonic qualities – distance effects' (Trail, 2010, pp. 71, 80). The distance effects – and direction effects, it should be added – are of pivotal importance in the stadium, and this is clearly illustrated, for example, by the significance of being seated nearby or far away from the away team supporters (as I shall demonstrate in further detail in Section 3.1).

Moreover, multimicrophone recordings do not decisively reflect the POA of any of the spectators who were there. Actually, the composite soundscape obtained through the synchronized recordings in Marra and Trotta (2019) expectedly bears closer resemblance to the soundscape offered through the televised broadcast than to any of the actual POAs in the stadium setting. While the adopted method indeed seems to serve the purpose of Marra and Trotta (2019), from the perspective of this book's approach, the contribution illustrates what is more generally the case when assessing the existing contributions' observations and sourcing of sounds. Firstly, the contributions have not paid much attention to the fact that the structure, distribution and significance of the sounds in the stadium setting are highly influenced by dimensions of sound distance and sound directionality. Secondly, and relatedly, the contributions have not systematically observed and examined the sounds in the stadium setting as distinctive when compared, for example, to the sounds of the televised broadcast.

As regards the question from where the observed matches and the sound-producing spectators have been drawn (see the columns 'Football' and 'Spectators' in table in the appendix), the contributions focus primarily on contemporary (at the time of the contribution's publication) matches at the elite level of national league football – exceptions to this tendency are a few examinations of sounds at historical matches (Hill, 2009; Nannestad, 2015) and at international matches (Back et al., 2001; Bell & Bell, 2020). The contributions represent a wide variety of national leagues and teams. While the contributions have focused primarily on matches including British and German teams, additional leagues and teams are increasingly represented including the sounds of spectators at football matches in Switzerland, Australia, Turkey, Denmark, Russia, Argentina, the United States, Brazil, Italy, Spain and France. The overview thus indicates that it is not (anymore) the case that 'they [football chants] have been most extensively investigated in the German speaking countries, thus focusing on German chants' and that 'other languages and cultures ... have been studied much less' (Lavric, 2019, p. 1). It might be the case that German scholars have focused primarily on German settings – this is indeed the motivation for Lavric's case selection which is focused on chants in the Romance languages – but, certainly, contributions in English include chants in languages other than German and English as well as a range of alternative national settings. Obviously, based on the language limitations of the present overview (as stated at the beginning of this chapter), it is not possible to identify and assess a possible body of contributions in other languages.

Furthermore, the contributions include both single-case studies – that is, studies relying on an examination of the sounds from one specific match (see, e.g. Fuller, 2016; Grøn & Graakjær, 2016; Jirat, 2007; Luhrs, 2007b; Power, 2011; Schoonderwoerd, 2011) – and multiple-case studies. A large proportion of the multiple-case studies does not explicate the exact number of matches, but examples from the studies that do specify the multiplicity include ten (Bell & Bell, 2020), fifteen (Morris, 1981), twenty-one (Marra & Trotta, 2019), twenty-three (Clark, 2006) and sixty-five (Robson, 2000). Predominantly, the contributions focus on the sounds of the home supporters of a specific team or a specific league. Only a few contributions focus on both the home and away supporters (see, e.g. Grøn & Graakjær, 2016; Luhrs, 2007b), and even rarer are comparative examinations of the sounds of supporters at matches including different teams and supporters. Certainly, among the multiple-case studies there are often different groups of supporters included, but the contributions do not usually perform a systematic comparative examination of the sounds of spectators – this is the case both when matches representing different teams in different leagues are included (see, e.g. Lavric, 2019) and when matches representing different teams in the same league are included (see, e.g. Back et al., 2001; Brunner, 2009; Fantoni et al., 2020; Luhrs, 2008). Beljutin (2015) thus represents the only contribution which includes a comparison of sounds of supporters at matches from two different national leagues (for a comparative examination of the sounds of supporters at matches played in the same league, see Howard, 2004). While Beljutin (2015) can thus be considered to represent a rare example of a synchronous study – that is, a comparison of the sounds from different settings and from approximately the same point in time – Tamir (2021) represents an equally rare example of a diachronic study, that is, a comparison of the sounds from different points in time and from the same setting.

From the perspective of the contributions' focus on sounds, there exists a predominant interest for the dimension of the lyrics of chants and songs which mirrors the previously mentioned trends of field of research. This particular focus might reflect the propensity of lyrics to lend themselves more readily to identification and scrutiny compared to other forms of (and aspects of the) sounds – for example, in contrast to other (aspects of the) sounds, there exists curations of (the lyrics of) chants and songs, and the lyrics are more disposed to retainment and representation. Apart from a few studies concentrating on a defined aspect of the linguistics of the lyrics (Argan et al., 2020; Daiber, 2015; McKerrell, 2021), the main focus is either on the role of the lyrics in establishing, maintaining and/or changing dimensions of identity pertaining to, for example, (in- and out-) groups, ethnicity, regionality, nationality and gender (see Bonz, 2016; Clark, 2006; Collison, 2009; Fantoni et al., 2020; Flint & Powell, 2011; Guschwan, 2016; Hill, 2009; Huddleston, 2022; Irak, 2021; Knijnik, 2016; Kytö, 2011; Luhrs, 2007b, 2008, 2014; Marra, 2021; Ricatti, 2016; Schiering, 2008; Zalis, 2021) or on the lyrics as a way to differentiate and categorize types of chants and songs (see Beljutin, 2015; Brunner, 2009; Khodadadi & Gründel, 2006; Lavric, 2019; Luhrs, 2007b; Morris, 1981; Pearson, 2012; Vilter, 2011). Examinations of other types and aspects of the sounds of spectators than (the lyrics of) chants and songs are much rarer, and insights are scattered across a number of contributions (most notably Bell & Bell, 2020; Boehm-Kreutzer, 2006; Fuller, 2016; Grøn & Graakjær, 2016; Herd & Löfgren, 2020; Herrara, 2018; Howard, 2004; Kopiez & Brink, 1999; Kytö, 2011; Lee, 2018; Marra & Trotta, 2019; Robson, 2000; Schoonderwoerd, 2011).

As already indicated by the specification of certain trends of the selection of case materials, the contributions mainly focus on what seems to be established practices and repertoires of sounds of particular supporters at particular clubs. Exceptions to this tendency are a few contributions on the formation of practices of singing in settings where no such practices have existed previously (Collinson, 2009; Daiber, 2015; Lee, 2018). Generally, although some contributions offer rather detailed insights into a specific (sub)group of supporters' idiosyncratic practices of sound production (see, e.g. Back et al., 2001; Kytö, 2011; Power, 2011; Robson, 2000), the focus of the contributions is mainly to make available generalizable insights. For example, while offering an insight into the 'the repertoire of the Oxfords United fans' (Morris, 1981, p. 315), the selection of chants and songs is viewed as 'a step' in the direction of unravelling 'the overall repertoire' (Morris, 1981, p. 306) of chants and songs at British football and the collection forms the basis for the proposition of a more widely applicable categorization.

In addition to scholarly contributions on the sounds of spectators in the stadium setting, several non-scholarly contributions and resources exist. Because some of these contributions and resources have been drawn upon by the scholarly contributions – also, some of them have inspired the subsequent examination (see Chapter 3) – a selection of non-scholarly contributions and resources will now be introduced. Compared to the preceding presentation of scholarly contributions, the overview of non-scholarly contributions is particularly selective and restricted. To give an impression of the diversity of contributions, among the types and fora of publications that are not considered here are the (mentions of and discussions on the) sounds of spectators in fanzines (see, e.g. Haynes, 1998), social media platforms (e.g. YouTube, Instagram and Facebook) and editorial media outlets (e.g. newspapers and websites; see, e.g. Hey, 2006; Storer, 2019). However, two types of contributions are of particular relevance from the perspective of this book.

The first type of publications could be coined chant curations. They offer a selection, organization and presentation of spectator chants and songs, and the publications are usually produced by and targeted for football spectators. One of the most comprehensive curations of chants is offered through the website www.fanchants.com, which exemplifies, as mentioned previously, how non-research sources can serve as archives for research publications (e.g. Daiber, 2015; Fantoni et al., 2020) – for a similar, although less comprehensive curation of chants, see the website www.fangesaenge.de, which has also been used by researchers for the selection of chants (e.g. Beljutin, 2015; Brunner, 2009). Based on submissions from 'fans from all over the world via the website, Android and iPhone apps' and offering more than twenty-six thousand chants for more than seven hundred clubs worldwide, www.fanchants.com aims 'to collect and archive all lyrics and audio of football chants past, present and future and to act as a forum for fans to share the wit, the banter and rivalry of the terraces'. While the sounds of chants can also be accessed through other media, for example, through spectators' uploads of chants from specific matches on YouTube, the website offers an extensive, accessible and searchable organization of the chants including a transcription of the lyrics. However, the website provides no visual accompaniment to the chants and no contextual indication on, for example, when, at what match, at what point in time during the match and from where in the stands the chants have appeared.

The organization principle of www.fanchants.com resembles that of several printed monographs which likewise offer curations of more confined selections of chants. Commonly, chants are grouped according to their national and club-related origin exemplified by Bulmer and Merrils (1992), Merrils (1997), Stein and Ruge (2018) as well as the extensive series published by Belchen Verlag in which each publication focuses on a specific club in Germany (for an example from the series, see Ohne Schiri, 2000). As regards the EPL, chant curations exist with respect to, for example, Chelsea (Worrall & Otton, 2017), Arsenal (Bazell & Andrews, 2019) and Tottenham Hotspur (Locken & Loughnane, 2009). Other publications include a wide(r) variety of clubs as, for example, the collection of German club chants in Gumpp et al. (2005) – which has incidentally served as an archive for the selection of chants in Khodadadi & Gründel (2006) – and British (national and club) chants in Bremner (2010), Hulmes (1998), Parker (2009) and Shaw (2011). In terms of providing indications on the contexts of the chants, the publications differ markedly: Some merely list the lyrics of the chants without no further information (e.g. Locken & Loughnane, 2009), while others offer sporadic information on the occasion for a particularly significant performance of some of the included chants (see, e.g. Bazell & Andrews, 2019; Portnoi, 2011; Scally, 2009). Some of these publications also exemplify how the meaning and function of the lyrics occasionally emerge as a supplementary organizing principle when grouping the chants; for example, the grouping of Arsenal chants includes 'Players', 'Support', 'Comebacks and celebration' and 'Spurs' (Bazell & Andrews, 2019).

Additionally, there exists a few examples of publications which position the chants in a broader historical and cultural context and thereby move beyond merely curating a specific selection of chants. For example, the curation of chants in Thrills (1998) is supplemented by insights into the history of football chants and how (new) chants are being created and distributed among spectators. Likewise, Marshall (2014) addresses British football chants from a historical perspective and includes numerous examples of chants that are generally contextualized in terms of their origin, meaning and function. A similar approach is adopted in Lawn (2020), where the purpose is to demonstrate 'how football chanting went from bespoke piano compositions in Victorian music halls via Cilla Black and wheelbarrows, to the cultural phenomenon that I today reviled and revered in equal measure' (Lawn, 2020, p. 12; see also Lawn, 2014). Moreover, specific chants have been the subject of particular historical interest; perhaps the most obvious example is *You'll Never Walk Alone* (see, e.g. Bensy, 2020; Oberschelp, 2013).

Generally, the publications here characterized as chant curations can primarily help suggest *what* has been chanted by spectators at football. However, the publications are inadequate in terms of both 'depth' and 'breadth' in the sense that the chants are rarely specified from the perspective of, for example, how, when and from where they appear at what particular match and with what relation to other chants, sounds and incidents from the actual match and/or possible prior matches. Moreover, from a research perspective, the publications' inclusion of chants is generally based on unsystematic, anecdotal and subjective criteria. For example, Marshall (2014) evaluates specific chants as 'sublime' (p. 175) and 'dire' – the latter evaluation incidentally refers to Tottenham Hotspur supporters' performance of the chant *Oh, When the Spurs Go Marchin' In* (see more in Chapter 3) – while the overall goal of Thrills' (1998) is to present 'a celebration of football songs and the culture that spawned them' (p. 11) and to provide a 'testimony to the endless wit and invention of football supporters' (p. 12).

The second group of contributions is represented by the numerous, mostly semi-fictitious representations of football and football spectatorship. In recent years, such representations have gained considerable scholarly interest, and several comprehensive overviews and taxonomies of selected types of productions are already available – types of productions include, for example, films and novels (e.g. McGowan, 2019; Piskurek, 2018; Schwab, 2006; Seddon, 1999), documentaries (e.g. Huck, 2011; Francis, 1964; Philipson, 2020) and autobiographies (e.g. Woolridge 2008; for an example from the perspective of a chant leader, see Lehmann & Knibbeche, 2019).

Of particular relevance to the present approach are publications which offer first-hand descriptions of the activities, experiences and immediacy of following a football club from the perspective of the spectator. For example, Hornby's (1992) personal memoirs – presented as an 'attempt to gain some kind of angle on my obsession' of being a fan of Arsenal – include an 'exploration of some of the meanings that football seems to contain for many of us' (p. 3). In addition to identifying a number of chants from various matches including Arsenal throughout the book, Hornby points to the more general pleasures of listening to/at football – 'I loved the different categories of noise: the formal, ritual noise when the players emerged ... the spontaneous shapeless roar when something exciting was happening on the pitch; the renewed vigour of the chanting after a goal or a sustained period of attacking' (p. 67). Regarding the spectator's role in the production of atmospheres, Hornby suggests: 'Part of the pleasure to be had in large football stadia is a mixture of the vicarious and the parasitical ... one is relying on others to provide the atmosphere; and atmosphere is one of the crucial ingredients of the football experience' (pp. 68–9). Generally, Hornby proclaims that for 'a match to be really, truly memorable' it should include a noisy crowd (p. 227).

Representing another significant example, Buford (1992) also identifies numerous (contexts for) specific chants at football throughout his descriptions of being part of crowds at football. In addition to provide insights into the experience – and the somewhat disturbing attraction – of taking part in violent crowd behaviour, Buford describes how the football stadium terraces offer 'not just the crowd experience but the herd experience with more intensity than any other sport, with more intensity than any other moment in a person's life – week after week' (p. 164). The experience seems to include a periodical lessening of the sense of individuality – 'I was ceasing to be me' (p. 165) – as the crowd emerges as an organic entity with close and clearly audible relations to the match, for example: 'A shot on goal was a felt experience. With each effort, the crowd audibly drew in its breath, and then, after another athletic save, exhaled with equal exaggeration' (p. 164). Similar experiences are offered in Arthur Hopcraft's (1968) attempt to 'explain something of football's compulsion' and to 'reach to the heart of what football is' (p. 10). He thus describes how a given player holds the capacity to 'silence the crowd instantly' and 'make it hold its breath in expectation'; and while 'the whole sound of the stadium changes from its baying or grumbling into an excited purr' the player's actions can sometimes result in 'a deep groan of disappointment' (Hopcraft, 1968, pp. 82, 85).

Although these examples and many others in a similar vein (for additional examples, see Gray, 2016; Irwin, 2006) are semi-fictitious or autoethnographic, as observed in Pearson (2012, p. 9), and thereby anecdotal, they can arguably help indicate and articulate potential aspects of the experience of spectatorship at football. From a research perspective, the examples can be seen as attempts to meet the recommendation that 'one needs not only to observe what is happening but also to *feel* what it is like to be in a particular social situation' (Marsh et al., 1978, p. 119). Also, the descriptions resonate believably with experiences as they have been documented in the few research contributions including qualitative insights into spectator's experiences. For example, during an interview in Marsh et al. (1978), a spectator explains: 'It's atmosphere really – it's sort of electric – it gets you going' (p. 94; see similar experiences offered through the interviews in Kopiez & Brink, 1999). Whereas chant curations generally lack information on the contexts of the chants as observed previously, these first-hand descriptions are usually richer when it comes to contextual information, even though validity of this information based on anecdotes should of course be considered with some reservation. However, examples of first-hand descriptions of the sounds in the stadium appear only sporadically in these texts which are not focused specifically on the sounds of spectators but on more general aspects of being a fan or a hooligan (for a comprehensive overview of this literature, see, e.g. Pearson, 2012, pp. 9–10). Moreover, dimensions of the sounds other than those subjectively experienced – for example, the sounds' structure, distribution and significance beyond the first persons' perceptions – are usually left undisclosed.

## 2.2 Contributions on sounds of spectators in the televised broadcast

Compared to the relatively large body of publications focused on the sounds – mostly the lyrics of chants and songs – of spectators in the stadium setting, research on the sounds of spectators in the televised broadcast is far scarcer. Consequently, the scholarly publications do not lend themselves practically to a schematic overview like the table in the appendix. The scarcity of research on the sounds of spectators in the televised broadcast could possibly come as a surprise given the fact that significantly greater numbers of spectators watch football through the televised broadcast than from within the stadium setting. One possible explanation for the scarcity of research could be that, generally, televised football – as an example of sports on television – have remained understudied. For example, 'for a sport that generates such an extensive volume of what we now call "media content", football has often been strangely absent in research coming out of media and communication studies' (Boyle, 2019, p. 179), and 'sports lack social as well as scientific legitimacy' (Bonnet & Lochard, 2015, p. 38; see similar arguments in Boyle, 2019, p. 179; Dahlén, 2008, p. 16, Gumbrecht, 2019, p. 36; Johnson, 2021, p. 5). Indeed, it is not uncommon for general studies on television (e.g. readers, handbooks and introductions) to pay no focused attention to sports programming. For example, *The Television Studies Reader* does not include sports programming as part of its objective to 'present contemporary work on a wide range of television modes and experiences' (Allen & Hill, 2004, p. 18). Similarly, while *The New Television Handbook* – written from the point of view of practitioners and those who want to become a practitioner – acknowledges that 'sport is a major input to television programming' (Holland, 2017, p. 51), sports do not feature among the television genres that the book offers an account of (including narrative, factual programmes and news). As a final example, in Bignell's (2013) *An Introduction to Television Studies*, which intends to describe 'some of the critical approaches to television that has become widely accepted in the subject' (p. 1), sports are not subjected to focused attention throughout the otherwise wide variety of included television genres and formats.

However, a closer inspection of the available contributions reveals that actually a body of research exists when it comes to the examination of various aspects of televised football – other than the sounds of spectators, that is. Firstly, it is possible to identify general studies on television which offer substantial insights into sports (hereunder football), and notable examples include Crisell (2006), Miller (2010) and Real (2005). Secondly, an additional body of research exists – actually, reference has been made to 'hundreds of studies' (Real, 2005, p. 338) on sports on television and the more general 'academic field of media and sport' has been characterized as 'enormous' (Gantz, 2014, p. 7) – which, for the present purposes, can be roughly divided into two broad categories: contextual studies exploring aspects of the wider circumstances of televised football and textual studies – representing the most relevant category for the present approach – focused on aspects of the audiovisual structure, distribution and significance of televised football or, in other words, on 'sports TV's distinctive textual aesthetics' (Johnson, 2021, p. 5).

As regards contextual perspectives, several book-length contributions have offered insights into various issues including, for example, the impact of media changes on the football industry (Boyle & Haynes, 2004), the politics of sports broadcasting (Dörr, 2000), the politics of football and television (Holz-Bacha, 2006), the history of the distribution and production of televised football in Germany (Grosshans, 1997) as well as political, historical, economical and sociological aspects of the relations between media (hereunder television) and sports (see, e.g. Billings, 2011; Boyle, 2014; Burk, 2002; Chisari, 2006; Dahlén, 2008; Goldsmith, 2013; Haynes, 1998; Milne, 2016; Neal-Lunsford, 1992; Raney & Bryant, 2006; Rowe, 2011; Sandvoss, 2003; Sterkenburg & Spaaij, 2016; Wenner, 1998; Whannel, 2009, 2014). Additionally, there exist anecdotal contributions on televised football from the perspectives of professionals working within the industry (see, e.g. Armstrong, 2019; Barwick, 2013) and experienced or experiencing spectators (Kelner, 2012), while several publications have focused on the production of televised sports (hereunder football) (see, e.g. Catsis, 1996; Deninger, 2012; Owens, 2021; Schultz, 2002; Schultz & Arke, 2016, Wittek, 2013).

As regards the research that has adopted a textual perspective on televised football it (still) seems fair to suggest that 'there is a scattered literature on this topic' (Scannell, 2014, p. 239) and that there exists only 'rare examples of TV studies scholarship that closely analyse the texts of sports TV' (Johnson, 2021, p. 58). These assessments hold particularly true when it comes to the textual element of the sounds of spectators. This situation of a scarcity of scholarly examinations of the sounds of spectators in televised football and sports can arguably be traced back to two seminal suggestions by otherwise textually oriented television scholars.

Firstly, Raymond Williams is widely cited (see, e.g. Boyle, 2014, p. 746; Hughson, 2014, p. 283) for having announced: 'Sport, is of course one of the very best things about television; I would keep my set for it alone' (Williams, 1968/1989, p. 34). Williams goes on to hint at what is for him the very best (and worst) elements of televised sports, and he suggests a rather drastic consequence: 'For a while one just snarls, "Get out of that box and try to run it yourself," and then, wisely, as with most sport on television, switches off the sound' (Williams, 1968/1989, p. 34). Practically, Williams identifies the visuals and the commentary – which he wants to, respectively, maintain and avoid in (t)his case experience – as the essential textual elements of televised sports and other sounds are not commented on. Obviously, Williams's approach is essayistic and idiosyncratic, but the fact that it has been widely cited in studies on televised sports suggests that it might have influenced subsequent researcher's perspectives on what (not) to focus on when it comes to a textual examination of televised sports.

Secondly, in a seminal scholarly contribution (Buscombe, 1975) – arguably representing a 'pioneering book about soccer on television' (Real, 2005, p. 339) – sounds are explicitly opted out from the focus of the examination. Buscombe thus suggests that '[at] the level of the sound track and in respect of the effect of these codes on the audience they do not seem nearly as important as the image track' (Buscombe, 1975, p. 24), and, as a consequence, 'while assuming that there are codes pertaining to the sound track, they will not be analysed further' (Buscombe, 1975, p. 24).

Seemingly, these discounts of the textual significance of the sounds of spectators have set the tone for subsequent textually oriented examinations of televised football. Illustratively, textual studies on televised football (and sports in general) have been 'specialized in and focused on either the verbal dimensions or the visual dimension of this [TV sportscasting] syncretic media discourse' (Bonnet & Lochard, 2015, p. 38). Although most studies offer some insights into both – as well as on the relation between them (for an obvious example, see the chapter on television and sports in Goldlust, 1987; see also Barnfield, 2013) – it seems possible to group most of the existing contributions according to their interest in examining either the visuals or the commentary of televised football or other comparable sports.

Examples of studies primarily focused on the verbal dimensions of the commentary would thus include Bryant et al. (1977), Comisky et al. (1977), Kennedy (2000), Lichtenstein and Nitsch (2011), Marriott (1996), Rose and Friedman (1997), Wren-Lewis and Clarke (1983) and several articles in Lavric et al. (2008). Examples of studies primarily focused on the visual dimension would include Hesling (1986), Morse (1983), Mullen and Mazzocco (2000, on televised US football), Raunsbjerg (2001), Scannell (2014), Schmidt (1981), Solvoll (2016) and Williams (1977; on televised US football). Furthermore, visual dimensions are the predominant focus in Siegel's (2007) discussion on television's (re)mediation of the large-screen video display in the stadium setting as well as in a recent examination of sports TV's 'formal properties or aesthetics' by Johnson (2021). Tellingly, a chapter entitled 'Sportvision' addresses 'the texts and techs of sports TV', and while acknowledging that 'the formal properties or aesthetics of sports TV are too vast to analyze comprehensively', the chapter focuses on 'a few critical building blocks of sports TV's formal grammar' including, for example, 'slow motion', 'instant replay', 'spilt-screen', 'video overlay' and the '180-degree rule' (Johnson, 2021, pp. 57–84) – that is, the focus is almost exclusively on examples of visual 'building blocks'. While these examples of previous contributions do not include a focus on the sounds of spectators at football, this does not mean that they are entirely irrelevant for the subsequent examination. Accordingly, many of them will help inform the examination in Chapter 4, which also draws upon a selection of theories on the textual structure of the sounds of television in general (e.g. Chion, 1994).

In summing up, it may not be the case (any longer) that televised sports lack scholarly legitimacy; also, it might not (any longer) be appropriate to maintain that 'television sound remain neglected in academic study' (Hilmes, 2008, p. 153). However, it seems fair to suggest that when it comes to televised sports, the textual element of sounds has been largely neglected except for the verbal, symbolic dimension of the commentary. The structure, distribution and significance of the sounds of spectators in televised football has thus not been subjected to focused, systematic examination (with the exception of a foray study of Graakjær, 2020a). Perhaps an explanation for this situation could be that whereas the sounds of spectators are differentiated, powerful and intrusive in the stadium setting, in the televised broadcast these sounds appear to represent an unassuming background to the commentary and largely appear undifferentiated and insignificant compared to the visuals. However, Chapter 4 offers a systematic examination of the structure, distribution and significance of the sounds of spectators in televised football, and the chapter will demonstrate that the sounds play a more refined role that what can be learned from the(se) existing contributions.

# 3

# The stadium setting

This chapter presents an exploration of the sounds of spectators in the stadium setting from the basic questions 'what?', 'where and when?' and 'why?'. The exploration begins by focusing on the structures (representing a reply to question of 'what'?) of the sounds, and subsequently aspects of the distribution and significance (representing replies to the question of 'where and when?' and 'why?', respectively) will be discussed.

## 3.1 What?

This section seeks to define the various types of sounds that exist at football in the stadium setting. The purpose is to introduce the full variety of the sounds of spectators at football including perspectives on the sounds of spectators beyond the lyrics of chants and songs (the primary interest of previous contributions). Obviously, the section focuses primarily on the sounds of spectators, but it will also include a presentation of the sounds among which the sounds of spectators emerge. The following examination is based on two typologies.

Firstly, the approach includes a typology of sounds from the perspective of the human participants who are responsible for the production and distribution of the sounds. This classification includes three types of sound:

- The sounds of spectators: Sounds produced by the attending spectators.
- The sounds of performers: Sounds created by players, additional club members (e.g. coaches, medics) and referees.
- The sounds of organizers: Sounds produced by the stadium staff providing security and service as well as delivering information and announcements over the public announcement (PA) system.

**Table 3.1** Overview of Creators and Types of Sounds at Football in the Stadium Setting

| Participants<br><br>Types of Sounds | Performers<br>(on the Field) | Spectators<br>(in the Stands) | Organizers<br>(via the Stadiums'<br>PA System) |
|---|---|---|---|
| **Music** | None | Chants, songs, rhythmic clapping and shouting | Music, commercials (before and after each half of the match) |
| **Vocal Sounds** | Shouts | Chatter, outbursts | Announcements, recorded sounds of celebrating spectators through highlights from previous matches |
| **Object Sounds** | Referee's whistle, ball strokes | Clapping, handling of objects | Referee's whistle, ball strokes, handling of objects |

Secondly, the examination relies on a typology of sounds (inspired by Truax, 2001; van Leeuwen, 1999) based on differences in the quality of the sounds.

- Music: Sounds characterized by defined rhythms, harmonics and/or melodies.
- Vocal sound: Sounds produced by the human vocal tract including talk and interjections.
- Object sound: Sounds produced by the motion and interaction of physical objects including human bodily parts other than the vocal tract.

Table 3.1 presents an overview and exemplification of how the two typologies of sounds combine.

## Sounds of performers and organizers

Performer sounds include both vocal sounds (e.g. screams, grunts, panting) and object sounds relating to the performers' interaction with physical objects (e.g. the ball, the pitch surface, the referee's whistles). Music is however not normally part of the sounds originating from performers throughout the match. The vocal and object sounds purportedly play a significant role for the players themselves. Players' vocal sounds thus include, for example, verbal encouragements to fellow team members as well as insults directed at the referee and opponent players. The object sounds can also provide feedback on the player's performance through, for example, the intensity of the corporeal sounds of exhalation and groaning and the sounds from striking the ball. The latter example illustrates the general capacity of object sounds to provide useful information on the physical characteristics of the object. For example, some performers are reportedly able to assess the quality of a shot or a pass by listening to the timbre from kicking the ball; apparently Johan Cruyff would criticize a player's technique based on sound alone: 'When he kicks the ball, the sound is wrong' (Cruyff in Winner, 2010, pp. 135–6). The capacity and effect of the sounds of spectators to drown out performer sounds generally implies that mostly spectators located very close to the pitch can hear these sounds. For example, apart from the piercing sound of referee's whistle (audible in all three case matches), the sounds of performers are only (occasionally) observable from my location at the Tottenham-Leicester match including the sounds of the ball hitting the crossbar – which has been described as 'the "donk" of ball-on-bar' (Gray, 2016, p. 21) – as well as ball strokes by the players (for a rare example of a spectator allegedly overhearing the performer sound of a tendon rupture, see Gumbrecht, 2021, p. 21).

Apart from the occasional individual communication from service and security personnel, the sounds of organizers emerge exclusively through the stadiums' PA system. For example, as this practice has apparently long been abandoned at football in England (see, e.g. Armstrong & Young, 1999, p. 180; Laing & Linehan, 2013, p. 315) there is no organizer-instituted musical band present at the case matches (for a present-day example from another setting, see, e.g. Zalis, 2021). In all three stadiums of the case matches, the PA system reaches the spectators from numerous speakers, typically hanging from the roofs and spread strategically throughout the grandstands to ensure that the sounds are distributed at about the same (high) level to all spectators (see also Cummins et al., 2019).

At the case matches, organizer sounds are distributed incessantly through the PA system both before and after the matches as well as in the pause between the two halves. As observed in the interval from approximately an hour before the match to half an hour after the match, the organizers offer an uninterrupted flow of sounds including commercials, highlights shown on the in-stadium jumbotrons from televised broadcasts of previous Tottenham matches – including the sounds of celebrating spectators – and an assortment of Top 40 musical tracks. Whereas this flow of sound has no specific connection to the activities on the pitch where the players can be seen warming up before the game, a closer relation between the PA music and the activities on the pitch can be observed when the match is about to begin and has just ended.

For example, at the case matches, an excerpt from 'Duel of the Fates' (John Williams) from *Star Wars* accompanies the players' ceremonial (re)entrance on the pitch in the minutes leading up to the match. The distribution of a specific piece of music to accompany the player's entrance as well as the consistent deployment of the same music across home matches potentially adds to the profile and brand of the club, and the music enhances the ritual and importance of the particular match. Similarly, a specific piece of music – a rendition of *McNamara's Band* – accompanies the players' re-entrance to the pitch leading up to the beginning of the second half. Moreover, at the Tottenham-Liverpool match right after the referee blows the whistle for the last time, the PA system distributes Dave and Chase's *Glory, Glory, Tottenham Hotspur* (1981) to celebrate that the home team has won the match (by the final score of 4–1). The song is based on the American Civil War song *The Battle of the Republic*, and, apparently, the song was first appropriated by the Tottenham supporters in 1961 during a European Cup match against the Polish team Górnik Zabrze. Following the first leg match the Tottenham team was characterized as 'no angels' by members of the Polish press due to what was considered a rough playing style. Subsequently, for the second leg home match, some of the spectators would wear angel costumes, display banners with spirited slogans and sing the chorus 'Glory, glory, hallelujah' as Tottenham defeated Górnik Zabrze 8–1. The recorded version by Dave and Chase – introduced as the B-side for the single 'Ossie's Dream' produced for the 1981 Cup Final – included the substitution of the original choruses' *Hallelujah* with *Tottenham Hotspur*, which reflects what supporters would early on have done themselves, as suggested in and by Finn (1963, p. 181). At the other two case matches which Tottenham did not win (1–1 against Leicester, and 0–2 against Chelsea), *Glory, Glory, Tottenham Hotspur* does not emerge and is substituted for (insignificant) tracks of music unrelated to the matches.

During the actual matches, organizer sounds appear only occasionally in the form of verbal announcements. For example, throughout the match, the stadium announcer identifies the players involved in substitutions, the goal scorers and the amount of stoppage time. These match incidents exemplify pauses in effective playing time – defined as the time when the ball is 'in play' – which also happens as the result of, for example, fouls, throw-ins, corners and players' injury. Such pauses amount to approximately 40 per cent of the duration of the case matches – a percentage consistent with the findings in Hamilton (2013) – and in the cases matches the pauses are not accompanied by music over the PA system. However, in subsequent home matches of Tottenham, the pause following the scoring of a home goal has apparently been accompanied by an excerpt from Darude's *Sandstorm* (1999), which, in addition to punctuate the flow of the match and enhance the goal celebration, potentially adds to the branding of the club and the ritual of watching matches at that specific stadium (comparable to the functions served by entrance and victory music).

Generally, the PA-distributed sounds have the effect of drowning out the sounds of spectators. This holds the potential to produce a conflict of interests between, on the one side, the organizer's attempt to auditorily invigorate and brand the event and, on the other side, the spectators' attempt to experience the pleasures of agency and empowerment related to their production of sounds; for example, spectators have experienced the necessity to 'compete with the deafening sound system' (Cloake & Powley, 2013, p. 226), and the music from the PA system might demotivate the production of sounds by spectators who face a futility in overpowering the PA system (see, e.g. Grøn & Graakjær, 2016). However, as the referee blows the whistle to signal the beginning of the match, the PA system is shut down and creates a stark contrast to the unaccompanied sounds of spectators now suddenly emerging in an auditory foreground. From this perspective, the auditory 'fencing in' of the sounds of spectators by the PA system has the effect of highlighting the immensity of the sounds of spectators at the specific moment when they come to prevail.

## The sounds of spectators

The focus on the sounds of spectators also begins by specifying a typology. The typology is inspired by Kopiez and Brink (1999, p. 15) who represent one of the very few existing typologies that do not focus exclusively on (the lyrics of) chants and songs. However, compared to the typology of Kopiez and Brink (1999), the present typology is non-hierarchical and finer grained as it includes five main types of spectator sound (as well as several subtypes) based on the previously mentioned tripartite classification of music, vocal sounds and object sounds.

Table 3.2 presents an overview of the typology, and the table indicates that while some examples of sounds unambiguously represent the characteristics of music, vocal or object sounds, there exists two intermediate or overlapping types of sound (i.e. 'musical vocal sounds' and 'musical object sounds'). The following

Table 3.2 Overview of Types of Sounds of Spectators at Football

| Types of Spectator Sound at Football | Vocal Sounds | Musical Vocal Sounds | Music | Musical Object Sounds | Object Sounds |
|---|---|---|---|---|---|
| Distinctive Examples | Talk (chatter), shouting interjections | Rhythmic shouting | Singing | Rhythmic clapping | Arrhythmic clapping |

sections will present in further detail aspects of the sounds of spectators from the perspective of the three main types (i.e. object sounds, vocal sounds and music).

## Object sounds

Clapping – that is, the relatively high-pitched percussive sound produced by spectators striking together the palms of their hands – represents the most significant subtype of object sound. This is arguably due to the specific traditions and regulations pertaining to the English setting of the case material. For example, Morris (1981) claims that 'continental and South American matches are played out to an almost non-stop deafening roar of massed drummers and hooters in the crowd. Few such instruments are taken into a British Stadium, so there is less background noise and more possibility for singing to be heard effectively' (p. 315). Illustratively, at Wembley Stadium, the list of articles not permitted in the stadium includes 'air horns' as well as 'trumpets, drums and other devices capable of causing a disturbance or nuisance' (Wembley, 2022). Accordingly, spectators' use of musical instruments or sound articles – which are prevalent in other settings (see, e.g. Fuller, 2016; Grøn & Graakjær, 2016; Jethro, 2014; Knijnik, 2016) – has not been observed at the case matches.

Although clapping 'might be considered an instrument' – and one that is 'cheap, portable, easy to maintain, and readily mastered' (Repp, 1987, pp. 1108–9) – generally, clapping 'is perhaps the most common audible activity of humans that is (a) intended to be heard by others and (b) does not involve either the vocal tract or a musical instrument' (Repp, 1987, p. 1100). Compared to, for example, singing, clapping 'can be sustained over longer periods of time because it is not constrained by the necessity to breath' (O'Connell & Kowal, 2008, p. 176). Furthermore, like the sounds of striking a football, the sound of clapping is indicative of the object and interaction that produces the sounds; specifically, 'the absence of a sex difference in clap spectra suggests that hand configuration, rather than hand size, is the most important determinant of the sound pattern' (Repp, 1987, p. 1104).

While individual clapping does appear sporadically, at football clapping mostly transpire as a collective activity, that is, as a phenomenon 'in which repeated interactions among many individuals produce patterns on a scale larger than themselves' (Sumpter, 2010, p. 9). Two sorts of collective clapping can be distinguished based on whether the clapping embodies prolonged synchronization or not. Synchronous clapping – or 'synchro-clapping' (Morris, 1981, p. 258) – emerges when a significant number of the spectators 'co-ordinate to act in unison' (Sumpter, 2010, p. 130) so that the tempo and rhythm of each of the individual's clapping conform to the same, distinct configuration. Morris (1981) argues that synchro-clapping is an 'English invention originating ... in the Liverpool Kop' and that it is performed in a distinct way 'with the hands held high over the head instead of the usual position in front of the chest' (p. 258). Furthermore, based on slow-motion film recordings, Morris observes how the degree to which the spectators are in synch when clapping 'is greater than 1/64th of a second' – a precision which is 'probably higher than that achieved by well-drilled military bands' (ibid., p. 258).

By establishing a distinct tempo and rhythm, synchronous clapping appears as 'musical object sounds', and this is furthered in cases where the clapping complements coordinated vocal expressions such as collective shouts and/or chanting. In the case matches an example emerges in the form of the shouting of a repeated four beat structure: *Yid Army, [clap], [clap]*. For a significant example in the existing contributions, Kopiez and Brink (1999, p. 71) identify the so-called 'Soccer-Rhythmus' ('the football rhythm') as originating from (the beginning of) the track 'Hold Tight' (released in 1966) by Dave Dee, Dozy, Beaky, Mick and Tich (1966). While this particular variant of rhythmic clapping is apparently pervasive throughout the case material examined in Kopiez and Brink (1999) – also, the rhythm is observed in the studies by Morris (1981) and Grøn and Graakjær (2016) – it has not been identified in the case material for this book.

Asynchronous clapping transpires when the simultaneous clapping of a significant number of spectators does not conform to a distinct temporal and rhythmic configuration. In contrast to synchronous clapping, asynchronous clapping does not include pauses or momentary auditory 'lacunae' of no clap impulses. Rather, the clapping appears to form a continuous flow or surge of sound. Compared to the more measured structure of synchronous clapping, asynchronous clapping includes a higher frequency of clap impulses. The tempo of everyone's clapping is thus more fast-paced compared to a slower frequency of the synchronous clapping.

## Vocal sounds

Vocal sounds here include all non-musical utterances originating from the human vocal tract ranging from talk (or chatter) to various forms of non-verbal utterances which in everyday communication often blend (see, e.g. Dingemanse, 2020, p. 188).

Whistling exemplifies a non-verbal utterance of particular relevance when introducing the vocal sounds of spectators at football. Although whistling is arguably 'not part of the English language', specific types of whistling can be seen as '"sound objects," which English speakers deploy systematically for implementing both initiating and responsive actions in social interaction' (Reber & Couper-Kuhlen, 2020, p. 164). At football, the specific variant of non-melodic (as opposed to melodic), 'small-smile' whistle (as opposed to the 'rounded lips' whistle; see, e.g. Shadle, 1983) appears as a high-pitched, highly air-pressed and piercing utterance – although not as piercing as the referees' (object of a) whistle and usually blending in with other sounds (and whistles) of spectators. This type of whistling is 'sometimes used as a substitute for booing, especially in Italy, but in England it is more often reserved for a plea to the referee to blow the final whistle and end the game' (Morris, 1981, p. 260) – indeed, it has been suggested that in Italy, 'in the stadium, fans will whistle at calls that go against their team' (Guschwan, 2016, p. 296); however, at the case matches no prolonged collective whistling has been observed.

Whereas the vocal sound subcategory of talk appears among spectators in close proximity – that is, the verbal communication represents an exchange of utterances at normal voice level – a widespread and distinct form of vocal utterances emerges as shouts and outcries performed by individuals or a group of individuals with a raised voice. At the Tottenham-Liverpool match an example of an individual outburst emerges as a specific spectator (seated four rows below my position) stands up, turns around and shouts 'Shit fans, sing up!' at fellow spectators in the same section who are not engaged in singing the chant *Come on You Spurs* as is rings from the stands with the most vocal supporters – the previously mentioned *Yid Army*, *[clap], [clap]* exemplifies a collective predominantly rhythmical shouting including clapping.

A particular recurrent form of vocal tract utterance can be referred to as response cries or 'exclamatory interjections which are not fully-fledged words. *Oops* is an example' (Goffman, 1981a, p. 99, italics in original; see also Ameka, 1992; Guschwan, 2016, p. 305). Existing contributions on interjections tend to focus on interpersonal communication (or public speeches) and interjections as a stand-alone utterance that do not normally enter as part of specific phrases or clauses from the perspective of syntax. Also, although clauses of collective interjections seem prevalent and significant at football, they are rarely examined or even observed. Exceptions from this trend include an identification of 'massed callings' (Morris, 1981, p. 260) in the form of booing, cheering, roaring, jeering, groaning and moaning as well as observations of 'a collective sigh of disappointment' and 'an intense burst of noise that sounds something like "yeah"' (Guschwan, 2016, p. 304). Moreover, clauses of collective interjections are indicated by the following 'chain reaction' which can follow when an attempt at scoring a goal result in the ball hitting the crossbar: 'It teases out a round-mouthed "aaaaawwwww" noises. Rueful hands are placed on heads but within seconds calamity has matured into motivation: teeth are gritted, hands smashed together at pace, and indecipherable yet hopeful cries of encouragement are hollered' (Gray, 2016, p. 21). Similarly, relevant descriptions exist in the anecdotal accounts of the sounds of the crowd as illustrated by the observations by Hopcraft (1968; see Section 2.1). Interjections here seem to transpire as collective phenomena both as stand-alone utterances and in distinctly produced clauses.

A recurrent and significant example of a stand-alone collective interjection at football is the noise-like, primary interjection of an intoned or pitched 'boo' (originating from fifteenth-century Middle English, according to O'Connell & Kowal, 2008, p. 123). Usually, individual spectators perform the boo beyond the normal breathing capacity of individuals. Booing thus normally emerges through a crescendo of intensity which is sustained at the climax for several seconds before it gradually decreases and fades away, and the prolonged sustain is achieved through the practice of staggered breathing. A significant example emerges at the Tottenham-Liverpool match as booing among the spectators gradually arises and slowly increases to a powerful climax as it is announced over the PA system that Dejan Lovren is about to be substituted for the former player of arch-rival Arsenal, Alex Oxlade-Chamberlain.

**Table 3.3** Examples of Variants of Segmented Collective Interjections at Football

| |
|---|
| A. Increase (moderate intensity) → Decrease (moderate intensity) |
| B. Increase (high intensity) → Break → Decrease (high intensity): 'Ooh' → Applause |
| C. Increase (high intensity) → Break → Further increase (high intensity, prolonged): 'Yeah!' |

Particularly dynamic and recurring examples of collective interjections emerge in various forms of segmented structures as hinted at previously. Based on the most recurrent types throughout the case matches, three distinctive structures (illustrated in Table 3.3) can be specified all of which begins by an accumulation of a mixture of interjections – for example, 'wow', 'that's it!', 'come on!', 'go!', 'yeah!' – which unfolds over a varying but usually relatively short period of time (a few seconds). As the interjections gradually increase in quantity, volume and pitch, the accumulation produces a general upsurge of the intensity of the sound produced by the spectators. In one variant – see variant A in Table 3.3 – the sound intensity increase is moderate and is replaced directly by a sound intensity decrease thus representing two segments.

The remaining two variants have in common a tripartite segmented structure and a more pronounced increase of sound intensity. At what turns out to represent the climax of its intensity, the accumulation suddenly ends and is followed by a break or what transpires virtually as quietness due to the notable contrast to the sound level of the (ending of) preceding segment. During this second segment, which is usually quite short and lasts less than a second, the (vast majority of the) spectators synchronously and literally draw in and hold their breath as the result of a shared and focused attention. Interjections here seem to emerge as collective phenomena both as stand-alone utterances and representing distinctly structured clauses.

For both variants, the third segment constitutes yet another striking contrast to the preceding absence of spectator sound. This segment is thus characterized by powerful and abruptly introduced interjections which appear to conform to a specific interjection thus contrasting the blend of interjections characteristic of the first segment. In one variation (see variant B in Table 3.3), the interjections conform to a synchronous 'collective exhalation of breath' (Gaffney & Bale, 2004, p. 29) – 'Ooh!' (or 'aaaaawwwww' as suggested previously) – embodying a prolonged descending pitch contour and expressing what appears to be disappointment. In another variation, the interjections articulate a relatively highly pitched 'Yeah!' expressing what appears to be jubilation.

While variant B is relatively short-lived and soon develops into a period of applause and further interjections, in variant C the jubilation is sustained for numerous seconds before it develops into a high-intensity mixture of additional interjections and clapping. This example – which transpired in the case matches after the scoring of home team goals – has been aptly described as 'a frenzy of noise' when a 'crush of screams and cries collects into a single roar' which might 'feel like an earthquake as bodies convulse and the stands shake' (Guschwan, 2016, p. 297).

## Music

In the case matches, the recurrent singing of *Oh, When the Spurs Go Marchin' In* clearly represents a case of music as it embodies a tonal sequence with a distinct rhythmic profile, pitch contour and tonal vocabulary or mode (Tagg, 2014, p. 179). By comparison, the rhythmic distinctiveness of clapping and shouting is not complemented by pitch contour, and the pitched booing is not complemented by a distinct rhythm. Moreover, singing embodies a more regular and recurrent pattern of accentuation, metre and periodicity than do speech (Tagg, 2013, p. 367). At football, the regularity is produced and supported by predominantly syllabic singing which means that each note is matched to a single syllable – melismatic singing, for its part, would indicate that several consecutive notes are sung over the same syllable.

Generally, the structure of sung melodies can be considered to represent 'melodic' tonal sequences as they are 'popularly understood, at least within a mainstream European or American context' (Tagg, 2014, pp. 179–80). Thus, melodic tonal sequences are characterized by:

- being easy to recognize, appropriate and to reproduce vocally.
- being perceptible as occupying durations resembling those of normal or extended exhalation (consisting of phrases lasting between about two and ten seconds).
- being relatively simple in terms of tonal vocabulary.
- tending to change pitch more by intervallic steps than by leaps.
- spanning rarely more than one octave.

Clearly exemplified by the singing of *Oh, When the Spurs Go Marchin' In*, these are structural features that make melodies 'cantabile' or 'singable'. It should then come as no surprise that very similar characteristics have been identified in the (few) previous studies which have sought to describe the typical structures of sung melodies performed by spectators at football. Most notably, Kopiez and Brink (1999) present a list of structural characteristics of 'the successful melody' (p. 191; translated by the author) – and the characteristics overlap almost entirely with the list presented above based on Tagg (2014). Kopiez and Brink (1999) suggest (perhaps with a tongue in cheek) that the relatively simple melodic features are characteristic of nursery rhymes and that this could seem to indicate that spectators at football 'have – at least regarding their singing abilities in the crowd – remained children' (Kopiez & Brink, 1999, p. 199; translated by the author). However, relatively uncomplicated melodic features are potentially characteristic of melodies from a wide variety of styles and genres, and such features reflect a practical necessity and 'the lowest common denominator' (Kopiez & Brink, 1999, p. 197; translated by the author) of the melodies that spectators – generally representing musical amateurs – can sing at football. Incidentally, Lee (2018, p. 377) exemplifies how spectators evaluate the melodic structure of a song as being too complex for them to sing in the stadium setting.

A distinction shall now be suggested between two main types of melodic structures: chants and songs. A 'chant' includes only one melodic motif, which is here defined as the smallest melodic unit possessing self-contained musical distinctiveness. The chant is relatively short and can be performed by a (few) lungful(s) of air. While chants represent a coherent and distinct sequence of notes, the structure is often musically open by ending melodically on a tone other that the main reference tone (i.e. the tonic or keynote) in the given mode. In addition to its shortness, this makes the structure of the chant particularly prone for 'reiteration' in the sense that the performance usually includes the 'consecutive recurrence(s) of a very similar or identical motif' (Tagg, 2014, p. 194). Therefore, although a chant embodies a short melodic structure, the practice of chanting usually extends over a lengthier period of time. These significant characteristics of the 'chant' are exemplified by the supporters' performance of *Come on You Spurs*, which emerges on several occasions in all three case matches. The chant lasts approximately four seconds (a lungful of air) and is repeated at least a handful of times. Melodically, it consists of five notes of which the four first is the same while the final, lower note is introduced melismatically as the syllable 'Spurs' is sung over a descending minor third.

Significant characteristics of the 'song' are exemplified by the performance of *Oh, When the Spurs Go Marchin' In*. The song thus represents a lengthier melodic sequence the performance of which extends beyond a lungful of air. Also, the song includes several motifs which combine to produce a coherent larger musical unit, that is, a musical period or section. Usually, songs include recapitulation in the form of recurrence of a particular motif (if not entire periods) after the intervening of different motifs – as illustrated by the (slightly modified) recapitulation of the lyrics 'Oh, When the Spurs Go Marchin' in' at the end of the chant after the intervening motif set to the lyrics 'I Want to be in that Number'. Consequently, songs generally represent rounded expressions in which the finishing tone usually represents the reference note of the given mode and thereby a terminal point.

Both examples of significant melodic structures exemplify that with the rare exception of the occasional solo performance by a neighbouring spectator – or the practices of a so-called *capo* or chant leader (see more below) – singing at football is performed collectively by groups of spectators in unison. This exemplifies how 'several participants together produce *notes of the same length at the same pitch and time* as each other' including the singing in parallel octaves 'as when men and women sing the same notes at the same time in different registers' (Tagg, 2013, p. 450, italics in original). Due to a usual overweight of adult male spectators at football, the lower octave is more pronounced – consequently, although the composition of spectators at football is mixed, the spectators' singing sounds as if it originates from a men's choir. While an octave doubling of the melody might be considered to represent a case of polyphony – as two sounds of differing pitch or timbre appear at the same time (see Tagg, 2014, p. 206) – the singing generally represents monophony in the sense that the melody is accompanied by neither additional melody lines (which could otherwise have constituted homophony or counterpoint; see Tagg, 2014, p. 453) nor musical instruments other than the vocal tract.

Occasionally, in cases not exemplified by the performance of *Oh, When the Spurs Go Marchin' In* and *Come on You Spurs*, spectators' singing of melodies might be distributed among more than one group of spectators and this practice exemplifies alternating singing or responsoriality, namely 'the exchange of musical material in a form resembling that of question and answer, or of statement and counter-argument' (Tagg, 2013, p. 470). Tagg distinguishes four subtypes based on whether the opening and/or the following statement is performed by an individual or a group of people (Tagg, 2013, p. 471). In the context of football, the most prevalent examples include the two subtypes characterized by a group 'answer' invited by either an individual or collective 'question'. The former type is illustrated by the practice of the capo (see Section 3.2), while the latter includes different groups of spectators exchanging shouts or chants to form a coherent expression. For example, Grøn and Graakjær (2016; see also Bonz, 2016, p. 152) provide the example of two groups of spectators taking turns in shouting *Come on AaB!* with the effect of a persistent, high-intensity vocal support. Although not available from my POAs in the stadium setting during the three case matches, on other occasions groups of Tottenham supporters positioned at the 'Park Lane' and at the 'Shelf side', respectively (referring to grandstands at White Hart Lane), have been observed taking turns in singing at/with each other. A group of spectators might also interfere with the vocal support of another group. For example, an encouragement for the away team – *Chelsea! Chelsea!* – has been observed to be transformed into a chant of insult by the home team's spectators who insert a new word in the chant's brief pauses: *Chelsea! (Shit!) Chelsea! (Shit)!* (Marsh et al., 1978, p. 66; for a similar example, see Davies, 1972, p. 122).

## Transtextuality

A significant aspect of the examination of what characterizes chants and songs is the musical origin – that is, from what the chants and songs originate. Compared to object and vocal sounds, music in the form of chants and songs represents a more diversified type of spectator sound. When focusing on from what chants and songs originate, the perspective is transtextual, as this term designates an interest for 'the ensemble of any type of relation, explicit or not, that may link a text with others' (Lacasse, 2000, p. 36). The term literally indicates the transformation (indicated by the prefix 'trans') of (an excerpt of) a particular sound event (the 'text') from one structure to another.

When examining the origin of the music performed by spectators at football, a basic distinction can be made between pre-existing and original music. Pre-existing music refers to music which has been produced and distributed prior to and outside the setting of a football match, whereas original music designates musical productions with no such pre-existence. Pre-existing music apparently predominates at football, but the previously mentioned chants *Yid Army, [clap], [clap]* and *Come on You Spurs* exemplify, as far as can be assessed, original music(al vocal sounds).

Sometimes the identification of a possible pre-existence of a chant or song is a relatively simple undertaking as when, for example, spectators' singing includes excerpts from a previously widely distributed and well-known piece of music as exemplified by the singing of *You'll Never Walk Alone*. Occasionally, however, it is often difficult to map the distributional 'career' of a particular piece of music – generally, 'in post-modern societies the destiny of the text is less predictable' (Tota, 2001, p. 121) – and not only can chants and songs in the stadium setting originate from pre-existing music, but they can also inspire new, 'post-existing' texts in other (e.g. political) settings (see, e.g. Dean, 2021; O'Brien, 2020). Illustratively, Kopiez and Brink (1999) refer to their examination of musical origins as being 'based on our recollection' (p. 174; translated by the author), although, currently, various forms of web-based media can facilitate the search for and identification of specific chants and songs (see Section 2.1).

However, even though pieces of music might obviously qualify as pre-existing, the specific origin cannot always be clearly identified – compare, for example, the identification of the origin of an accredited, historically specified recording of *You'll Never Walk Alone* (see, e.g. Schoonderwoerd, 2011, pp. 127–8) with the identification of the origin of *Oh, When the Saints Go Marchin' In*. The latter song represents an uncredited, undated and originally orally transmitted spiritual which possibly 'originated as a 19th century Protestant hymn and remains a message of revelation and redemption' (CBS News, 2013). Among the most popular early recordings of the song is a version by Louis Armstrong (1938), and subsequently the song has been recorded by numerous artists.

In addition to establishing the origin of the song from outside the setting of football, a further complication of examining songs from a transtextual perspective is the specification of the first performance and subsequent circulation of the song within the setting of football matches. Generally, 'the vast majority of songs are common to virtually all football grounds, with slight variations' (Marsh et al., 1978, p. 67; see also Canter et al., 1989, p. 70). Specifically, *Oh, When the Saints Go Marchin' In* has been described as 'part of the repertoire of all clubs for the last 20 years. Almost universally adaptable with innumerable variations in circulation' (Kopiez & Brink, 1999, p. 84; translated by the author; see also Back et al., 2001, p. 43). Indeed, a wide variety of versions and performers of the song has been observed (see, e.g. Collinson, 2009, p. 22; Luhrs, 2007a, p. 260; Schoonderwoerd, 2011, p. 130; Thrills, 1998, p. 136; Vilter, 2011, pp. 35, 79). Moreover, the case of *Oh, When the Saints Go Marchin' In* illustrates that within the setting of football matches, 'the origins of the chants are contentious' (Fuller, 2016). For example, the song has been said to be introduced in the beginning of the 1960s by supporters at Liverpool 'to honour one of their star players, Ian St John' (Morris, 1981, p. 305), but around the same time, the song was allegedly performed by supporters at both Southampton (Merrills, 1997, p. 14) and Tottenham (as implied in Finn, 1963).

While examples can be offered of spectators having performed 'preexisting music on football' – that is, music which originally and explicitly includes reference to football (see examples in Lawn, 2020, pp. 34–5; Nannestad, 2015, pp. 323–4) – based on the case matches and observations in the available contributions, 'preexisting music *not* on football' clearly predominates among the chants and songs performed by spectators. Evidently, this tendency cannot be explained by a scarceness of available musical candidates – for example, the website www.45football.com offers a curation of well over one thousand examples of songs on (various aspects of) football in the form of musical tracks distributed by record labels from around the world (see also Buchanan, 2002; Laing & Linehan, 2013; Paytress, 1996). Rather, the predominance of 'preexisting music not on football' might represent a reflection of a more general aspiration among spectators to demonstrate and experience some level of ownership, spontaneity and creativity through their singing performances at football matches.

When focusing on spectators' inclusion of 'preexisting music not on football', as suggested previously, the pre-existing source material embodies an expansive range of musical types and genres, including (but not limited to) hymns, nursery rhymes, classical music, rock, pop, jazz, musicals and television music (e.g. commercials and title tunes; for examples, see Back et al., 2001, p. 62; Thrills, 1998, p. 33). This illustrates what has been hinted at previously that the decisive criterion for the inclusion of pre-existing music into the 'repertoire' of spectators at football is the 'sing(-along-)ability' of the melodies. However, an additional criterion – although relevant in some cases more than others – is the specific potentials of meaning which the origin and pre-existence of a particular piece of pre-existing music offer the spectators to 'play with' as part of their performance. Questions as to how and why particular musical works are chosen and reworked for chants and songs to be performed at football are not well documented in the existing contributions. It has been suggested that the practice is similar to that of and within the context of performance of 'folk-music' where musical expressions 'circulate predominately orally, exist in many variants, and their authors are unknown' (Herd & Löfgren, 2020, p. 13; for examples of how specific chants and songs are developed, see Guschwan, 2016, p. 305; Kopiez & Brink, 1999, 167; Lee, 2018, p. 376; Pearson, 2012, p. 65; Thrills, 1998, 50).

## Rearticulations: Adoptions and adaptions

Generally, the spectators' performances based on pre-existing music can be considered to represent rearticulations as the spectators' performances give new or further expression to the pre-existing music. The collective unison singing thus represents a new stylistic expression compared to the music's prior distribution outside the setting of the football match. This also implies that the performance represents de- and recontextualizations in the following sense: 'If an element is taken out of a specific context, we observe the process of de-contextualization; if the respective element is then inserted into a new context, we witness the process of recontextualization' (Reisigl & Wodak, 2015, p. 28). Generally, spectators' de- and recontextualization of pre-existing music epitomizes what has been termed the 'iterative force of music' (Derrida in Gilbert, 2004, p. 3) – that is, music holds the capacity to escape its original setting and becomes realizable in others. Two types of rearticulations can be specified: adoptions and adaptions.

I propose the term 'adoption' to account for a rearticulation of (an excerpt of) pre-existing music without significant (lyrical) modifications, and I suggest the term 'adaption' to refer to a rearticulation of (an excerpt of) pre-existing music including a significant 'relyricisation' (Lacasse, 2000, p. 57) – or, if the pre-existing piece of music is instrumental, a 'lyricisation' (see, e.g. Dean, 2021; Herd & Löfgren, 2020). Alternative terms for 'adaptions' include 'copsais' (an acronym for 'customisation of popular songs as sung in stadia', as proposed by Laing & Linehan, 2013, p. 314) and 'contrafactum' (see, e.g. Kopiez & Brink, 1999, p. 169; Millar, 2016, p. 311; O'Brien, 2020, p. 120).

From the perspective of the case matches and the existing contributions, adaptions seem far more common than adoptions. Rare examples of adoptions include the Liverpool FC supporters' performance of the previously mentioned song *You'll Never Walk Alone* and Rangers FC supporters' adoption of 'Rule Britannia' (McKerrell, 2015, p. 624). Spectators' adoptions of (excerpts of) music without lyrics seem even rarer, but a remarkable example is provided by various supporters' adoption of the seven-note bass guitar riff that features throughout the track 'Seven Nation Army' (2003) by The White Stripes (for specific examples of adoptions, see Dean, 2021; Sandgren, 2010). However, there are no examples of adoptions in the case matches, which corresponds with the evaluation that adaptions – or contrafactums – are widespread and predominate at football 'almost without exception' (Kopiez & Brink, 1999, p. 167).

Obviously, *Oh, When the Spurs Go Marchin' In* exemplifies an adaption as the melody is retained while 'Spurs' represents a relyricization of the song's original 'Saints'. Moreover, the adaption of the song can be seen to exemplify a signature song – also termed a 'signature tune' (Morris, 1981, p. 306) or a 'club anthem' (Back et al., 2001, p. 49) – as it is the most repeated song with the most powerful following throughout the case matches (also, the song serves to identify Tottenham when playing for the team in the football simulation video game of FIFA; see more in Section 4.4). For example, observed from my POA the song emerges significantly (with a substantial following) on seven occasions throughout the Tottenham-Liverpool match, and the song has been described as 'the classic Spurs song of the modern era' (Duggan, 2012, p. 207). Indeed, other possible, and perhaps even more original candidates are not performed with the same degree of regularity and pervasiveness – for example, the (somewhat controversial) chant *Yid Army, [Clap], [Clap]* appears regularly but with a limited following; and while 'Tottenham had its *Glory, Glory, Hallelujah, The Spurs Go Marching On*' as an example of a chant 'of their own' (Morris, 1981, p. 306; see also Merrills, 1997, p. 56) it does not appear regularly throughout the case matches. Arguably, this is influenced by the fact that the song already appears manifestly as organizer music (as mentioned in Section 3.1) which challenges the spectators' possible experience of ingenuity and spontaneity.

However, as already hinted at, the song *Oh, When the Saints Go Marchin' In* is not exclusively adapted by Tottenham supporters. Most notably, the song has long been 'inextricably linked with' and currently serves as the 'Southampton club anthem' (Merrills, 1997, p. 14) – incidentally, as 'Saints' is the nickname for the football club Southampton, the adaption does not include an actual relyricization but rather what could be seen as a resymbolization. In addition to the substitution of 'Saints' with 'Spurs' – as well as a possible connection with the spiritual theme (and the lyrics' inclusion of *Marching* at the end) of the victory music *Glory, Glory, Tottenham Hotspur* – what distinguishes Tottenham supporter's adaption of the song is the way in which it is performed regarding the tempo and structure. The performance thus typically includes two relatively slow renderings of the eight-bar verse (accompanied by the supporters raising their hands towards the sky) followed by a fast rendition of the verse introduced and accompanied by rhythmic clapping. This style of performance – described as 'slooooowwwww' before 'they speed up' – is arguably idiosyncratic and originating at Tottenham: 'As far as I can tell, Spurs fans started it' (Marshall, 2014, p. 201).

An opportunity for a direct comparison between styles of performance incidentally presents itself in the case match between Tottenham and Liverpool as the Liverpool supporters also introduce an adaption of *Oh, When the Saints Go Marchin' In*. Apart from a substitution of 'Saints' for 'Reds', the tempo is markedly higher than the Tottenham supporters' versions. Interestingly, the tonality of the Liverpool supporters' performance is identical to the typical tonality of the performance of Tottenham supporters (i.e. the key of B major). While the existing contributions on singing at football have not examined this specific aspect, a comparable examination is offered in a study on chanting at college basketball where the observation is made that crowds 'all over the country, spontaneously chanting Air Ball, start on the musical note F above middle C, plus or minus one piano key' (Heaton, 1992, p. 83). Rather than a reflection of an ability of absolute pitch among the supporters (who are representing musical amateurs, as previously observed), the tonal consistency is explained by feasibility as that particular pitch range allows the chant to 'be comfortably sung by persons of both genders and all vocal ranges' (Heaton, 1992, p. 83) – a similar explanation might apply for the tendency of tonal consistency observed in the case matches.

Another type and significance of adaptions emerges in cases in which the adaption can be seen to refer to a previous (dissimilar) adaption at football matches. Compared to the signature song, this type includes a modification of the structure or performance of previous variants at football matches. Whereas the signature song maintains a stable reference to the pre-existing music due to the unvarying performance, this type arguably blurs or weakens the relation due to the subjection of the music to at least two phases of modification – first, the music is introduced in the setting of football, and second, the music is rearticulated with reference to its introduction in the setting of football. This process illustrates how the 'original meaning' of a song and chant can indeed be sometimes 'nearly lost and become irrelevant' (O'Brien, 2020, p. 117). It might also help explain why 'the tone of the songs often has no relation to the mood of the message. The fans may sing savage threats or gross insults in a tone of voice which is joyous, friendly, or even sentimental, according to the tune on which it is based' (Morris, 1981, p. 307). For example, at the Tottenham-Liverpool match, the song *One Season Wonder (He's Just a One Season Wonder)* emerges among Tottenham supporters to the melody of *Guantanamera* shortly after Harry Kane has scored his second goal of the match. Rather than drawing on and referring to the possible meanings and circumstances of the original song – which has been extensively adapted at football from at least the 1960s (conceivably influenced by the commercially successful version by The Sandpipers from 1966; see, e.g. Laing & Linehan, 2013, p. 314) – the song alludes to previous, lyrically identical versions sung by supporters of opposing teams. Harry Kane was thus tagged and taunted with the *One Season Wonder* song in the beginning of the season following his breakthrough season (i.e. 2014/2015) in a (short) period of time when the goals were few(er) (Rosser, 2017).

## 3.2 Where and when?

Generally, this section is inspired by the suggestion that 'no sound event, musical or otherwise, can be isolated from the spatial and temporal conditions of its physical signal propagation' (Augoyard & Torgue, 2005, p. 4). The focus is here confined to the 'intra-stadium space' and not the stadium's position within the 'intra-urban space' – let alone 'the sport's locational dynamic' (Bale, 1993, p. 6). Generally, the three case stadiums embody characteristics of the latest stages of stadium designs (see, e.g. Bale, 2003a; Flowers, 2017; Paramio et al., 2008) reflecting reactions to a number of fatalities at stadiums during, especially, the 1980s (see, e.g. King, 2002) as well as 'tendencies towards confinement, control, surveillance and territorialization in society at large' (Bale, 1993, p. 6). The stadiums thus exemplify how the design has become increasingly motivated by concerns relating to the 'comfort, control and discipline of crowds' (Bale, 1993, p. 7). Also, the cases exemplify how stadiums have become 'multi-functional' (Paramio et al., 2008, p. 527) and defined by 'media technology, consumerism and commercialization' (Turner, 2017, p. 126).

From the inside, all three stadia appear enclosed and separated from the outside environment. The stadiums are thus 'shut off from the outside world to focus attendants on the inside space and increase of noise' (Bonz, 2016, p. 149). The grandstands of the stadiums are all roofed, and they include a possibly floodlighted pitch as well as jumbotrons and a PA system. Moreover, the stadiums include sectioned seating for spectators – hereunder designated, far-apart sections exclusively for the away supporters and for the most partisan home team supporters. However, the three stadia appear somewhat dissimilar when it comes to the general design and size. The relatively small rectangular White Hart Lane can be seen as a representative of the following description: 'The oddity of the shapes of the different grandstands gives … a sense of special location and provides each ground with its own characteristic identity' (Morris, 1981, p. 42).

The stadium thus includes unusual features and marked differences between the four grandstands. For example, the east end includes supporting pillars, whereas 'no stadium in the world has a control suite like White Hart Lane's' housed in an 'octagonal capsule suspended from the roof in the south west corner' – fittingly described as 'Tottenham's space saving oddity' (Inglis, 1996, p. 372; for overviews of the history and redevelopments of White Hart Lane, see Inglis, 1996, pp. 364–72; Powley & Cloake, 2016). By comparison, both Wembley and Tottenham Hotspur Stadium exemplify newly (re)developed, big(ger) bowl-like structures. While these structures might seem like 'soulless concrete bowls that look much like any other concrete bowl' (Inglis in Bale, 1993, p. 44), there are distinguishing features. For example, the Tottenham Hotspur Stadium is particularly distinguished by an asymmetric structure 'arranged as a horseshoe meeting the all-important South Stand behind the home goal' (Buxton, 2019). This 17,500-seater single-tier South Stand is purportedly the most notable feature for creating a 'wall of sound' and an 'atmosphere inside' which 'has been widely praised' (Buxton, 2019). By comparison, 'reporters have always waxed lyrical about the noise and the atmosphere once you get 36,000 inside White Hart Lane' (Welch, 2013, p. 333), whereas Wembley has not regularly been highlighted positively for its potential as a setting facilitating 'atmosphere' – for example, 'what it seems to lack [the new Wembley Stadium] is atmosphere' (Goldblatt, 2014, p. 274).

Obviously, at the most general level, spectators are all positioned in grandstands around the pitch, and the sounds of spectators thus emerge from the grandstands among the spectators themselves. Generally, because there are no periods of (absolute) silence – and as 'auditory phenomena penetrate us from all directions at all times' (Rodaway, 1994, p. 92) – the sounds of spectators appear ubiquitously irrespective of an individual spectator's specific position within the stadium setting. Moreover, given the relatively large scale of the football pitch as well as the fact that spectators are positioned all around the pitch, the sounds of spectators will inevitably be experienced as originating from different directions and distances. By comparison, most of the performer sounds will not be heard by most of the spectators, whereas the only occasional organizer sounds will be available to all spectators in almost equal measure. The sounds of spectators are thus a predominate source for offering spectators a spatial experience implying both 'a sense of the place' – inspired by the observation that 'sound is a vital component in the development of a sense of place' (Gaffney & Bale, 2004, p. 30) – and a 'sense of being placed (within that place)'.

## A sense of place

An auditorily encouraged 'sense of place' can be seen as a reflection of the basic fact that 'sounds fill spaces and when they are present give character to particular places' (Rodaway, 1994, p. 92). Generally, insights into the significance of the build environment for the production and dispersal of the sounds of spectators are scarce in the existing contributions on the sounds of spectators. Illustratively, it has been proposed: 'The question remains: What is the relationship between the architectural form of the stadium and the degree of energy felt within it? This is the material for another, longer book' (Gumbrecht, 2021, p. 74). Also, studies on the acoustics of the stadium design often focus on other sounds than the one produced by spectators, for example, the distribution of sounds via the PA system and the possible use of the stadium for pop concerts (Fitzgerald & Trim, 1998; Griffiths, 1998). However, the example of Tottenham Hotspur stadium exemplifies how the design of the stadium also seeks to accommodate for the sounds of spectators (Buxton, 2019).

Although the significance of the build environment has not been regularly and thoroughly examined, previous contributions occasionally hint at the acoustic significance of the stadium design. Based on the general observation that 'stadium architecture ... helps shape the football soundscape', Fuller (2016) refers to the example of Stadium Kanjuruhan of Malang in East Java and observes how 'the sound easily dissipates, as there is no roof upon the stadium' (Fuller, 2016). Similarly, Edensor (2015) provides the example of spectators' creation of a 'deafening noise that the roof intensified' (p. 86), and it has been observed how 'a low roof and an enclosure which packed fans together produced more concentrated noise than those occasions when the fans were loosely collected on some open-air terrace' (Armstrong & Young, 1999, p. 201). Moreover, as New York City Football Club temporarily played their home matches in Yankee Stadium (normally used for baseball), it has been observed how the stadium's 'seating is concentrated in one corner, while the opposite end is uncovered and allows large amounts of sounds to escape' (Lee, 2018, p. 369).

These examples point specifically to the significance of (the existence and location of) the roof, the type and extend of the build enclosure and the distance between spectators at different ends and sides of the stadium. The distance between fans at Wembley stadium is greater than at both Tottenham Hotspur Stadium and especially White Hart Lane. Illustratively, at the Tottenham-Liverpool match at Wembley, the sounds of spectators appear relatively blurred and somewhat muffled, possibly as the result of the relatively long distances to/ between the spectators and no proximate reverberation for a large proportion of the sounds (as the roof is far above most of the spectators). For example, frequently the soundscape includes what is, on the one hand, noticeably particular melodies (specifically, *Guantanamera* and *Hey Jude*), but the lyrics are, on the other hand, not decipherable. By comparison, the sounds of spectators produced at White Hart Lane appear more focused and concentrated, arguably resembling the previously cited experience of 'more concentrated noise'. Whereas the large distance between (most of the) seats and the roof construction at Wembley results in a large, open space for sounds to be dispersed within, the sounds do not travel (as) far at the White Hart Lane where the relatively proximate roof construction has the effect of a more immediate reverberation.

The reduced distance between spectators at Tottenham Hotspur Stadium is not only due to the smaller capacity of the stadium compared to Wembley stadium. Also, the distances between the pitch and the surrounding seats are minimized. At White Hart Lane, the distance is further reduced as the surrounding seats are even closer to the pitch and the pitch itself is smaller than at both Wembley and Tottenham Hotspur Stadium. In addition to representing a (much) smaller venue, an impression of closeness to other spectators is reinforced by a lesser distance between seats and row of seats; that is, there is less elbow- and legroom in the seats of White Hart Lane compared to the other two stadiums, although the seats at Tottenham Hotspur stadium have been described as 'compact rather than generous in depth and width' (Buxton, 2019). These characteristics exemplify how the build environment of the stadiums 'helps shape' (as referred to previously) the soundscape of the stadiums. Inspired by the concept of 'territory sound' – which Chion offers to account for sounds that 'serve to identify a particular locale through their pervasive and continuous presence' (Chion, 1994, p. 75) – the stadium can be considered as a 'sound territory' or a 'place for sound' which influences the quality of the specific sounds which emerge in that locale or setting.

## A sense of being placed

In addition to offering 'a sense of place', the sounds of spectators also offer a 'sense of being placed' within the stadium. While the general characteristics of the build environment represent a common precondition, the specific location of the spectators markedly differentiates the experience of the sounds of spectators.

Obviously, like the fact that 'no two people see the same thing (because no two people can occupy exactly the same place)' (Bale, 2003b, p. 88), no two people hear the same thing – indeed, 'the sounds of the stadium are as varied as the places within the stadium' (Gaffney & Bale, 2004, p. 31). Although spectators' location is not entirely fixed during a match, the following examination will focus on the rather stable location of spectators as they have been placed within the stadium setting, and the focus is on POAs from different locations in the open-air grandstands (thereby excluding, e.g. the glass-covered VIP boxes from where the experience is fundamentally different; see, e.g. Gumbrecht, 2021, p. 16).

As with the available perspectives on 'a sense of place', perspectives on the significance of spectators' location are sporadic in the existing contributions. Illustratively, it has been suggested that the 'examination of the particular spatial qualities of sound in the varied spaces of the stadium is a subject of further study' (Gaffney & Bale, 2004, p. 31). However, a few notable exceptions from this tendency exist – as when, for example, the finding that 'away fans counted for 28 while the home fans accounted for only 2 chants' is explained in the following way: 'It is vital to take into account that the chants were collected in the away end with Barnsley fans who were very vocal, making it difficult to hear the Notts County fans and their songs' (Luhrs, 2007b, p. 105). This explanation clearly indicates what should be considered as a basic condition: what you hear is highly dependent on from where you are listening within the stadium setting. Moreover, the explanation hints at the significance of stadium sectioning as well as the presence of at least two groups of spectators, that is, home and away supporters.

An important condition for spectators' experience of the sounds of spectators is the location of their POA in relation to the location of the home and away supporters. The three cases illustrate three different locations from where I have spectated and carrier out my observations, and these differences significantly influence the observations. At the Tottenham-Leicester match, although I am not seated among/with the away supporters (as was Luhrs, according to the previous quote), my position at the South end of the West stand is neighbouring the away section in the curve between the South and West Stand. From my POA, the sounds from the packed away section dominate the soundscape almost entirely. The supporters are singing powerfully – reinforced by the relative low roof construction which makes the sound resonate at close range – and the sounds produced by the Tottenham supporters are largely drowned out: The sounds of the home supporters from the nearby South Stand cannot effectively penetrate the 'sound barrier' by the intermediate away section, and the sounds from the North and East stand are too far away not to be masked. Moreover, the spectators in the section in which I am positioned do not produce sounds at levels to compete with the volume of the away support – that is, the West Stand has been described (appropriately, based on my observations) as mostly occupied by 'VIP seats' where 'not many of the nearly 6000 people … get all that involved in the singing or chanting on a match day' (Football Stadiums, 2022).

While it seems reasonable to suggest that generally: 'From outside the crowd the most noticeable feature is the sheer noise. From inside the words become clearer and more salient' (Canter et al., 1989, p. 70), my experience indicates how being 'outside' a specific group of spectators does not necessarily imply that the words or lyrics (of the songs and chants) of this crowd are unclear. From my location, every sung word by the away supporters was audible, whereas the lyrics of all other chants and songs by groups of spectators from other locations within the stadium setting were often indistinct. Obviously, had I been seated in another section of the stadium, the observations of the sounds of spectators had been markedly different.

The observational POA of the two other case matches differs markedly from the one adopted at the Tottenham-Leicester match. In both cases, I observe the sounds from a location far away from the away supporters and I am only occasionally able to distinguish the away supporters' contribution to the production of the overall soundscape. However, at the Tottenham-Chelsea match, the sound production of the away supporters emerges distinctly when the two Chelsea goals are scored. Particularly, when the penalty goal is scored (to 0–2 by Willian in the injury time of the first half), the celebration sounds of the away supporters penetrate the soundscape significantly. Sonically, the sounds are highlighted by the absence of potentially masking sounds of the home team supporters. As Willian takes steps towards the ball at the penalty spot, most spectators seem to hold their breath, and as the ball enters the goalmouth the spectators in my and the neighbouring section express uncoordinated and rather subdued sounds of frustration and displeasure. Visually, the 'sounds are highlighted' as the source of the sounds seems to 'light up' after the goal has been scored. Already, before the scoring of the goal, the away supporters have taken on a visually distinct appearance seen from the viewpoint of my seat (highly placed at the curve in the opposite end of the stadium).

The visual appearance of the away supporters at this particular match – played in the dark late afternoon of December 22 (2019) – is thus intensified by the operation of floodlights (widely introduced at stadiums in England from the 1950s; see Steen, 2014, p. 28). It might be the case that the operation of floodlights has the effect of 'highlighting the action of the field' and that 'if the number of visual elements is reduced … the potential for enjoyment is also reduced' (Bale, 1993, p. 45). However, the experience of watching the goal scored by Willian rather suggests that the floodlights help create a state in which 'senses are heightened' (Gray, 2016, p. 57) to appreciate also sounds and visual elements outside (or in the periphery) of the perimeters of 'the field'. Because the away supporters are placed in a section close to the pitch, they are clearly illuminated by the floodlights. Moreover, by being enclosed by rows of stewards in bright yellow vests and by wearing predominately blue shirts, the away supporters stand out from both the above dark (not illuminated) sections and the adjoining sections of predominantly white-shirted spectators.

Consequently, the bodily expressions of celebrations – which from a distance appear as myriads of highly dynamic micromovements (of supporters jumping up and down with their hands in the air) – are clearly distinguishable from the inactive and inconspicuous bodily movements of the adjoining spectators. Accordingly, the sonically and visually highlighted (source of the) sounds seem to emerge as a 'ray' or 'beam of sound'. This impression is intensified by the fact that from my position – well over a hundred meters from the away supporters – the sounds 'arrive' with a 'delay' illustrating what has been generally suggested: 'Fans are spread over such a large area that acoustic delays become important' (Howard, 2004, p. 78). Thus, the myriads of micromovements are visually perceptible in a moment (for about half a second, it seems) before the distinguished sounds of roaring celebration 'hit' the section in which I am seated.

The preceding examples generally indicate that the sectioning of the stadium intensifies differences between (groups of) spectators' vocal activity and the experience hereof. Previous contributions have occasionally alluded to the existence of one big, all-inclusive group of sound-producing spectators. For example, reference has been made to spectators at football as 'one big soundbody' (Lavric, 2019, p. 2; translated by the author) and as 'many-as-one attuned to the nature of the occasion that all are in. All for one, and one for all' (Scannell, 2019, pp. 121–2). Certainly, on rare occasions, apparently and practically all spectators in the stadium might join in on a particular chant or song – for example, when opposing supporters can join in chants towards a common third-party enemy (see, e.g. Lawn, 2020, p. 196). However, such occasions arguably represent exceptions from the general tendency of the presence of more than one group of spectators as suggested by the previous examples drawn from the case material.

The examples drawn from the case material suggest, firstly, that not everyone is equally engaged in singing. This observation hints at the differentiation between (mere) spectators and the explicitly partisan and vocally supporting spectators (see, e.g. Canter et al., 1989, p. 10). Secondly, the vocally supporting spectators should be distinguished based on their partisanship. This observation hints at the differentiation between (at least) two vocally explicit, partisan groups of spectators (supporting the home or away team) – or, if one should use the previously referred to analogy to the human body, 'two antagonistic bodies' (Gumbrecht, 2019, p. 48).

Conceivably, spectators can occasionally find themselves immersed in the production of sounds to such an extent that it offers 'the impression that every person inside the stadium was singing at once' or 'feels like the whole world is singing' (Gray, 2016, p. 96). Correspondingly, it has been observed how songs and chants 'would reverberate from all around the ground at times, giving the impression that every person inside the stadium was singing at once' (Pearson, 2012, p. 67). However, these experiences are highly dependent on the given POA, and they do not seem to reflect that, regularly, from at least the 1960s in England, two opposing groups of supporters will be present (for an example of a context with no regular presence of away supporters, see Goksøyr & Hognestad, 1999, p. 208). A pertinent example of this is offered through the following observations at a match between Coventry and Tottenham Hotspur (in the 1971–2 season). After having noticed how 'the noise was deafening echoing up to the roof as they chanted it [the chant *What a Load of Scrubbers*] over and over in unison' (incidentally also exemplifying the significance of the stadium roof, mentioned previously), Davies decides to move to another section of the stadium to see if the group within which he had been located 'could be heard throughout the ground' (Davies, 1972, p. 121). Subsequently, from outside the group and from a distance, Davies observes that 'looking at them from a distance they seemed so puny. When you're with them, you fell you've taken over. But they hadn't taken over anything, just been corralled into one part of one stand and tolerated' (Davies, 1972, p. 125).

While it is of course possible to offer a more detailed differentiation of spectators – for examples based on differentiations of subgroups of home teams supporters including difference in ground locations (see, e.g. Giulianotti,

1999, p. 69; Marsh et al., 1978, p. 58) – the proposed distinction highlights the minimal yet most relevant distinction when it comes to understanding differences in spectators' production of sounds at football. Moreover, the attendance of at least two opposing groups of spectators has been considered as a basic condition for the emergence of 'atmosphere'. If ' "atmosphere" is always both warmth and distance' this points to the significance of a confrontation between opposites; therefore, 'fixtures lacking this tension of warmth and distance, perhaps were there are no "away" fans in attendance, where home fans turn up in low numbers … are said to lack this atmosphere' and 'the spatial organization of the ground … plays an important part in constructing "atmosphere" ' (Giulianotti, 1999, p. 69).

## Points in time

The examination of the sounds of spectators at football from a temporal perspective basically includes two intertwined perspectives: On the one hand, the perspective of so-called diataxis specifies 'the extensional ordering of events of durations exceeding that of the extended present' (Tagg, 2013, p. 385), and, on the other hand the perspective of syncrisis addresses the 'arrangement of structural elements inside the extended present' (Tagg, 2013, p. 417).

From the 'horizontal' perspective of diataxis it is generally characteristic of the sounds of spectators that they are ever-present during the case matches. The intensity of the sounds – in terms of the frequency and dynamics of auditory impulses – generally changes throughout the matches, as the sounds of spectators will normally wax and vane. As already observed, moments including 'auditory lacunae' emerge by the abrupt and striking contrast in sound production that results from when spectators 'hold their breath'. Also, more prolonged periods of time might be characterized by a relatively low intensity of the sounds of spectators – illustratively, previous contributions have exemplified how spectators are occasionally 'too nervous to create noise' (Pearson, 2012, p. 67) and how, when the opposing teams score a goal, 'the majority of home fans say little beyond muttering angrily under their breath' (Guschwan, 2016; see also Plenderleith, 2018).

Moments of what approximates silence among spectators can occasionally be observed right before a match, for example when requested as part of some sort of dedicatory ceremony. An example transpired in the case match between Tottenham and Leicester, where spectators remain inaudible as a trumpeter performs a rendition of *The Last Post* as part of the Remembrance Day ceremony held by all EPL clubs at matches in the week leading up to 11 November (the date of the armistice of the First World War) to commemorate members of the armed forces who have died in the line of duty. Further examples (not exemplified in the case matches) include a period of silence to commemorate a person who has recently passed away (for an example, see Robson, 2000, p. 161; this practice is sometimes substituted for a period of applauding).

Whereas short periods of silence occasionally emerge before matches, during the match examples of silence – or attempts of silencing – are few and do not clearly result in the same degree of quietness among spectators. For example, as the Japanese top division allowed (a restricted number of) spectators to attend matches during the Covid-19 pandemic under the following conditions: 'J. League side Vissel Kobe have told fans not to sing, chant or wave flags in their season-opening clash with Yokohama FC in order to help contain the spread of coronavirus' (Duerden, 2020), sounds did emerge in the form of 'an occasional crinkle of a food wrapper or a spontaneous burst of applause' (Rich, 2020). Attempts of silencing the spectators can also originate from the spectators themselves as exemplified by a 'silent protest' organized on three match days up to 12 December 2012, including spectators at all matches in the German top two divisions (Stieler et al., 2014; for further examples of self-imposed silencing among spectators, see Herd & Löfgren, 2020, p. 16; Lawn, 2020, p. 183; Uersfeld, 2018; Zalis, 2021).

From the perspective of syncrisis, most of the time the sounds produced by spectators are clearly foregrounded. Furthermore, the sounds of spectators are layered in the sense that different types of sounds emerge at the same time with a varying and normally gradually changing degree of predominance. For example, *Oh, When the Spurs Go Marchin' In* usually emerges gradually from a background of sounds which could be described as 'a simmering, skin-pinching aural fuzz' or a 'seething white noise' (Goldblatt, 2007, pp. 672, 673). The example indicates that although singing can in fact be heard throughout the match as part of the simmering background – arguably representing a continuous 'musicalization' of the soundscape (see a similar observation by Nyman in Redhead 1997, p. 71) – singing is not always predominant. Occasionally, individual or collective shouts clearly emerge in an auditory foreground as exemplified previously by a spectator's call for fellow spectators to 'sing up!'. The examples indicate how the 'seething white noise of the crowd' can indeed be 'set alight by the sparkling cries of relief, surprise and acclamation' (Goldblatt, 2007, p. 673).

The gradual emergence of *Oh, When the Spurs Go Marchin' In* exemplifies the typically gradual emergence of chants and songs compared to the usually prompter introduction of interjections and clapping. This can be partly explained by intrinsic differences between the two types of sound. Whereas the non-musical sounds of spectators in the form of interjections and clapping need no further motivation or coordination other than a specific match incident – for example, clapping 'can be achieved without a leader or centralized control' (Sumpter, 2010, p. 130) – the practice of collective singing seems to need some sort of additional coordination. Collective singing thus represents a more varied and vocally demanding type of sound: firstly, a particular song or chant must be somehow agreed upon, and secondly, the chosen chant or song must be introduced in (musical) terms of pitch and tempo – although, when it comes to the recurrent signature song (exemplified by *Oh, When the Spurs Go Marchin' In*), the coordination demands seem less urgent compared to other instances of chants and songs.

Another explanation for the gradual introduction of songs and chants is the absence (as far as can be assessed from the observations I carried out) at the case matches of the capo, which translates (from Italian) roughly to a 'leader' and allegedly originates from Italian football (Goldblatt, 2007, p. 555). A capo operates as a sort of 'conductor of the crowd-as-orchestra or choir' (Fuller, 2016, p. 7) and coordinates (often by use of a megaphone) the introduction, continuance and ending of specific collective expressions. In addition to temporally structure the expressions, the capo might engage in patterned 'call and response' sequences (as hinted at in Section 3.1) when the capo 'calls' a group of spectators by shouting out a short motif and a group of spectators 'respond' collectively to that particular call (see, e.g. Bonz, 2016, p. 152; Jirat, 2007, pp. 115–16). Also, the capo might be assisted by musical instruments. For example, it has been observed how 'fans may join in with a song which has been started by the use of a musical instrument, in particular bass drum, but also including hooters, saxophones' (Bell & Bell, 2020, p. 11; for further examples of the operation of a capo, see, e.g. Grøn & Graakjær, 2016; Lehmann & Knibbiche, 2019).

The absence in the case matches of a formalized, clearly identifiable and 'conducting' capo implies that songs and chants seem to be introduced rather spontaneously among the spectators – although certain sections of the stadium (and groups and individuals herein) are clearly more active in instigating singing than others as already illustrated by the sectioning of the away and home supporters. For example, in an English setting, the 'chant leader', usually positioned in the section behind one of the goals, has been specified as a more informal initiator of singing, and it has been observed how 'quite a lot of fans, at one point or another, succeeded in starting of chants and songs, but few could do so consistently' (Marsh et al., 1978, pp. 66, 67). Morris (1981) suggests that 'the fans are their own composers and their own conductors' (p. 252) and observes how some chants are seen to be 'triggered off ... by some kind of "internal display energy" from the terraces themselves' (Morris, 1981, p. 306). Similarly, Kopiez and Brink (1999) suggest that 'the predominant form of singing is marked by an uncontrollable spontaneity' and that singing often 'originates from small cells of two or three spectators' (as observed by a football spectator in an interview in Kopiez & Brink, 1999, pp. 51, 180; translated by the author; see also Gray, 2016, p. 95; Pearson, 2012, pp. 66–7). In the case matches, almost all observable and sustained instances of singing originate from the stands comprising the most partisan supporters, whereas sporadic and unsuccessful efforts to introduce songs can be observed in other parts of the stadium. For example, at the Tottenham-Liverpool match, on several occasions one or two spectators can be registered in my section to attempt to introduce a specific chant or song – including the otherwise popular exemplars of *Oh, When the Spurs Go Marchin' In*, *Yid Army, [clap], [clap]* and *He's One of Our Own* (to the melody of *Sloop John B*). However, as no one joins in on the singing, the attempts are soon ceased.

## Couplings

In addition to an examination of when the sounds emerge from the perspective of the initiating spectators, the introduction of sounds can be seen from the perspective of their relatedness to actions and incidents at and in the match. The sounds of spectators can thus be temporally distinguished based on the degree to which they are coupled with specific match-related incidents including the actions of performers, organizers and spectators. The sounds of spectators might occasionally emerge as coupled with incidents outside the setting of the match as exemplified by the previous example of a 'silent protest' and by the spectators' reaction to the broader political situation as examined in Irak (2021). However, there are no such examples during the case matches and based also on observations in the existing contributions they seem rather rare. The focus is thus here on couplings between the sounds of spectators and match incidents, and from this perspective three degrees of temporal couplings can be distinguished: loose coupling, moderate coupling and close coupling.

In light of the distinction offered in Morris (1981), loosely coupled singing can be considered to consist of chants and songs which are 'independent of moment-by-moment incidents on the pitch' and emerge 'seemingly of their own accord, when nothing special is occurring on the field' (p. 306) – an extreme example offered by Morris is the 'boredom chorus' which might transpire as 'deliberately irrelevant songs' when the match 'lacks excitement' (Morris, 1981, p. 307; see also Fuller, 2016). Further examples of loosely coupled sounds can be observed when the singing is motivated by a particular point in match time regardless of how the current match is progressing. For example, in Bell and Bell's (2020) study on spectators at matches including the Northern Ireland national team, this practice is observed as one of the 'significant factors which influence collective vocalisations at matches' as singing emerges 'at the beginning/end of a match' (p. 10; for further examples, see Daiber, 2015, p. 138; Lee, 2018, pp. 388–9; Power, 2011, p. 103). The case matches, as well as several observations in previous contributions, suggest that loosely coupled singing is predominant. Correspondingly, Morris (1981) observes that 'roughly 60 per cent of all chantings are unrelated to influences from the game' (p. 306). Also, the signing of *Oh, When the Spurs Go Marchin' In* exemplifies a 'loose coupling', as the song's appearances seem unrelated to specific match incidents – rather, the song appears as a general reaction to the basic condition of Tottenham playing a match.

An intermediate level of 'moderate coupling' is observed when spectators produce sounds which, on the one hand, embody a reaction to a specific incident but, on the other hand, are not in detailed synch with that incident – for example, when spectators clap to show their appreciation of a match incident just passed. Following Morris (1981), examples of singing that are moderately coupled with specific match incidents can be termed 'event-timed' (p. 306), because they emerge as a reaction to a specific 'event' (or incident) – for example, when the team 'scores/concedes goal' or is 'playing well and there is a break in play (e.g., a corner or free-kick)' as observed in Bell and Bell (2020, p. 10). In the case match between Tottenham and Liverpool, an example of a moderate coupling can be observed as the previously mentioned song *One Season Wonder* emerges as a reaction to the (second) goal scored by Harry Kane at about one minute after the goal has been scored and celebrated.

The sounds of the spectators are 'closely coupled' when they are approximately 'in synch' with the developments of specific match incidents. For example, the sudden decrease of intensity when spectators 'hold their breath' closely parallels the progression of an attempt at scoring a goal. The subsequent reaction of the spectators will likewise be synchronized in detail, as the specific moment in which the attempt at goal has succeeded (or not) will be promptly accompanied by collective interjections. While this example illustrates spectators' abrupt and highly accentuated or rhythmic production of sound, other cases of 'close couplings' exemplify a more gradual progress of the intensity of the sounds. For example, in the Tottenham-Liverpool match, when a player for Liverpool approaches the sideline from the players' bench to replace a player on the pitch, the (home-supporting) spectators produce an increasingly powerful 'boo' which culminates as the player runs onto the field – the spectators build up the intensity of the sounds to offer him (a former player of arch-rivals Arsenal, as previously mentioned) a cold reception. Another example transpires in the Tottenham-Leicester match when spectators' increased booing and whistling accompanies the away team's goalkeeper attempt to stretch the period of time used for preparing a goal kick – the majority of the spectators disapprove of this practice of 'stealing time', as they, conceivably, want the ball to be put into effective play as soon as possible so as to accelerate the action and the chances for the home team to score a goal.

Table 3.4 provides an overview of the three types of couplings. Although exceptions and ambiguous cases exist, the table indicates how collective non-musical sounds of spectators tend to be more closely coupled to actions in the stadium setting than examples of singing.

Table 3.4 Overview of Types of Couplings between the Sounds of Spectators and Match Incidents

|  | **Loose Coupling** | **Moderate Coupling** | **Close Coupling** |
| --- | --- | --- | --- |
| **Temporal Relation between the Sounds and Match Incident** | No relationship to specific match incidents | Delayed (by several seconds) response to specific match incidents | Practically synchronous |
| **Predominant Type of Sound** | Chants and songs | Chants, songs and applause | Interjections |
| **Examples** | *Oh, When the Spurs Go Marchin' In*, *Yid Army*, [clap], [clap] | *One Season Wonder*, applause after scoring a goal | Segmented collective interjections |

## 3.3 Why?

This section examines *why* spectator sounds emerge at football. By focusing on the functions of the sounds of spectators the section basically examines what the sounds 'do' and to what, for whom and in what way the sounds have significance. The section takes as its starting point the semiotic perspective of communicative factors and functions introduced by Jakobson (1960) – although the circumstances and setting of the sounds of spectators at football necessitate a broadening of Jakobson's perspective which is focused primarily on the poetic function of verbal communication from a single addresser. The sounds of spectators in the stadium setting are thus part of a 'social situation' defined as 'the full physical arena in which persons present are in sight and sound of each other' (Goffman, 1981b, p. 136). Jakobson's perspective is here adopted as a general outline – or a 'cursory description' (Jakobson, 1960, p. 357) – of communicative factors and functions which arguably 'provides a powerful framework for discussing and understanding all kinds of texts' (Danesi, 2020, p. 103). Encouragingly, the approach has been widely used and elaborated within studies on music and sound (see, e.g. Middleton, 1990, pp. 241–2), although it has hitherto only marginally inspired contributions on the sounds of spectators at football (see the reference to the phatic function in Back, 2001; see also Khodadadi & Gründel, 2006).

Jakobson specifies six 'constitutive factors' which are 'inalienably involved' in any act of communication, namely the addresser, the context, the message, the contact, the code and the addressee (Jakobson, 1960, p. 353). Each of these six factors are then shown to correlate with a function which specifies what the act of communication serves to do. Normally, any act of communication will fulfil more than one function and hence embody a 'hierarchical order of functions', and the following examination is inspired by the recommendation that acts of communication 'must be investigated in all the variety of its functions' (Jakobson, 1960, p. 353).

### The emotive function

From the perspective of communicative functions, the singing of *Oh, When the Spurs Go Marchin' In* obviously serves an expressive or 'emotive function'. The lyrics imply a focus on the addresser and serve to 'produce an impression of a certain emotion whether true or feigned' (Jakobson, 1960, p. 354). Furthermore, the singing can be seen to include a 'direct expression of the speaker's attitude toward what he is speaking about' (Jakobson, 1960, p. 354) – given that 'speaker' and 'speaking' are here substituted by 'singers' and 'singing'. During the singing of the lyrics – including the segments *Oh, when the Spurs go marchin' in* and *I want to be in that number* – each of the singers subscribes to the 'I', who 'want' to be associated with and participate in ('be in that number') the activities ('marchin' in) of the football club of 'Spurs'. Following the categorization of constellations of addresser-addressees in Lavric (2019; inspired by the participation framework offered by Goffman, 1981b; see more below), the example indicates a variant of the addresser as a 'fictious single' and 'exemplary ... fan ("I")' (Lavric, 2019, p. 20; translated by the author). Further possible addressers who are likewise able to express their attitudes and emotions include, for example, subsections of supporters and 'real fans as opposed to lukewarm associates' (Lavric, 2019, p. 19; translated by the author).

The example of *Oh, When the Spurs Go Marchin' In* illustrates how the emotive function often transpires as a significant part of the functions of the signature song. The signature song basically serves to indicate aspects of the addresser's appreciation, admiration and loyalty to the club. Comparable to the idiosyncrasy of the (individual) handwritten signature, the (collective) 'auditory signature' of the signature song embodies a distinguishing expression that confirms the supporters' presence and approval.

Also, the rhythmic shouting *Yid Army, [clap], [clap]* embodies an emotive function. Although the proportion of Tottenham supporters with a Jewish origin (implied by the term 'Yid'; see Poulton & Durrell, 2016, p. 732) is not obviously extraordinary compared to, for example, the supporters of Arsenal (see Waddington et al., 1998, p. 167), a practice has emerged of associating Tottenham supporters with a Jewish origin (see an example of a taunting chant against the perceived Jewish origin of supporters of Tottenham in Armstrong & Young, 1999, p. 192). The rhythmic shouting exemplifies a reclamation of this association by Tottenham supporters themselves, and their intentions for doing so have been found to include '*value reversal* (to transform the negative into a positive); *neutralisation* (to expunge its injurious meaning and so render it ineffective); *stigma exploitation* (to highlight the stigma)' in addition to the possibility that the term has become 'simply a football term and, in the words of one fan, a "Spurs thing"' (Poulton & Durell, 2016, p. 730). Furthermore, the emotive function appears prominently among previous contribution's categorizations of (the lyrics of) chants and songs which often serve to present spectators' positive or negative attitudes towards various referents and addressees (see, e.g. Luhrs, 2007a, 2007b; Morris, 1981, pp. 307–8).

The emotive function is also characteristic of spectators' interjections. Generally, Jakobson indicates that interjections represent the 'purely emotive stratum' in language (Jakobson, 1960, p. 354). Incidentally, the singing of *Oh, When the Spurs Go Marchin' In* includes an interjection in the form of an 'Oh' representing an '*audible glee*' as coined by Goffman (1981a, p. 106; italics in original). Further examples of interjections at football can be described as 'a natural overflowing, a flooding up of previously contained feeling, a bursting of normal restraints, a case of being caught off-guard' (Goffman, 1981a, p. 99). Such interjections transpire at football most expressively in the form of the segmented collective interjections as illustrated in Section 3.1. These sounds clearly exemplify how 'emissions from a source inform us about the state of the source' and the intensity of the 'closely coupled' sounds can be seen as 'evidence of the alignment we take to events' (Goffman, 1981a, p. 100). In contrast to the more intentional practice of the (introduction of) singing, the segmented collective interjections present 'a case of exuded expressions, not intentionally sent messages', which suggests that 'one might better refer to a "vocalizer" or "sounder" than to a speaker' (Goffman, 1981a, p. 100). The emotive functions of interjections – exemplified by the different segmented collective exemplars – furthermore illustrate how football spectatorship potentially involves the experience of a wide variety of emotions within a relatively short period of time.

The actualization of the emotive function is basically dependent on the spectators' ability to express themselves without having their production of sounds censored, prescribed or instructed (or 'spoon-fed' as referred to by Morris, 1981, p. 313) by an authority other than the spectators themselves. Such outside influence potentially deprives spectators the opportunity to establish and maintain a self-image and presentation of themselves as spontaneous, empowered and creative performers. From the perspective of the 'production format' in Goffman (1981b), the spectators are (or seek to appear as) simultaneously animators ('a body engaged in acoustic activity'), authors ('someone who has selected the sentiments and the words in which they are encoded') and principals ('someone who is committed to what the words say') (pp. 144–5). For example, it has been suggested that 'clubs pride themselves on the originality of their lyrics and the breadth of their repertoires' (O'Brien, 2020, p. 121). The existing contributions provide numerous examples of spectators' attitude towards and reactions against being 'pushed' towards producing (or not) specific sounds at specific times and places. For example, Arsenal Football Club attempted to provide its supporters with 'an "approved songbook" from which their fans could select chants'; however, the book 'contained no profanities or songs that abused local rivals Tottenham Hotspurs' and the 'songbook, or the idea of having one never caught on' (Lawn, 2014, n.p.). Another example illustrates a more implicit attempt by the organizers to encourage spectators to (co)produce sound:

> A simulated artificial crowd noise was transmitted over a large speaker at the back of the North Stand. The mass of supporters behind the goal were not subsequently invoked to sing or generate noise which was perhaps the perceived intended outcome, rather responded with sheer bewilderment leading some fans to register official complaints with the club. (Turner, 2017, p. 121; for further examples, see Morris, 1981, p. 315; Powis & Carter, 2019, p. 396)

## The conative function

The 'conative function' denotes an 'orientation towards the addressee' and finds 'its purest grammatical expression in the vocative and imperative' (Jakobson, 1960, p. 355). The chant *Come on You Spurs* exemplifies an act of communication which obviously includes a connotative function as it addresses the 'You' of 'Spurs' (arguably designating both the performers and supporters of Spurs) who are encouraged to 'Come on', that is, to join in and engage themselves further in the match and the support. Also, the individual shouting of 'sing up!' at the Tottenham-Liverpool match referred to previously exemplifies the conative function.

The conative function is also relevant from the perspective of previous contribution's categorizations of (the lyrics of) chants and songs. For example, the categorization of Luhrs (2007a, 2007b) indicates how 'integrative' chants and songs are usually directed towards members of – and aspects pertaining to – the in-group (the club, the players and managers, the location and the supporters themselves). From this perspective, *Oh, When the Spurs Go Marchin' In* represents an example of an 'integrative club chant' (Luhrs, 2007a, p. 260), and the song thus includes aspects of the conative function as well. So-called 'divisive' chants and songs are, for their part, usually directed towards members of – and aspects pertaining to – an out-group (the club, the players and managers, the location, the away supporters, the referee and the police) – although the category of 'Criticism of

Home Club' suggested by Morris (1981, p. 309) exemplifies how home supporters' animosity can sometimes be directed at the home team. Additionally, although not exemplified by the case matches and the existing categorizations (e.g. Lavric, 2019; Luhrs, 2007a, 2007b; Morris, 1981), examples can be offered of spectators targeting the media personnel (Robson, 2000, p. 181), the television audience (Thrills, 1998, p. 130) and political authorities (Irak, 2021; Jack, 2021; Power, 2011). From the perspective of Goffman (1981b), these examples illustrate that any utterance or act of communication on behalf on the spectators will not just include an 'addressed recipient' but also 'unaddressed recipients', that is 'the rest of the "official hearers", who may or may not be listening' (Goffman, 1981b, p. 133).

A further dimension of a conative function of *Oh, When the Spurs Go Marchin' In* can be identified if the song is seen as a musical performance to and for the performing spectators themselves – this would imply a broadening of Jakobson's (1960) focus on non-musical acts of communication between a distinctive addresser and addressee. Musically, the function is partly reliant on the rather simple, cantabile melody, exemplifying how the conative function can 'also be associated with ... "imperative" rhythms, which set bodies moving in specific ways, and, in a general sense, with mechanisms of identification whereby listener's self-image is built into the music' (Middleton, 1990, p. 242). Lyrically, the spectators can be heard to communicate to themselves a message that they already know, thereby embodying an 'I-I' direction of communication and thus an overlap of the addresser and the addressee (Lotman, 1990, pp. 20–1). Such examples of autocommunication are said to be 'connected with a very wide range of cultural functions' including 'a sense of ... existence' and 'self-discovery' (Lotman, 1990, p. 29). The supporters' awareness that the song is heard by a great number of attending unaddressed recipients – for example, the opposing team's players and supporters, referees and the television audience – (re)affirms the supporters' existence and adds to the establishment and intensity of their self-esteem. It might be argued that spectators in this case 'seek some response from those who can hear ... but not a specific reply' (Goffman, 1981b, p. 136).

## The referential function

The 'referential function' indicates 'a set ... towards the referent, an orientation toward the context' or 'someone or something spoken of' (Jakobson, 1960, pp. 353, 355). Although in 'numerous messages' it is 'the leading task' (Jakobson, 1960, p. 353), the singing of *Oh, When the Spurs Go Marchin' In* indicates that the referential function is not always the predominate one. Obviously, the singing of *Oh, When the Spurs Go Marchin' In* includes aspects of the referential function through the critical reference to the football club of 'Spurs' (as opposed to, e.g., the 'reds' or the 'Saints', as exemplified previously) as well as the stated activity of 'marching'. Moreover, an orientation towards the context is implied when acknowledging that the song represents an adaption and emerges as a signature song. Usually, the referential function is an implied part of the criteria for establishing categories of chants and songs. For example, the previously mentioned categories rely on the differentiation of a referent – or a 'someone' – who is 'spoken of' (or 'sung about') in a way which usually both expresses the attitudes and emotions of the sender (the emotive function) and appeals to a certain reaction on behalf of the addressee (the conative function).

However, the referential function is not confined to verbal communication and the lyrics of songs and chants. For example, the various forms of 'couplings' (see Section 3.2) include aspects of the referential function, because the sounds refer – with varying degrees of temporal precision – to circumstances and incidents at/in the match. Some of these sounds are clearly coded as they usually reflect the (mis)fortunes of the involved teams through their intensity, type (e.g. 'Yeah' or 'Oh') and locational origin (e.g. among the home or away supporters). The function is operative most obviously when the sounds of spectators refer to incidents that other spectators have not noticed. For example, the increased booing at the Tottenham-Liverpool match potentially informs that something to the dissatisfaction of the home team supporters is happening at the match (i.e. a preparation of a substitution of a former Arsenal player) even though the Tottenham team is doing well, is in ball control and attacking (which would normally not result in booing). Also, the sounds of spectators might include information on the progression of match incidents even for those who cannot see the match – they might be visually impaired (as referred to in the introduction) and/or positioned in a service section of the stadium or even outside the stadium: 'People who live near football arenas ... can guess what is happening in the game through sound: the crowd uproar means the home team scored; silence means it lost the match' (Marra, 2021, p. 41).

## The poetic and metalingual functions

Compared with the referential function's relevance in terms on *what* is being communicated, the 'poetic function' highlights the significance of *how* an act of communication is structured and performed: 'The set (*Einstellung*) toward the message as such, focus on the message for its own sake, is the poetic function of language' (Jakobson, 1960, p. 356; italics in original). While the poetic function is usually dominant in verbal art, 'in all other verbal activities it acts as a subsidiary, accessory constituent' (Jakobson, 1960, p. 356). The substitution of 'Saints' (of the original lyrics) for 'Spurs' embodies aspects of a poetic function. The substitution implies that some aspects of the original (sound of the) word is maintained while others have changed. 'Spurs' echoes the basic structure of 'Saints' by representing a one-syllable word which begins and ends with the same letter; however, 'Spurs' includes only one vowel (as opposed the diphthong or gliding vowel of 'Saints') as well as a bilabial plosive ('p') at the beginning of the word. Arguably, 'Spurs' holds the potential of a more distinct performance as the bilabial plosive allows for a highly air-pressured and rhythmically marked introduction of a fixed and clear vowel sound. Consequently, inspired by the example of a verbal substitution which 'just sounds smoother' (Jakobson, 1960, p. 357), 'Spurs' could appear to sound 'tighter' than 'Saints'. Incidentally, this might help explain why the song has emerged extensively among the supporters of Tottenham Hotspur even though the song has a closer (verbatim and historical) association to Southampton Football Club.

The example illustrates that generally the poetic function can be seen to emerge as part of the production of contrafactums. For example, rearrangements of the lyrics of a specific song – usually involving the 'two basic modes of arrangement used in verbal behaviour, *selection* and *combination*' (Jakobson, 1960, p. 358; italics in original) – can include metaphors (see, e.g. Argan et al., 2020; McKerrell, 2021), humour and self-irony (see, e.g. Herd & Löfgren, 2020, p. 19). This is often established by reference to aspects of the context in which the contrafactum emerges and/or to aspects of the relation between the (original) melody and the rearranged (or added) text – as observed by Morris (1981): 'This contrast between style and content, in which sweet ballads are sometimes employed to convey a message of death and mutilation to the enemy, adds considerably to the formalized nature of the whole performance and enhances its ritual atmosphere' (p. 307).

At football, most examples of spectator sounds are not regularly and primarily incorporating a 'metalingual function', that is: 'Whenever the addresser and/or the addressee need to check up whether they use the same code, speech is focused on the code: it performs a metalingual (i.e., glossing) function' (Jakobson, 1960, p. 356) – Jakobson furthermore specifies the metalingual function from the perspective of a distinction between two levels of language, that is, '"Object language" speaking of objects and "metalanguage" speaking of language' (Jakobson, 1960, p. 356). However, the function is arguably operative in cases where spectators are 'singing about singing' (if not exactly 'speaking of language'). For example, when chanting (*You only) Sing when You're Winning* to the tune of *Guantanamera*, the spectators hint at a code of singing: when and why to sing and the meaning of singing as such. Specifically, the song taunts the opposing fans (implicating also the conative function) for their lack of support and engagement when, for example, their team has conceded a goal (see, e.g. Warner, 2011).

## The phatic function

The contact or 'phatic function' (a term inspired by Malinowski) denotes a 'physical channel and psychological connection between the addresser and the addressee, enabling both of them to enter and stay in communication' (Jakobson, 1960, p. 353). Jakobson furthermore specifies that 'there are messages primarily serving to establish, to prolong, or to discontinue communication, to check whether the channel works ("Hello, do you hear me?"), to attract the attention of the interlocutor, or to confirm his continued attention ("Are you listening?")' (Jakobson, 1960, p. 356). The phatic function is usually part of chants and songs oriented towards a designated addressee. Essentially, these chants and songs include an attempt to connect with the addressee by attracting and maintaining the addressees' attention and awareness of the message – be it in the form of praise and support or animosity. However, the sounds of spectators might serve the function to disrupt and 'discontinue communication' (as suggested in the previously referred to quote by Jakobson). For example, whereas chants and songs include words, 'when produced by a crowd, these words develop an additional power, that of noise, which shifts or doubles the work of words with a non-referential dimension … it disturbs perception, it does not "mean"' (Trail, 2013, p. 320). The sounds of spectators can thus emerge also as a 'sonic phenomenon mustered to attack the referential and symbolic, opening a dimension of sound production that is not *for* communication, but rather to shut it down' (Trail, 2013, p. 320; italics in original). For example, the spectators' production of sounds holds the potential to 'shut down' the opposing supporters' communication of support to their preferred team as well as their animosity towards the opposing participants. For example, it has been observed how 'at every game, fans compete to be the loudest, cleverest and most passionate supporters and to defend the honour of their team against their rivals' (Guschwan, 2016, p. 291).

While the preceding examples have focused on addresser-addressee constellations, the phatic function of the sounds of spectators might also be seen from an intragroup perspective. Such a perspective could be seen as a form of – and as a potential to refine the understanding of – the so-called 'intra-audience effects' which refer to 'reactions spectators have to other spectators' and which arguably represent 'a major factor contributing to the excitement, the arousal, and ultimately the entertainment value that result from sports spectatorship' (Hocking, 1982, pp. 100–1). An intragroup perspective has already been hinted at through the autocommunicative function of singing, but the sounds of spectators arguably include functions beyond communication which consequently reside 'close to the limits of a semiotic approach' as they 'have less to do with meaning than with processes in themselves, less with signs than with *actions*' (Middleton, 1990, p. 243; italics in original). The perspective is here introduced as a supplement to the perspective of Jakobson (1960), and it is inspired by the suggestion that 'the phatic function is the leader' when music performs the task of 'creating solidarity' (Middleton, 1990, p. 253). Also, the pertinence of non-communicational intragroup functions has been hinted at in existing contributions. For example, it has been suggested that songs and chants can be 'meaningful *beyond* text and *beyond* genealogy' (Herrera, 2018, p. 472; italics in original), and that spectators' production of sound is part of a 'ritualization' in which 'participation is focused less upon saying/describing anything than activating a state of being' (Robson, 2000, p. 171; see also Hoy, 1994, p. 24).

Some of the existing contributions seem to suggest that non-communicational functions are typical of certain type of chants and songs. For example, Morris (1981) establishes a specific category of 'atmospheric chants … concerned with creating an atmosphere without any specific message being transmitted' (p. 315). In a similar vein, Robson (2000) offers a binary distinction between so-called 'saying songs' which 'contain explicit discursive messages' and 'doing songs' 'bereft … of instrumental semantic elements' and representing a 'renunciation of propositional discourse in favour of illocutionary force' (p. 177). Furthermore, Back et al. (2001) suggest that 'mass singing of club anthems possessed a phatic quality, it revealed shared feelings and established an atmosphere of sociability rather than communication … they were not about conversation, rather they were about being affective' (p. 49).

Possibly, certain structures and practices of chants and songs can be considered to gravitate towards representing acts of communication more (or less) than others. For example, in the Tottenham-Liverpool match, the communicative functions of the moderately coupled song *One Season Wonder* seem generally more pronounced when compared to the communicative functions of the loosely coupled *Oh, When the Spurs Go Marchin' In*. This might indicate that non-communicational intragroup functions are particularly associated with the recurrent signature song or 'club anthem' as referred to in the quote above (for a similar case, see Gumbrecht, 2021, p. 73).

However, all instances of collective singing arguably hold the potential to serve non-communicational functions when the experience of collective singing is seen as 'an oscillation (and sometimes as an interference) between "presence effects" and "meaning effects"' (Gumbrecht 2004, p. 2); while the latter highlights processes of interpretation and communication, the former specifies our relations with 'things in the world' which 'have an immediate impact' (Gumbrecht, 2004, xiii) with respect to bodily and sensory experiences. At football, presence effects will emerge collectively when (sections of the) spectators develop a type of sociability or form of assembly referred to as 'mystical bodies' incorporating 'a sense of communal elation … out of the transitive attention of laterally associated individuals on a physical event' (Gumbrecht, 2021, p. 78). In attempting to explain the emergence of 'mystical bodies', Gumbrecht points to 'rhythms' and 'intensity'.

Rhythms 'can give the crowd its temporal form', and while 'the singing of fans is particularly effective' (Gumbrecht, 2021, p. 89), collective rhythms can also be produced through shouting and clapping (as examined in Section 3.1). The significance of collectively produced rhythms arguably relies on the capacity of humans to establish 'interactional synchrony' which 'suggests the sharing of emotion' (McParland, 2009, p. 121) or, similarly, 'muscular bonding' (McNeill, 1995) which 'can endow groups with strong senses of solidarity' (Herrera, 2018, p. 482). In defining the origins and characteristics of intensity, Gumbrecht highlights the crowd's 'pent up movement' and argues that the 'transitive perception of certain movements on the playing field … can lead to explosions of intensity' and that 'dramatic developments within a game release energy, thanks to the lateral presence of many bodies' (Gumbrecht, 2021, pp. 82–3).

Like the significance of others for the potential positive consequences of autocommunication, Gumbrecht (2021) suggests that the sense of communal elation is heightened by the 'awareness of the opposing fans' who 'contributes to the process of intensity' and 'triggers a paradoxical simultaneity of aggressive impulses along with the desire to withdraw into our own collective body' (p. 84). This suggestion echoes the previously proposed precondition for the emergence of 'atmospheres', that is, the attendance of two opposing groups of spectators (see Section 3.2). If 'atmosphere is what relates objective factors and constellations of the environment with my bodily feeling in that environment' (Böhme, 2017, p. 1), then the experience of rhythms and intensity can help not only to discriminate and reinforce the opposition between spectators. The experience also indicates ways in which 'objective factors' and 'constellations' relate to spectators' 'bodily feelings'. Correspondingly, atmospheres at football are typically described from the perspectives of intensity and emotional valence. For examples of the former, atmospheres have been reported to be generally 'lacking' (Armstrong & Young, 1999, p. 211), 'in continuing decline' (Power, 2011, p. 102) and 'electric' (Hoy, 1994, p. 296). As regards emotional valence, atmospheres have been described as 'fervent' (Robson, 2000, p. 181), 'joyful … carnivalesque' (Knijnik, 2016, p. 472), 'cold' (Marra & Trotta, 2019, p. 87), 'toxic' (Robinson & Clegg, 2019, p. 300) and 'intimidating and threatening' (Clark 2006, p. 500).

Atmospheres and communal elations at football are arguably potentially satisfying as they offer 'rituals of presence in an environment that has almost systematically done away with such things' (Gumbrecht, 2019, p. 44). Similarly, Scannell (2019) suggests that the 'the many-as-one is … one of the greatest shared experiences that is available to us … being attuned, being given over to the event as a common, collective shared, unforgettable experience' (p. 121). Obviously, the emergence of atmospheres at football relies on numerous additional, mutually influencing factors (see, e.g. Canter et al., 1989, p. 127; Edensor, 2015; Uhrich & Benkenstein, 2010), but the present perspective highlights the functions and capacity of the sounds of spectators to establish and reinforce rhythms, intensity, communal elation and an opposition between groups of spectators.

Singing and other forms of musical sounds produced by spectators (e.g. rhythmic clapping and shouts) might seem particularly significant when it comes to the production of rhythms, intensity, communal elation and atmospheres. However, some of the collective interjections are also highly relevant in this respect. Clearly, they can be rhythmical and implicate a temporal ordering of the crowd. Also, by comparison with the typically loosely or moderately coupled chants and songs, some examples of collective interjections are closely coupled with 'certain movements on the field' and 'dramatic developments' – thereby, interjections can be considered to contribute significantly to bring forth an experience of collectively focused intensity. Also, arhythmical interjections are significant; arguably,

> the most intense and significant form of verbal activity engaged in by fans at a football match is not even the chant, but the wordless or semi-articulate cheer: an activity at once expressive and affective, but without *meaning* as such. (Gilbert, 2004, p. 11; italics in original)

The collective, arhythmical clapping and interjections of jubilation embody a kind of 'sensory buzz' constituted by the intensity and pervasiveness of myriads of impulses throughout the stadium – similar to fizzing sound from the myriad of bursting bubbles produced by sparkling wine being poured in a vessel (Graakjær, 2021b) – with the possible effect of evoking the sensation of what is popularly described as bodily goosebumps. Fittingly, the sociologist Émile Durkheim offered the concept of 'collective effervescence' (1912/2001, 157) to account for the heightened arousal – or communal elation – associated with certain forms of group-based interaction.

4

# The setting of the televised broadcast

This chapter presents an exploration of the sounds of spectators in the televised broadcast. In mirroring the structure of Chapter 3, the exploration begins by focusing on the structures (representing a reply to the question of 'what'?) of the sounds, whereas aspects of the distribution and significance (representing replies to the question of 'where and when?' and 'why?', respectively) will be discussed subsequently.

## 4.1 What?

This section offers a reply to the question: What sounds appear in the televised broadcast? The section concentrates on the sounds of spectators, but it will also include a presentation of other types of sounds among which the sounds of spectators emerge. The focus is restricted to the sounds from what could be termed the 'complete coverage' (Goldlust, 1987, p. 86) or the 'live sports coverage' (Milne, 2016, p. 146) of the football match – representing a case of 'actuality sportv' (Goldsmith, 2013, p. 59) – and other forms of televised sports presentations are opted out (for an overview of alternative forms of sports programming, see Goldsmith, 2013; Milne, 2016, pp. 146–7). Consequently, when compared to the four audio components of the live televised broadcast suggested by Goldlust (1987, p. 91), the overview excludes the sounds of pre-prepared (pre- and post-match) programming, hereunder the music which accompanies the titles sequences and credits. Instead, the overview includes the components of commentary and so-called 'international sound' – a term used to account for 'the "natural" sound emanating from the stadium event itself' that can 'provide the home viewer with some sense of the sounds and noises experienced by the spectator in the stadium' (Goldlust, 1987, p. 91).

The typology and subsequent examination of the sounds is based on the characteristics of the empirical material. Generally, the distributed sounds are influenced by the setting in which the empirical material has been obtained and examined, because 'if you see a Premier League match outside the UK then you will be watching a PLP output' (Milne, 2016, p. 62). PLP – that is, Premier League Production, set up in 2004 and operated by IMG sports Media – 'receives a clean feed (match coverage minus Sky Sports and BT sport commentators, graphics and other embellishments such as the station identification)' (Milne, 2016, p. 65) which is in turn made available for the extensive number of Premier League international licensees around the world; for example, 'at the start of the 2013–2014 season, Premier League Production delivered content to Premier League Licensees in 212 different territories' (Milne, 2016, p. 61). The distributers in the Danish setting (the channels 6'eren and YouSee) are thus examples and representatives of international licensees which offer a personalised – or 'channelized' – version to their Danish audience including commentators in the Danish language. This situation implies that the Danish commentators have no influence on the production of the visuals during the match the way that Sky Sports and BT sport commentators seem to have. For example, during the Tottenham-Leicester match, conceivably influenced by the verbal focus of the local commentators, the camera focuses for a considerable period of time (approximately six seconds) on representatives of the Leicester club owners; in the Danish broadcast, the commentators do however not refer to anything related to this specific visual focus at any point in time.

This particular process of production and distribution of the empirical material implies that the examination cannot take into account what has reportedly been made possible in some other settings, namely the audiences' potential interaction with the televised broadcast; for example, 'BskyB' digital service … has a facility that allows viewers to choose their own camera angles and frames … As a Premier League game is being played, viewers can edit the coverage while placing bets in incidents in the game' (Schirato, 2007, p. 132). Also, a number of experiments have been performed to test how the user might be able to navigate and create their own unique soundscape when watching a match – for example, Mann et al. (2013) explore the potential of enabling the viewer to choose the audio balance between the crowd and the commentators, and Oldfield et al. (2015) test how to allow users to navigate the (soundscape of the) match based on the detection, extraction and localization of ball-kicks and whistle-blows. The present examination will however concentrate on an exploration of the case matches based on the 'end product' of the channelized Danish versions.

Based on these premises, Table 4.1 provides an overview of sounds in televised football including two main types which I term 'football television sounds' and 'televised sounds at football'. 'Televised sounds at football' basically include the three subtypes of 'sounds at football' already presented as part of Table 3.1 in Section 3.1). The category thereby also includes the previously referred to international sound, and the sounds of this category are representative of the clean feed, which appears identical across international settings. Typically, this part of the broadcast soundscape differs only marginally across international settings in cases (like the present ones) where the international broadcasters have their own commentators present in the stadium – as the commentators' microphones are also operative in capturing the sounds of the stadium event (e.g. the sounds of spectators), the specific placement of the commentators' microphones in the stadium press section influences the soundscape (illustrating the significance of spatiality, as examined in Section 3.2). While this category of sounds is also available to the spectators in the stadium setting, the televised representation of the sounds influences the sounds' structure, distribution and significance. Table 4.1 attempts to indicate this by illustrating how the sounds are embedded within the distribution of the football television sounds.

| *Football television sounds* | | |
|---|---|---|
| Sound creators | Television production team(s) | |
| | Commentators | Sound designers |
| Examples | Speech | Music, sonic signals |

| *Televised sounds at football* | | | |
|---|---|---|---|
| Sound creators | Participants at the venue | | |
| | Performers | Spectators | Organizers (PA system) |
| Examples | Speech, object sounds | Music, speech, object sounds | Speech, music |

**Table 4.1** Overview of Sounds from the Televised Broadcast of Football

The sounds at football distributed by the televised broadcast thus differ markedly when compared to their original appearance in the physical setting of the stadium. Accordingly, the televised broadcast has long been seen as a constructed version of the actual match; for example, 'the televised version of the game has its own structures, its own unity, and provides points of reference and emphases which are unique to the medium event' (Williams, 1977, p. 139), and television 'does not simply *transmit* a sporting event; it carefully *constructs* it' (Siegel, 2007, p. 189; italics in original). However, whereas the constructed version of the televised broadcast has been examined from the perspectives of visual and verbal creations of narratives, dramas, discourses and ideologies (see, e.g. Goldlust, 1987, p. 87), spectator sounds have not been subjected to systematic examination in this respect – which further exemplifies the general inattention to sounds in existing textual contributions on televised football (see Section 2.2). Consequently, if it is the case that 'TV does not merely make available to many more pairs of eyes in faraway places than those in the sporting arena can see for themselves: it *transforms* what they can see' (Crisell, 2006, p. 103; italics in original), the present section examines how the broadcast transforms what the television audience 'can hear'.

'Football television sounds' indicate the sounds of the broadcast which appear as a creation of a television production team and hence originate from the television channel. Following Williams (1977), football television sounds can be seen as the auditory part of the 'medium event' which supplements and includes both the 'game' and 'stadium events' to establish the 'total telecast' (p. 135). While the televised sounds at football are practically identical across international settings (by representing the clean feed) – although the specific placement of the commentators within the stadium can influence what the commentators' microphones pick up from the surrounding spectators, as already hinted at (and see more below) – football television sounds represent additional sounds which differ across international settings depending on the sound production of the given television channel. Football television sounds include the subtypes of commentary (obviously in the form of verbal sounds) and musical sound signals – or 'stings' defined as examples of a 'brief musical or visual insert or punctuation' (Holland, 2017, p. 297) – which accompany the occasional, superimposed graphical announcement of a goal scored in another match relevant to the one being watched (e.g. because the other match is part of the same league). Incidentally, the sliding 'bumpers' that frame the visual introduction of slow-motion replays (see the visual shots 3 and 5 in Table 4.2) are not accompanied by sound.

Football television sounds are made available only to the audience of the televised broadcast and as such they are not a regular, public feature of the soundscape at the stadium during the match. This does of course not rule out the possibility that some spectators might keep 'an ear' to the progress of other, simultaneously played football matches via personal mobile technology. However, spectators are not collectively and publicly able to access the sounds from the televised broadcast, because, although the in-stadium jumbotrons tap into the broadcast television feed for their visuals during the case matches, they do not do so for its audio (see also Siegel, 2007, p. 191). Therefore, if it seems reasonable to argue that 'the experience of watching top level football in stadia filled with giant screens has become more mediated' (Whannel, 2014, pp. 773–4), this experience is most pronounced before, in between the two halves and after the actual match when the jumbotrons offer an audiovisual flow of various texts. Consequently, whereas the visual redistribution of the televised broadcast in the stadium setting 'complexifies this picture by multiplying Williams' embedded layers to the point that they resemble nothing so much as a set of Chinese boxes' (Siegel, 2007, p. 195), Williams's perspective is still applicable when it comes to an understanding of the distribution of sounds.

**Table 4.2** Overview of a Selection of Shots from the Live Televised Broadcast of Tottenham-Leicester Match (on 6'eren, 29 October 2016)

| Visual shot | Time | Visual contents | Commentators (1 and 2) | Sounds of spectators |
|---|---|---|---|---|
| 1 | 23:51 | The camera, situated high in the middle of the grandstand, presents a real time, panning long shot of the movement of the ball. The shot captures the ball possession and build up by the home team and it ends by showing an attempt to score a goal by the player Victor Wanyama. | (1) *Rose, once again he is on the attack, that's a nice cross.* *Son picks up the ball, tries to serve it up for himself.* *Then here comes Wanyama and takes over.* | From the outset of the shot, scattered and indistinct shouting, clapping and singing emerge. Then, towards the end, the sound level increases and culminates in a collective outburst of disappointment. |

(*continued*)

**Table 4.2** Overview of a Selection of Shots from the Live Televised Broadcast of Tottenham-Leicester Match (on 6'eren, 29 October 2016) (continued)

| Visual shot | Time | Visual contents | Commentators (1 and 2) | Sounds of spectators |
|---|---|---|---|---|
| 2 | 24:00 | The camera, now situated in a lower angle, presents a real-time panning medium close-up shot of Victor Wanyama running back to his original midfield position. | (2) *Yes, it is excellent. They have been successful, I think, in changing the play from one side to the other, Tottenham.* | Forceful applause. |
| 3 | 24:05 | On a white background, a dark blue lion's head (a part of the Premier League logo) slides across the screen. | | |
| 4 | 24:06 | The camera, situated high in the stand behind the goal, presents a slow-motion, panning medium long shot of the movement of the ball. The shot captures the attempt to score a goal also shown at the end of shot 1 (see above). | (2) *Now, also an attempt at goal has happened, but they have been shooting at goal from outside the penalty area.* | The applause gradually transforms into disapproving booing and whistling, and the sound level further increases. |
| 5 | 24:13 | On a white background, a dark blue lion's head (a part of the Premier League logo) slides across the screen. | | |
| 6 | 24:14–24:21 | The camera, situated high in the grandstand, presents a real-time, panning medium close-up shot of the referee moving while being followed and questioned by one of the away team players. | | The disapproving booing and whistling continues while a two-note chant emerges. |

## 4.2 Where and when?

Basically, apart from the (rarely appearing) studio- and superimposed sonic signals, the sounds from the televised broadcast of football offer the audience a sense of an 'auditory access' to the stadium setting. The sounds thus somehow assist in generating a sense of 'being there from a distance' (inspired by Rowe & Baker, 2012, p. 305), illustrating how television can be viewed as ' "a medium-that-channels" that which is out of reach' (Siegel, 2007, p. 188).

Obviously, the televised distribution of sounds implies a positioning of the audience which differs markedly from the position of spectators attending the match in the stadium setting. While each spectator occupies a unique position or POA within the stadium setting – a position which may not be very different from the position of spectators in the neighbouring seats but which is nevertheless unique and considerably different when compared to most other spectators in the stadium – there is not normally a differentiation of POAs among the televised audience (although this might possibly change as indicated by the previously mentioned experiments). The listening position made available through the televised broadcast is only comparable to the various POAs in the stadium setting in the general sense of being largely fixed throughout the match (depending on the possible mobility of the spectator in the stadium setting). Compared to each possible POA in the stadium setting which implicates a sense of distance and directionality, the soundscape of the televised broadcast does not offer such impressions – at least, this seems to be the case of the production of the case matches and the examination of the sounds based on a television set with integrated speakers.

As the sounds of the commentators appear in an auditory foreground, it could appear as if the audience is positioned close the commentators, who are apparently at the stadium themselves. Specifically, the voices of the commentators (who are invisible throughout the broadcast of the match) could 'seem to emanate … somewhere *close behind* and to the sides of the television viewer. It is as if the viewer were an eavesdropper on two magnificently informed experts and fellow fans, just outside his field of vision' (Morse, 1983, p. 53; italics in original). This impression is furthered by the fact that, occasionally, sounds from other spectators clearly transpire through the commentator's microphone, and this offers the audience an experience comparable to the experience of overhearing shouts of neighbouring spectators in the stadium setting (as exemplified by the example of a spectator's attempt to influence fellow spectators to sing up; see Section 3.1). For example, during the Tottenham-Liverpool match, a child can be heard shouting from what appears to be a position very close to the commentators' microphones: 'Come on!' This exemplifies how the exact position of the commentators' microphones in the stadium setting influences the soundscape of the different international broadcasts when broadcasters have their commentators present within the stadium.

A further (and unusual, it seems) example is provided by the broadcast of a match at the African Nations Cup in 2006 in which the soundscape of BBC's coverage was significantly influenced and disrupted by a drummer 'about ten feet from Mark Fisher's commentary point' – consequently, throughout the match, the commentators were 'frequently the wrong side of audible' (Smith, 2006). Interestingly, Eurosport's coverage of the same match was not affected by the drummer, which could indicate that the commentators were either 'in another part of the ground' or in 'another part of the world' – the latter would exemplify an absence of sounds sourced from the commentators' microphones (Smith, 2006). Incidentally, the case indicates that implications of distance and direction also pertain to the placement of the commentators in the stadium setting: 'A balance needed to be struck with the position of the microphones, too close to the crowd risked being able to pick up individual voices, with the broadcasting of bad language a possible consequence; too far, and the feeling of "being there" would have been removed' (Mann et al., 2013, p. 13).

## Sound sourcing

Compared to the possible and occasional sense of placement offered through the sounds sourced from the commentators' microphones, the sounds of spectators do not offer a clear sense of distance other than appearing in the background to the voices of the commentators. For example, when *Oh, When the Spurs Go Marchin' In* emerges in the televised broadcast, the sounds cannot be located in terms of either their proximal or lateral origin within the stadium setting. Moreover, regularly and without any obvious relation to how the game is proceeding (e.g. where the ball is at), the televised soundscape includes performer sounds in the form of, for example, the ball being stroked by the players. This implies, somewhat paradoxically, that the far-away television audience is offered a more intimate auditory contact with specific match incidents than are most of the spectators in the stadium setting.

The televised broadcast thus generally offers a composite soundscape that does not, for example, position the audience as listening from one identifiable POA. Instead, the broadcast can be considered to offer the audience access to a 'zone of audition' (inspired by Chion, 1994, p. 90) constituted by several different, yet simultaneously accessible POAs including sound sources which appear both relatively far away and at close range – exemplifying, respectively, the 'observational POA' and the 'active POA' as coined by Høier (2012). Apparently, based on the available insights into the processes of production, this blend of POAs corresponds to the use of microphones within the stadium setting. To give an example focused on the production of performer and spectator sounds, an 'ambitious example of miking a soccer game' has been demonstrated to represent 'an audio mix' comprised of sounds obtained from at least seventeen microphones (Wittek, 2013). Expectedly, this number illustrates an increase of microphones in use – for example, a previous study has indicated that 'a mixture of five sound sources was used' (Williams, 1977, p. 136). However, the development of use of microphones is not as well described as the historical increase of cameras at football – for example, whereas Milne (2016, p. 44) exemplifies the increase in the use of cameras, no such information is provided regarding the uses of microphones.

Based on the textual structure of the sounds and available descriptions of production processes, it seems reasonable to suggest, though, that at least the following types of microphones are operational: main microphones 'placed in a centralized location' and 'often suspended from the roof', ambience spot microphones 'placed in front of the spectator sections' and so-called shotgun microphones (possibly supported by parabolic reflectors) which, with the 'sharpest possible directionality', can add a 'hyper-real, exaggerated loudness and clarity of sound' by 'picking up the sound of the ball' (Wittek, 2013; see also Oldfield et al., 2015; Owens, 2021, p. 100). As regards the latter type of microphone, a 'typical microphone setup' for the EPL has been said to include '12 highly directed shotgun microphones' arranged around the pitch – also, whereas the 'ambient crowd noise' (i.e. the sounds of spectators, following the present terminology) embodies a 'static surround signal', the shotgun microphones are 'panned to the front of the mix' as an engineer is responsible during the match for 'raising and lowering' the signals according to play so that only those microphones picking up sound near to the action are active at a given point in time (Oldfield et al., 2015, pp. 2718–19). This use of microphones seems to illustrate how sports broadcasting is no longer 'always in aural long shot' as once argued by Chion (1994, p. 160) – actually, in the case matches, there is a continuous inclusion of aural 'close up shots'. The case matches do not observably offer further close-up performer sounds. Such sounds could, in principle, be made available through so-called 'lavaliere' microphone clipped unto clothing – thereby offering the audience an individual POA (as coined by Høier, 2012) – or placed, for example, on the goal posts similar to its common use 'on basketball back-boards to pick up the sounds of the ball hitting the hoop or the sound of the ball going through the hoop' (Owens, 2021, p. 103). However, there is no indication of such practices assessed against the soundscape of the televised case matches.

The composite soundscape of the televised broadcast thus includes a complex mixture of different sound sources: superimposed, foregrounded sounds 'from the studio' (the sonic signals); foregrounded sounds of the commentators from a specific, permanent location inside the stadium; 'middle grounded' sounds of performers (striking the ball) from specific, changing locations on the field; and backgrounded sounds of spectators from a variety of unspecific locations all around the stadium stands. Consequently, from the perspective of the available sounds, the television audience is offered a privileged access to the match compared to the spectators in the stadium setting: The soundscape of the broadcast includes types of sounds (i.e. performer sounds) not accessible to most spectators in the stadium setting, and it offers a wide-ranging sourcing of the sounds of spectators from all around the stadium setting. However, the facts that the televised sounds of spectators comprise a blend of the sounds of spectators from all around the stadium, reside in an auditory background and lack locational specificity imply that especially the chants and songs emerge differently and deficiently compared to their appearance to spectators in the stadium setting. Firstly, television viewers are not positioned to appreciate the spatial dimension of the sounds of spectators in terms of offering 'a sense of (being) placed'. Secondly, and related thereto, television viewers are not able to appreciate with much nuance the venue as an example of 'aural architecture' that allows for a specific quality of the soundscape to emerge. Thirdly, only chants and songs which attract a substantial following do clearly emerge during the televised broadcast.

Most evidently, *Oh, When the Spurs Go Marchin' In* emerges in all three case matches as it represents the frequently introduced signature song of the home team supporters who massively outnumber the away supporters. By comparison, only a small proportion of the numerous chants and songs introduced by the away supporters can be heard in the televised broadcast. Illustratively, while the chants and songs originating from the away team supporters predominate the soundscape at the Tottenham-Leicester match (as experienced from my location inside the stadium), the chants and songs only transpire occasionally throughout the televised version of the match. Moreover, when a chant or a song from the away team supporters emerges, the television audience is oftentimes offered merely the contours of a melody without being able to decipher the accompanying lyrics. Illustratively, when the lyrics of the away supporters do exceptionally emerge in the televised broadcast, it has been highlighted as an unusual case: 'The chant was one of the loudest sung by the away end of around 4,000 and the tune and final line was clearly audible on television coverage' (Pearson, 2012, p. 66).

An example of a more routine condition of the distribution for the sounds transpires in the Tottenham-Leicester match as a two-note chant (embodying a repeated descending interval from the note g to e) emerges among other sounds of spectators as indicated in Table 4.2 (see shot 6).

The televised version of the sounds offers no potential of specification, but from my position in the stadium setting, it is discernible that the chant is sung over the syllables 'Schmei-chel' (i.e. the surname of the away team's goalkeeper). The example also illustrates that in addition to not being able to position the sounds as originating from a particular location inside the stadium setting, the television audience is regularly not able to determine, from listening to the specific (melody of) chant or song alone, from where and whom it originates. More generally, the example reveals the difficulties and limitations of relying on the televised broadcast for the identification and examination of chants and songs in the stadium setting (see, e.g. Sandgren, 2010, pp. 135, 142; and see Howard, 2004, for similar challenges regarding an examination of the sounds of spectators based on the radio broadcast).

## The visual accompaniment

In addition to the preceding examination of the sounds from the available listening positions, the whereabouts of the sounds must also be explored from the perspective of their relation to the visuals of the broadcast. What is immediately striking, then, is how the editing of the visuals appears highly dynamic and flexible when compared to the rather fixed edit of the sounds – indeed, the visuals include 'a range of standpoints' (Crisell, 2006, p. 103) or 'points of view' (POVs). Although one specific camera perspective is predominant and recurring – that is, in all three case matches, represented by a 'prime camera' (Scannell, 2014, pp. 161–2) positioned high and in the middle of one of the sideline grandstands and panning right and left to cover the action – the visuals include the following variabilities: a relatively high frequency of visual cuts from one camera setting to another (Table 4.2 exemplifies the frequency of cuts over a short period of time), a high variety of different POVs in terms of distance and direction, an almost constant panning of the camera (usually following the location of the ball on the pitch) and a frequent incorporation of recorded material in the form of slow-motion replays (see more later in the text on the latter examples of temporal variations of the visuals).

Table 4.3 presents an overview of these features and how they relate to the broadcast of the sounds of spectators. Generally, the table indicates that the composite soundscape (resulting from the deployment of multiple simultaneously operating microphones) does not correspond to what the viewer would be able to hear if the viewer was in fact positioned as suggested by the camera.

When examining the sounds from the perspective of the visual content, firstly, a significant proportion of what can be heard cannot be seen. The sources of the sounds thus often appear off-screen or reside at the borders of the off-screen and on-screen division (Chion, 1994, p. 74). For example, the commentators are not presented visually, and the spectators are rarely focused upon and appear mostly in the background or the periphery of the screen. Also, the sounds of the spectators heard through the broadcast do not obviously originate from the spectators shown on screen. Instead, the cameras predominately focus on the playing field where they follow the movement of the ball and interactions

Table 4.3 Overview of Chosen Relations between the Sounds and the Visuals in Televised Football

|  | Visuals | Sounds |
| --- | --- | --- |
| **Perspective** | Several specific points of view | One unspecific 'Zone of audition' |
| **Shot** | Single; one transmitting camera at the time | Composite; multiple, simultaneously transmitting microphones |
| **Cuts** | Numerous | None |
| **Recorded Material** | Frequent slow-motion replays | None |

between performers at the ball. This focus illustrates that, secondly, a significant proportion of what can be seen on-screen cannot be heard. Although a small selection of performer sounds transpires regularly – for example, the referees' whistle and ball strokes captured by shotgun microphones, as mentioned previously – most visualized (inter)actions among the performers remain inaudible.

The sounds of spectators can also be positioned from the perspective of diegesis here defined as 'the space-time continuum of the scene on screen' (Chion, 2009, p. 474). However, it is not entirely clear how to delimitate this 'space-time continuum of the scene' as the 'medium event' includes both the 'game event' and the 'stadium event' (following Williams, 1977, as mentioned previously). The 'game event' could perhaps be considered to constitute a distinct part of the diegesis: 'The game on the field becomes a closed, diegetic world represented by switching cameras' (Morse, 1983, p. 48). However, the relevant 'space-time continuum of the scene' can arguably be broadened to include the 'stadium event', which could seem to be the suggestion of the following observation: 'Both players *and* crowd are part of the diegetic world of the game established through regular alternation of video cameras' (Morse, 1983, p. 51, italics in original); moreover, televised 'natural crowd noise' has been referred to as 'diagetic [sic]' (Real, 2014 p. 20). Although the spectators are only partly and sporadically seen on-screen, spectators are thus part of the diegetic world as constituted by the 'stadium event'.

From the perspective of the diegesis of the 'stadium event', the sounds of spectators occupy a somewhat ambiguous position. On the one hand, as already indicated, the 'zone of audition' offered through the television production is not realistically available to any of the participants of the space-time continuum of the scene on-screen. For example, as shown in Section 3.2, spectators in the stadium setting will perceive the sounds from individual POAs which will necessarily implicate a sense of direction and distance. On the other hand, the sounds clearly originate from the space-time continuum of the 'stadium event', as described previously. Although each participant's POA differs both from the soundscape of the televised broadcast and from that of other participants' POA, the sounds of spectators are heard by all participants in the stadium setting. Moreover, the sounds of spectators have a diegetic role to play, as they can influence and be influenced by match incidents; for example, when a goal is scored, the celebration emerges as a 'co-production' of both players and spectators usually gesticulating at and among each other. The celebration is thus not confined to a closed, diegetic world represented exclusively on/by the field. Also, the spectators in the stadium setting will occasionally directly address the television audience through their production of sounds, which arguably provides a further manifestation of the 'diegetic existence' of stadium spectators. An additional indication of why it seems reasonable to view the sounds of spectators as part of the diegesis presents itself by the deployment of recorded spectator sounds in televised matches during the Covid-19 pandemic, where the sounds are extra-diegetic as the source of the sounds is clearly not part of the space-time continuum of the scene on-screen. The visuals reveal the absence of spectators by including footage of empty grandstands, and the sounds of spectators obviously represent an editorial add-on designed for the television audience (see more in Section 4.4).

An editorial manipulation of the sounds of spectators during live televised sports is not entirely unheard of. For example, when working on the television production of sounds for American car racing (NASCAR), the sound designer was faced with the problem that the cheering crowd could not be heard, because 'the noise from the engines bounced around and masked pretty much every other sound' (Andrews, 2012). Consequently, the sound designer 'went to his sound library and found a suitable recording of crowd swell', and the next time the race would come to an end, he would 'snuck in this pre-recorded crowd, mixing it to sound just right against everything else' (Andrews, 2012). Similarly, practices of 'sweetening' (Butler, 2012, p. 336) the sounds of live televised sports have been reported with respect to other types of sounds; for example, during the live broadcast of a ski jump competition, the sound operator decided – in a process not unlike the workings of foley artists – to use 'a sampler and keyboard to trigger different sounds, synchronized with the visual movements … produced live and on the spot' including the 'sounds of ski jumpers taking off and landing, and … noise from the audience, bells, a dog barking and more' (Høier, 2012, p. 7; see also Williams, 1977, p. 138). However, whereas examples can thus be provided of the deployment of added, extra-diegetic sounds of spectators, there is nothing from the case matches – assessed against the observations made in the stadium setting – to indicate that (some of the) sounds have been added.

With respect to the sounds originating from the television production team (excluding the televised sounds at football), the sonic signals are clearly extra-diegetic by representing superimposed sounds not available to the participants at the stadium event. The sounds of commentators arguably 'exist in a dual relation to the diegesis, both part of it and narrating it' (Morse, 1983, p. 53). On the one hand, commentators might be seen as extra-diegetic in the sense that they perform a role comparable to that of a voice-over, which cannot be heard by the participants of the space-time continuum of the scene on-screen and which has no direct impact on the showed narrative, actions and incidents. On the other hand, the commentators can be viewed as diegetic 'super-spectators' who are at the stadium event and to whom the television audience is offered an 'aurally privileged access'. Also, the commentary can principally (depending on rights and access) be retrieved through stadium spectators' personal media use. The commentators might not have a direct and obvious influence on the stadium event. However, the stadium spectators will occasionally address the media production personnel explicitly, and a more implicit address might be considered from the perspective of spectators' attempt to stimulate the commentators' acknowledgement of the sounds produced by the spectators – thus obtaining some, approximately, unbiased recognition which potentially nurtures the emotive function of the sounds of spectators (as introduced in Section 3.3).

## Temporal perspectives

As already indicated, the televised broadcast of football offers a modified version of the sounds of spectators compared to their appearance in the stadium setting. From a temporal perspective – focused on when the sounds of spectators emerge – the television production team asserts an influence on when the sounds of spectators are (not) to be heard by the television audience.

At the most general level, the mere presence of the television production team can occasionally inspire spectators to activate certain chants and songs. In addition to influence when specific chants are there to be heard by the television audience, the television production can influence when chants and songs are *not* to be heard. Again, the case match does not provide obvious examples beyond the general tendency of the television production to drown out chants and songs that do not attract a significant following. However, an example transpired as Falkirk and Celtic met in 2009 in Scottish league on Remembrance Day (shortly introduced in Section 3.1). While the spectators inside the stadium complied to perform the expected one minute of silence, a group of spectators outside the stadium apparently attempted to disrupt the ceremony: 'At the corner between the two stands where Celtic fans were watching the game, around 40 people sang republican songs during the tribute to the fallen' (Mathieson, 2009). However, based on the alleged ability (according to an Sky insider) 'to mute any chants or songs which could cause offence', the 'sound levels were brought to a minimum to cover up the sound of chants from outside the ground' – whereas the sounds were thus not distributed through the televised broadcast, 'the crowd disruption was audible on radio coverage and was later also revealed on additional footage posted on video-sharing website YouTube' (Mathieson, 2009). Another example is referred to by Lawn (2020): 'Abuse at one ground was so bad that BBC Sussex had to turn off a crowd microphone' (p. 132).

When focusing on their more detailed televised integration, the sounds of spectators appear incessantly and dynamically as they wax and wane throughout the programme. By comparison, the commentary, although also usually a continuous feature throughout the match, is filled with (mostly short-lasting) pauses, while the sonic signals appear only sporadically. From the perspective of syncrisis (introduced in Section 3.2), the sounds of spectators are layered both within the sound type itself and in its relation to other sounds. Moreover, the sounds vary with respect to their salience and forcefulness. For example, during some sequences of the broadcast the sounds will reside in an auditory background to the commentators (see, e.g. shot 1 in Table 4.2), whereas in other sequences, the sounds appear more powerful, which in turn can stimulate the commentators to raise their voices. This happens, for example, when spectators either begin to chant collectively (see shot 6 in Table 4.2) or react compellingly to specific match incidents (see shots 2 and 6 in Table 4.2).

While the unceasing appearance is comparable to the distribution of the sounds in the stadium setting, the televised broadcast's visual and verbal accompaniment implies that the sounds contribute to an occasional multilayered temporal structure. This happens when the visuals move from live coverage and into the mode of slow-motion replay. For example, during the Tottenham-Liverpool match, slow-motion replays emerge on fifty-five occasions, and they make up a total airtime of 9′ 46″ equivalent of approximately 10 per cent of the programming time devoted to the actual match (i.e. 1h 37′ 17″). Such occasions have been described as 'a fusion of the "live" – commentary and ambient sound – and the non-"live" – anachronistic visual material' (Marriott, 1996, p. 83). Similarly, based on the premise that 'sight and sound, inseparable "in reality", are deconstructed via the communicative technologies of television that simultaneously transmit and record live events. They are recombined to create a multi-dimensional spatiality and temporality for viewers' (Scannell, 2014, p. 175),

Scannell identifies a 'doubling of time and space' (Scannell, 1996, p. 172) and the emergence of a 'magic doubled moment: the now of the background ambient sound of the on-going game in real time, and the then of the visually displayed moment just now past to which the foregrounded words of the commentator speak' (Scannell, 2014, p. 175).

Whereas Marriott does not explore in further detail the structure of the sounds of spectators, Scannell suggests that these sounds (variously termed background ambient sound) must be distinguished according to two different conditions. In one condition, during a 'quick replay' following 'fouls and near misses', 'the coverage is designed to hold in focus where the action is and to allow the commentary and the ambient sound to convey to the viewer a sense of how the game is going' (Scannell, 2014, p. 162). In another condition, prompted by the scoring of a goal, 'television's visual structure moves into a different gear. It no longer follows the action' (Scannell, 2014, p. 162). Furthermore, Scannell argues, 'viewers hear but do not attend to the background sound because they are listening to the foreground commentary which addresses a different moment' (Scannell, 2014, p. 175). The temporal implications of the structure of the sounds of spectators can be elaborated by reconsidering the implications of the sounds during these two conditions.

To refine the understanding provided by Scannell of the significance of quick replays it seems relevant, firstly, to specify that the slow-motion visuals hold in focus where the action *was*, while the effective playing time of the match is momentarily paused. This is exemplified in shot 4 (see Table 4.2), where the attempt at goal is shown in slow motion right after the ball has passed the goalmouth resulting in a goal kick to the away team. Secondly, the commentators do not always refer to the visually displayed moment during slow-motion replays as Scannell seems to suggest – probably due of Scannell's focus on replays of the scoring of goals. While such examples of what could be coined 'audiovisual counterpoints' (inspired by Chion, 1994, p. 37) arguably 'occurs on television every day, even though no one seems to notice' – the previously mentioned mismatch between the visualized owner representatives of Leicester City and the commentators' focus on something else has already provided an example – they emerge 'especially in replays of sports events, when the image goes its own way and the commentary goes another' (Chion, 1994, p. 37). For example, during the Tottenham-Leicester match (see shot 4 in Table 4.2), in addition to the commentators' reference to the action visualized by the slow motion, the commentators summarize more general aspects of the match as it has progressed so far.

The visuals and the commentary thus include reference to two different temporalities: the visuals refer to a specific point in time that has just passed, whereas the commentary includes reference to an extended period of time that has preceded the specific point in time specified by the visuals. Basically, the commentary conveys to the viewer a sense of how the game has been going. The spectator sounds, for their part, arguably refer to yet another point in time, that is, how the game is going right now – as observed by Scannell 'the background sound of the real-and-present moment' can indicate 'further eventful happenings' through 'a roar from the crowd' (Scannell, 1996, p. 172). For example, in the sequence referred to in Table 4.2, in the stadium setting it is obvious that the away team's goalkeeper is trying to stretch the period of time used for preparing the goal kick. From this perspective, the two-note chant emerges as a support to the goalkeeper from the away team's supporters. Consequently, shot 4 in Table 4.2 exemplifies how, actually, a 'tripled moment' can emerge during the broadcast, as the spectator sounds refer to a 'time zone' – (1) now – that is dissimilar to that of both the visuals and the commentary referring to (2) just before and (3) until now, respectively.

So far, the examination has indicated that the televised sounds of spectators embody the most prevalent example of a live and match incident-focused element of the broadcast. Contrary to the occasional broadcast of recorded visuals, the sounds of spectators are continuously live in the sense that the production of the sounds coincides with the distribution of the sounds throughout the broadcast – although the televised distribution represents a significant modification of the sounds, as shown previously. Moreover, although the commentary is live, it oftentimes refers to past and future (e.g. expected or hoped for) incidents within the given match or even issues unrelated to specific match incidents (e.g. the career of managers and players). As for the accompanying graphic sounds, they appear recorded in the sense that their production has preceded their distribution – yet, they might be appreciated as ' "live" in the limited sense that the time of transmission coincides with the time of reception' (Marriott, 1996, p. 70).

The temporal structure of the sounds of spectator can be further specified by assessing them from the perspective of synchronicity or 'synchronized sound' defined as 'sound that is shot simultaneously with the picture and matches exactly' (Holland, 2017, p. 298). Specifically, the segmented, collective interjections (see Section 3.1) illustrate how the sounds of spectator can be closely in synch with specific match incidents. The relations between the televised visuals and sounds might not qualify unambiguously as so-called 'synch points' which denote 'a salient moment of an audiovisual sequence during which a sound event and a visual event meet in synchrony' (Chion, 1994, p. 58). Firstly, the sounds of spectators are 'detached' from the object(s) that causes the sounds (e.g. the players' passes, dribbles and shots at the goal). By comparison, the televised performer sounds of, for example, a player striking the ball represent an intrinsic connection between the sound and the object from which the sound emerges. Secondly, and relatedly, the sounds of spectators emerge as a social reaction to match incidents rather than as a physical effect of, for example, the striking of a ball. Nevertheless, although the sounds of spectators, exemplified by the segmented, collective interjections, do not necessarily coincide precisely with the given match incident, to 'the naked ear' there appears to be no noticeable delay of the spectators' reaction. Indeed, there are 'degrees of synchronism', and from this perspective, the televised reproduction of the sounds of spectators tends to gravitate towards being tightly rather than 'loosely' synchronized (Chion, 1994, p. 65).

Remarkably, as the televised soundscape does not include the same degree and type of distance and directionality effects compared to the experience of the sounds of spectators in the stadium setting, the synchronization of the televised visuals and sounds appears tighter in the televised broadcast than in the stadium setting. Most intensely, a 'loose synchronization' can be experienced in the stadium setting when a small and clearly demarcated group of spectators situated in a distant section of the stadium reacts distinguishably to a specific match while the rest of the spectators do not react or react in a much less distinguishable manner – as exemplified by the Chelsea supporters' cheering of the goal scored on penalty (see Section 3.2). In the televised broadcast, there is no delay effect of these sounds, as they are picked up by (also) the microphones in relatively close proximity to the away fans.

## 4.3 Why?

The communicative functions (Jakobson, 1960, introduced in Section 3.3) served by the sounds of spectators in the setting of the televised broadcast differ notably from the functions of the sounds in the stadium setting. This is due not only to the obvious fact that the television audience is not placed in the setting of the origin of the sounds. Also, as shown in the previous sections, the televised broadcast embodies a modification of the sounds. Firstly, the television production distributes the sounds of spectators as part of the 'televised sounds at football' which implies that the sounds offer no clear sense of spatiality and are accompanied by the performer sounds of ball strokes. Secondly, the sounds of spectators are embedded within the 'football television sound' where they emerge in the background of the foregrounded sounds of the commentators and the (occasional) sonic signals. Consequently, in the television broadcast the sounds are largely indistinguishable when it comes to determining 'who says/sings what to whom?' Accordingly, the significant emotive, conative and referential functions of the sounds transpire only vaguely through the modified distribution of the sounds. As the functions of the sounds pertaining to addressers and addressees inside the stadium setting are thus markedly lessened, the televised sounds of spectators should additionally be examined from the perspective of the television production – that is, the programme and channel – representing the addresser and the television audience as representing the addressee.

## The emotive function

From the perspective of the emotive function, at first glance the sounds might appear irrelevant. For example, the sounds are not exclusively distributed by the given channel, and thereby the sounds do not distinctly serve as an expression of the 'speaker's attitude' nor as a potential contribution towards branding the specific programme and channel – although, in a broader perspective, the sounds could be considered to brand the televised broadcasts from precisely the EPL. By comparison, the sounds of the commentors and the sonic signals hold the potential to serve an emotive function and appear as sound brands, because they are usually uniquely produced for and distributed by the given channel. However, the sounds of spectators can be seen to serve an emotive function to the extent that the sounds add a sense of occasion to the broadcast (see, e.g. Deninger, 2012, p. 111; as referred to in the introduction to this book). The continuous distribution of the sounds also serves to help indicate (in addition to the visuals and the commentary; see, e.g. Comisky et al., 1977) that the programme is constantly exciting while preventing 'auditory lacunae' – approximating instances of 'dead air' – to emerge whenever there is a pause in the commentators' verbal address. Without the masking sounds of spectators, such pauses could indicate that nothing (interesting) is going on. Furthermore, if the sounds of spectators were not there, the pauses in the commentators' address would allow, for example, for performers' shouts and interjections to resonate and emphasize the unengaging, 'lifeless' surroundings of an empty stadium. The emotive function of the sounds of spectators thus pertains especially to the enhancement of the programme as an expression of the 'stadium event' (following Williams, 1977, as referred to previously).

Whereas this function of the sounds has been suggested by producers – for example, main goals of microphone arrangement in sports broadcasting have been said to include offering a 'quasi-cinematic dramatization of events' (Wittek, 2013) – it has been regularly overlooked in scholarly contributions; for an example (although focused on American football): 'While television excels in covering the "game event", it does a poor job of covering the "stadium event" of which audience response is the most important part' and 'a content analysis of camera shots used in television coverage of football games found that shots of the crowd represented only three percent of all shots' (Hocking, 1982, p. 106). As implied above, a focus on the sounds (and not merely the visual appearance) of spectators would reveal that the crowd is sonically ever-present and included in 100 per cent of all shots. Therefore, if it is reasonable to suggest that the stadium can be seen as a 'huge television studio' and that 'the supporters in the stadiums (in space) become … just a piece of the scenery for television coverages' (Penz, 1990, p. 164), the sounds must be considered to play a critical role.

## The conative function

From the perspective of the conative function, the sounds of spectators in the stadium setting rarely include an explicit address of the television audience. However, the sounds of spectators can be considered to function implicitly to suggest specific responses from the audience. While the sounds serve to express 'a sense of occasion' from the perspective of the emotive function, from the perspective of the conative function, they serve to help guide how the audience can and should react to the occasion. From this perspective, the sounds bear a resemblance to 'one of the most distinctive aspects of television sound', namely 'the audible inclusion of an audience' (Lury, 2005, p. 82). The sounds from an internal audience have long been deployed on television and, before that, on the radio. For example, so-called 'laugh tracks' have been organized to guide viewers' responses and promote the illusion of sociability during sitcoms (Lury, 2005, p. 83). Reportedly, the use of laugh tracks is 'falling out of use in recent years, due in no small part to the fact that the "liveness" of television is increasingly being de-emphasized' (Birdsall & Enns, 2012; see also Smith, 2008). However, granted that liveness is still important for televised football (see more below), a characterization of spectator sounds in the light of laugh tracks seems appropriate.

Obviously, although the stadium could be considered as an enormous television studio, the sounds of spectators in the stadium setting differ markedly from 'laugh tracks' in sitcoms. Firstly, the sounds of spectators are continuous (and not merely occasional) and can function unobtrusively as a guide to the audience throughout the entire match. Secondly, the sounds of spectators include appeals to the experience of both satisfaction and dissatisfaction – as well as the experience of 'attention summoning' segmented collective interjections – and the sounds thereby appear varied compared to the normally more limited repertoire of responses characteristic of the 'laugh track' (where laughing predominates). Thirdly, the sounds of spectators appear more authentic in the sense that they originate from actual spectators – that is, the spectators have paid an admission fee to attend the match and they would have arguably been there irrespective of the intervention of a television production team. Fourthly, contrary to the responses of a live studio audience (or the prior construction of a recorded, or 'canned', version), the sounds of spectators are normally relatively unaffected by editorial control and management – with the reservation that the television production exercises some level of influence on the production of the sounds, as exemplified previously. Finally, the audience reactions embodied by the so-called laugh track (whether 'canned' or 'live') are usually clearly extra-diegetic in the sense that the performers do not interact with the sounds' creators who are also usually entirely invisible to the television audience – by comparison, the performers (players) often interact with spectators in the stadium setting, and spectators are said to influence the performance – for example, following the common-sense understanding of the effect of the spectators representing a twelfth man at/in the match.

Although the sounds of spectators have been considered marginal in this respect – for example, Scannell argues, 'viewers hear but do not attend to the background sound because they are listening to the foregrounded commentary' (Scannell, 2014, p. 175) – a few studies have indicated the 'realization' of aspects of the conative function of the sounds of spectators. These studies also suggest that – contrary to a previous suggestion: 'the football game on television is received in privacy by an isolate, usually male viewer who must forego the pleasures of the crowd' (Morse, 1983, p. 47) – televised football is often watched and responded to in groups: 'Sports is the type of television most often consumed in a social context' (Harris, 2004, p. 167). For an empirical example, as part of a linguistic study on the appropriations of live televised football matches, it was found that viewers, for example, laugh, sing, clap, mourn, sigh, dance and jump up and down more or less synchronized with the televised spectator sounds (Gerhardt, 2014, p. 217). While the suggestion has been made that 'television sports coverage is constructed in order to invite the viewer's involvement through offering patterns of reaction to the sport directed by the commentator' (Bignell, 2013, p. 110), this study indicates that the televised sounds of spectators have a role to play alongside that of the commentator(s). Arguably, the sounds of spectators are thus part of an 'imaginary dialogue between the viewer and the programme' which 'lays out codes in which the viewer's response should take place'; whereas it seems reasonable to assume that 'throwing cans of beer at the screen are not expected', actually 'singing football songs' (Bignell, 2013, p. 110) has been shown to be part of the response repertoire of the television audience. Similarly, and perhaps more expectedly, the singing of songs in synch with the televised sounds of spectators has been observed in larger, (semi-)public gatherings (Kytö, 2011, p. 82; see also Bonz, 2015; Weed, 2007, 2010; Whannel, 2014).

## The referential and metalingual functions

As regards the referential function, the sounds of spectators have already been suggested to offer an indication of the atmosphere in the stadium setting implied by the emotive and conative functions of the sounds. Obviously, the televised sounds represent merely an indication and conveyance of the atmosphere. This is arguably illustrated by the commentators' occasional reference to the atmosphere in the stadium setting. It might be so that 'announcer comments describing crowd response to the game event are rare' (Hocking, 1982, p. 107; although see Comisky et al., 1977), but they do appear as indicated by their prominent appearance in the televised football simulation video game FIFA (Graakjær, 2020b). Whereas the commentators' reference to the 'atmosphere' of the stadium event might be considered to illustrate a metalingual function, the sounds of spectators do not seem to do so through the televised broadcast (where the possible verbal feature of the sounds is largely inarticulate).

It has been argued that 'the external "acting out" of fan identification tends to be more extreme in the arena or stadium experience, but the television viewer may experience emotions that are every bit as powerful and excruciating' (Real, 2005, p. 349; see also Gantz, 1981, p. 271). While this might represent a realistic illustration of spectator responses to the 'match event', when it comes to the 'stadium event' it seems fair to assume that the experience of being there (in the stadium) and the experience of 'being there' from a televised distance are 'only remotely related' (Hoy, 1994, p. 293). The embodied, participating and potentially 'sound-overwhelming' – as I experience it during the Tottenham-Leicester match – presence in the stadium setting offers a 'sheer sense of atmosphere that television can only partly capture' (Crisell, 2006, p. 104); indeed, 'what you get (which you cannot get from seeing the game on television) is the atmosphere, the mood in the ground, the sheer physical presence, in every way, of the crowd' (Scannell, 2014, p. 174).

Even though the televised sounds of spectators are the result of the intervention of a production team (as explored previously), they might be appreciated as 'a stamp of authenticity' (Raunsbjerg, 2001, p. 216) and, likewise, as capable of creating 'a sense of authenticity' (Haynes, 1995, p. 149). Whereas the continuously changing visual perspectives are obviously unrealistic in the sense that they are ever-changing and frequently include POVs not possibly accessible to spectators in the stadium setting, the sounds thus seem to offer the television viewer a more real sense of access, which gravitates, more than the visuals, towards bringing the audience 'into the atmosphere of the event', as this has been stressed as another one of the main goals of microphone arrangement at football (Wittek, 2013). Accordingly, the sounds of spectators can help satisfy the 'overriding obligation (that all accept) to bring it off and make it happen as a case of "the real thing"' (Scannell, 2014, p. 160) – similarly, it has been argued that a 'pretence of realism remains a powerful professional ideology of sports broadcasting' and that an 'ethos of realism prevails' (Haynes, 1995, p. 149). This obligation seems especially characteristic of the production of European football as, for example, the production of American football has long been characterized by a high(er) degree of 'stylization' (Morse 1983, p. 383). Conceivably, the lack of graphic sound to accompany the sliding 'bumpers' in the case programme (mentioned previously) presents a textual absence, which has the effect of not emphasizing the introduction of an 'unreal thing'.

While providing an indication of the atmosphere pertains especially to the 'stadium event', the sounds also serve a referential function with respect to the 'match event'. From this perspective, the reference is indirect, as the sounds of spectators are not an intrinsic part of the 'match event' and offer information on match incidents in the form of what might be termed 'vicarious evaluations'. Normally, only the occasional performer sounds of ball strokes and the referees' whistle transpire as direct sonic manifestations of aspects of the 'match event'. By comparison, the visuals offer a more direct 'access' to match incidents. This does not imply that the match is made visually available in its entirety for the television audience, although some observers seem to suggest so; for example: 'The variety of camera angles used during a single broadcast allows a viewer a chance to see all aspects of the game from a better vantage point than had he or she been in the best seats in the stadium' (Hocking, 1982, p. 100), and 'television enables us to see and understand endlessly more about any athletic event' (Gumbrecht, 2019, p. 47). Rather, following a seminal contribution on televised American football, the visuals of the televised broadcast 'simultaneously reveals too much and too little in a football game' (Oriard, 1981, p. 37). Whereas 'too much' refers to the highlighting and making logical and understandable specific match incidents – thereby denying 'the true fan's pleasure … in making such judgements' (Oriard, 1981, p. 37) – 'too little' refers to the fact that by 'focusing primarily on the ball', the visual production 'denies the viewer any knowledge of entire portions of the game that take place away from the ball' (Oriard, 1981, p. 37; for a similar argument, see Mumford, 2019, p. 238). Consequently, by 'watching the game on television he [the television viewer] is too dependent on the camera's eye (and, worse, the announcer's mouth) for his information' (Oriard, 1981, pp. 37–8). However, as previously implied, the television audience need not rely exclusively on the visuals and the sounds of commentators for information on match incidents and developments.

When acknowledging that the sounds of spectators can convey a sense of how the game is going, the sounds might be likened to a meticulously match-monitoring 'auditory seismometer'. The meticulousness shows most significantly through the various closely coupled interjections which represent the promptest auditory information on decisive match developments during broadcast football; for example (although the example refers to radio broadcasts): 'The crowd are much quicker than the commentators – the roars and groans precede the descriptions of the action by several seconds' (Hornby, 1992, p. 110). The sounds can thus provide the audience with a sense of how the match is going even if the relevant match incidents are not shown on-screen – a function also referred to from the perspective of production, as the purpose of microphone arrangement is said to include 'providing information about occurrences, not all of which are visible in the picture' (Wittek, 2013). As the home team supporters are usually the predominant suppliers of televised spectator sounds (as the away team supporters are significantly outnumbered), these sounds not only indicate that 'something' is happening. By embodying an additional emotive function, that is, expressing the current emotional state and attitudes of the spectators, the sounds also indicate the relevance and certain distinguishing features of the specific incidents. Television viewers can usually rely on a code when they adopt such a mode of what could be coined 'listening-in-search' (Truax, 2001, p. 21). The code is usually operational based on the tendency for home supporters to be positively inclined towards the home team and, simply put, the code goes like this: negative booing indicates either home team impediments (as exemplified in shot 4, Table 4.2) and/or away team fortunes and, of course, vice versa, when spectator sounds are positive and celebrating (as exemplified in shot 2, Table 4.2).

To further the understanding of this particular code, it is instructive to briefly compare it to the spectator sounds from another example of televised sports. During an examination of tennis – suggested to represent 'the acoustic sport par excellence' – Chion (1994) identifies the stroke of the ball as 'the sonic signature of the sport: the thump with a dry echo' (p. 159); parenthetically, one might add that the vocal sounds of performers are also distinctive for the sport of tennis (see, e.g. Goffman, 1981a, pp. 112–13; Powis & Carter, 2019, p. 393). Chion goes on to observe how the absence of the thumping sound of hitting the ball is also significant. Television viewers can 'hear' when a ball is not struck, as the 'thump' becomes conspicuous by its very absence. Chion does not specify the role of the spectators, but viewers of televised tennis also seem to be able to rely on a code – albeit a different one when compared with televised football. In tennis, where the players do not regularly play at what could be seen as 'home stadium settings' – which in turn implies that the attendance is not regularly characterized by a majority of 'home player supporters' – the sounds of spectators are less recognizably partisan. Nevertheless, the sounds of spectators might indicate whether the absence of the sound of a ball stroke is due to a ball being placed successfully out of reach of the opponent (which usually results in approving cheers) or to a ball being placed unsuccessfully outside the lines of the tennis court (which usually results in disappointing 'oohs'). The sounds of spectators at tennis are thus normally not a resource that television viewers can use to identify who is winning/advantaged and who is losing/disadvantaged. Spectator sounds of televised football, by comparison, accurately provide this type of information, which indicates that – contrary to the point made by

Chion: 'you could not follow along with your ears if you were watching soccer' (1994, p. 159) – actually you are able to 'follow along with your ears' (even without paying attention to the commentary) when watching televised football including the sounds of spectators. Clearly, the commentary can also play a role by conveying information on decisive match incidents when the audience might not focus visually on the match; for example, spectators in 'the kitchen getting a beer' can find themselves suddenly informed on match developments by 'an announcer screaming' (Altman, 1986, pp. 50–1).

## The phatic and poetic functions

The uninterrupted distribution of the sounds of spectators at football indicates that they can help establish a sense of continuity and hence serve a phatic function of upholding contact with the television audience. Although Scannell does not focus explicitly on the role played by spectator sounds – rather, Scannell suggests, 'When we turn to television coverage of live events we find that continuity is achieved in the first place through visual presentation backed up with its spoken commentary' (Scannell, 2014, p. 159) – the sounds of spectators are arguably critical in creating continuity and 'a smooth flow from shot to shot' (Scannell, 2014, p. 159). This function also hints at a possible poetic aspect of the sounds. Although – or perhaps because – the lyrics of the chants and songs only transpire rather indistinctly, the melodic feature of the sounds is overriding. Consequently, the sounds can be heard as a sort of 'background music' or a constant 'musicalization' of the broadcast.

Given that the achievement and maintenance of continuity is 'a fundamental aspect of the management of liveness' (Scannell, 2014, p. 158), spectator sounds should be considered to play an important role in this respect as well. For televised football, 'liveness' is crucial. Generally, 'television's recording of sport has a short shelf-life: there is a "zone of liveness", after which the liveness effect will have expired' (Crisell, 2006, p. 99), and football illustrates vividly 'the unique and overlapping strengths that television possesses: *spectacle*, the primary source of its ability to provide entertainment; and *liveness*, the presentation of something which is happening now and will have an unknown outcome' (p. 98; italics in original). Specifically, the liveness of televised football 'offers the real sense of access to an event in its moment-by-moment unfolding' (Scannell, 1996, p. 84), and it recovers 'as far as possible, the "nowness" of the whole event through recency' (Crisell, 2006, p. 99).

The sounds of spectators offer a continuous support for the experience of liveness not only when the game itself might not be all that exiting; indeed, often, as Scannell (2014) observes, 'there will be stretches of time when nothing much seems to be going on' (p. 168). The dynamic visual production could perhaps be seen to help sustain the viewer's sense of liveness (see, e.g. Willoughby, 1989, p. 73); however, the sounds are in a sense privileged as they hold the potential to act as the essential 'lifeline' – or 'live line' – between the programme and the audience. This function is particularly operational in cases where the audience is visually distracted – for example, when looking away from the screen, feeling drowsing or momentarily located in another room (as exemplified above) – or visually 'impaired' as when the visuals do not include a specific incident to which (a large proportion of the) spectators in the stadium setting react. An example of the latter emerges in the Tottenham-Liverpool match, when the 'target' of the spectators' booing is not visually disclosed for a prolonged period of time until the actual substitution of the former Arsenal player is visually introduced (an incident also referred to in Chapter 3).

## 4.4 Football matches with no spectators in the stadium setting

Prior to the Covid-19 pandemic televised broadcasts of elite football in stadium settings without spectators were rare and usually appeared as the result of the home team being penalized for some type of spectator misbehaviour at a previous match. However, as part of the precautionary measures to help prevent the spread of the Covid-19 virus in the beginning of the 2020s, spectators' access to elite football matches was suspended around the world. Meanwhile, leagues, organizers and broadcasters worked to secure matches were nonetheless played and made available for television audiences. The suspension of spectators presented itself as a challenge for broadcasters and television executives. They expressed 'a serious concern over what that [people seeing banks of empty seats and people hearing no noise and no audio effects] would do for people's enjoyment of the matches' and the situation was seen to 'probably devalue the product' (according to a senior Sky source in Edwards, 2020). The absence of the sounds of spectators was considered particularly challenging, as the broadcasters could no longer benefit from spectator sounds' proclaimed attractions as referred to in the introduction and exemplified throughout the preceding sections in this chapter. Consequently, to help avoid offering viewers a devalued product, in some settings broadcasters would add pre-recorded spectator sounds to the televised broadcast to simulate the soundscape which would otherwise have been produced by the attending spectators. For example, when the EPL resumed in June 2020 after a period of complete suspension of matches, EPL broadcasters Sky Sports (among others) offered its viewers a soundtrack of recorded sounds of spectators.

The practice of adding sounds of spectators to the televised broadcast from stadiums without spectators might represent an extraordinary case. However, it was widespread during the stated period, and in addition to its historical and potential future relevance, a closer examination of the sounds can assist in profiling the structure, distribution and significance of the sounds of spectators in 'regular' cases of televised matches (as examined so far in this chapter). Therefore, based on observations from a textual examination of a case match between Tottenham and Liverpool (introduced in Section 1.2) played during the Covid-19 precautions in front of an empty stadium and broadcasted with added spectator sounds, these sounds of spectators shall now be examined from the perspectives of the 'what?', 'where and when?' and 'why?' questions already introduced.

As regards the 'what?' question, the sounds are reportedly supplied by EA Sports (since 1993 the producer of the football simulation video game series of FIFA): 'In partnership with *EA SPORTS FIFA*, Sky Sports has created a range of bespoke and team-specific crowd noises and chants to bring the vibrant atmosphere of the Premier League to the restart' (Sky Sports, 2020). The sounds were produced from previous recordings – used in the game series of *FIFA* – of spectators at previous, 'pre-Covid-19' matches between the involved teams. The process of collecting recordings of spectator sounds began with the creation of *FIFA 15*, when the FIFA team gained 'exclusive access to Premier League clubs' allowing not only for the construction of 'detailed photography of all 20 stadiums so they could be authentically recreated' but also for 'realistic audio to goal reactions, misses, whistles and over two hours of crowd-specific songs' based on recordings of 'cheers, chants and sounds of more than 20 Premier League matches' (EA Sports, 2014). The televised broadcast offered both an 'audio carpet of flat crowd noise' and 'special sounds for penalties, goals and fouls' (Yusha, 2020) drawn from a collection of more than eight hundred different sound clips. According to an EA Sports sounds producer and designer, 'there is nothing simulated or generic. It is all club-specific content' (Andrew Vance in Lerner, 2020).

When it comes to the specific types of sounds included in the televised broadcast with added sounds of spectators, the soundscape differs considerably from the normal televised broadcasts as these have been explored in the previous sections of this chapter. Firstly, the spectator's singing is represented only by signature songs which do not refer to specific match incidents or contextual aspects, like, for example, the history of previous matches between the two clubs or the career of specific players and managers. For example, during the case match, *Oh, When the Spurs Go Marchin' In* emerges on numerous occasions, whereas other melodies including possibly more 'topical' (exemplified by the emergence of *One Season Wonder*) are absent. Secondly, while the lyrics of the sounds of spectators generally transpire only vaguely through the televised broadcast, some of the potentially controversial sounds which occasionally emerge in the televised broadcast are entirely absent from the case match. For example, the case match does not include the chants and shouts with reference to 'Yid' (e.g. *Yid, Yid, Yid* and *Yid Army, [clap], [clap]*, which are otherwise regular features of the televised broadcasts of matches including Tottenham Hotspur) – tellingly, the reproduction of singing provided by EA Sports was said to include only 'some of the more family friendly chants' (Quinn, 2020). Thirdly, the soundscape does not include interjections and shouts of individuals, duads or smalls groups which would normally emerge through the commentator's microphones. Finally, possibly as the result of the absence of the otherwise (normally) masking sounds of spectators in the stadium setting, performer sounds – especially the sounds of ball strokes – are more pronounced throughout the case match.

With respect to the questions of 'where and when', the added sounds of spectators in the case match are distributed exclusively through the televised broadcast and are therefore not accessible to the performers in the stadium setting – in some settings, television viewers were offered the opportunity to switch off (and on) the added recorded sounds (see, e.g. Pugh, 2020). While this seem to represent the most prevalent procedure during the Covid-19 pandemic, alterative procedures have been reported. For example, the English Championship clubs (i.e. clubs from the second highest division in English football) were given the option to provide recorded sounds of spectators at their stadiums during matches as exemplified by the home matches of Queens Park Rangers. Here, the sounds were arranged by the theatre sound company Autograph in collaboration with the production company Entourage and www.fanchants.com. The distribution of different sounds from twelve different zones around the stadium was meant to simulate the variation in sound production of attending spectators (Andrew, 2020). Also, in some settings, where a limited number of spectators were allowed access to matches, the added recorded sounds of spectators would mix with the sounds of the attending spectators in the television broadcast (Pugh, 2020). In the case match, in contrast to the frequent appearance of spectators in the background or periphery of the visuals during normal broadcasts, the spectators are entirely absent from the visuals, and from the perspective of diegesis, the sounds of spectators are thus clearly extra-diegetic.

When it comes to the question of 'when' the sounds of spectators emerge, the procedure is, as far as can be assessed, comparable to the one previously described by reference to the deployment of a sampler and keyboard. Thus, during the case match a sound operator controls 'a mix board and sound board where he can hit the button for reaction from a tackle from an away player or a shot from the home team' (Andrew Vance in Lerner, 2020; similar processes of adding spectator sounds have been reported in the context of, e.g., American football and baseball; see Baccellieri, 2020 and Roehl, 2021, respectively). However, on numerous occasions throughout the match, the added sounds of spectators' reactions do not temporally match the progression of specific match incidents. The observed mismatches do not seem to include what has previously been described as (occasional) mishaps – as when, for example, a 'routine save ... saw a huge roar generated that felt incredibly out of place' (Marland, 2020) or when the sound operator 'mistook a near-miss ... for a goal and let off the "goal" sound, before quickly switching to "miss"' (Allen, 2020). Incidentally, similar 'mishaps' might transpire in the stadium setting, when a particular section of the spectators – from their particular point of view – can mistake a near-miss for a goal (e.g. when the ball moves speedily past the post and into the net from the backside of the goal); however, the deployment of multiple, simultaneously operating microphones in the televised broadcast will often level out this reaction, as the cheering sounds will blend with the sounds of disappointment from the part of the stadium's spectators who are actually able to see that a goal has not been scored.

Consequently, rather than actual mishaps, temporal mismatches emerge when the sounds are not timed and tempered in detail to the action on the pitch. For example, in the case match, when the home team goal is scored (in the 1–3 defeat), the action is accompanied by cheering only after approximately half a second of delay, while roughs tackles against home team players are not accompanied by strong outbursts of displeasure – which would be an expected reaction observable through the televised broadcast of the sounds of spectators in the stadium setting. Objectively, the delays might seem negligeable, as they last less than a second. Nonetheless, from the point of view of the television viewers, who are used to an experience of tight synchronization, the delay is quite conspicuous. The significance of even a small temporal inconsistency in the relation between the visuals and the corresponding sounds could perhaps be likened to the case of 'lip synch', where viewers 'accustomed to a tight and narrow synchronization' will object to 'a looser and more "forgiving" synchronization that's often off by a tenth of a second or so' (Chion, 1994, p. 65).

It is not entirely clear why the delays in the observed match emerge. The absence of obvious mishaps could seem to indicate a relatively well-versed sound operator. However, the sound operator will inevitably be constrained by the specific point of view from where the match is observed. By comparison, the spectators at a match embody a kind of 'collective omni-viewer' in the sense that no matter what happens at the match, at least a portion of the spectators will have privileged visual access to the incident, which they immediately (with no distance delay) come to communicate to the television audience through the multi-microphone production of the sounds. Moreover, whereas performer sounds of ball strokes and the sounds of ski jumpers taking off and landing (see the example referred to previously) include relatively predictable incidents and interactions of physical objects or synch points, the sounds of spectators represent social reactions to more impulsive and erratic match incidents and developments. However, regardless of the reason for their introduction from the perspective of production, the emergence of delays creates a textual positioning of the sounds of spectator which temporally differ markedly from the regular televised broadcast. Parenthetically, when it comes to the temporal introduction, the sounds of the video game of *FIFA* (from which the excerpts of sounds originate) resemble the regular televised broadcast more than does the sounds of the televised broadcast of matches with no spectators in the stadium setting – apparently, the game's algorithms produce a much more reliable in-synch introduction of the sounds of spectators compared to the capability of a human sound operator (Graakjær, 2020b).

Arguably, the practice of adding sounds of spectators who are not attending the match epitomizes that 'live TV sport is a confection processed just like any BBC, HBO or Netflix drama' (Rowe, 2020). Inspired by this perspective, the comparison between the added sounds and the 'laugh track' seems to become even more applicable (see also Newman, 2020). Compared to the regular televised match, the sounds of spectators in the case match are less varied, editorially controlled and originate from imaginary spectators with whom the performers do not (and cannot) interact. Additionally, and perhaps more appropriately (since 'laughs tracks' are not a regular part of current television dramas), if the sounds of spectators can indeed be heard as a sort of 'background music' or 'musicalization' of the broadcast, the added sounds resemble the use of extra-diegetic background music in films and television to, for example, suggest the general mood of a scene (for a similar observation, see Carter, 2020).

Relatedly, the practice of adding recorded sounds of spectators could be considered to indicate a possible modification of the significance of the sounds' role to serve as 'a stamp of' and being capable of conveying a 'sense of authenticity'. As noted previously, prior examples of editorial manipulations of the sounds of spectators during live televised sports predominantly aim to uphold a sense of authenticity from the perspective of the viewer (Andrews, 2012). For example, the soundtrack of the crowd swell used at the NASCAR broadcast – likely to have been recorded in another setting than at a car race, where the sounds, in the nature of things, would be difficult to apprehend in the first place – seems to match the visualized cheering crowd. This arguably illustrates that, although the production of the sounds is manipulated, what matters is whether the sounds are verisimilitudinous; that is, they have the appearance or semblance of something which could have expectedly transpired in the visualized setting. However, the case match blatantly abandons such an appeal as the television viewers are offered sounds which they cannot see in – nor infer from – the visualized setting. Whereas the added, recorded sounds have routinely been referred to as 'fake' (Hughes 2020) and as representing 'a fake soundtrack' (Rowe, 2020), it should thus be stressed that the sounds were never 'real' to begin with – that is, in the first, televised instance. As elaborated previously, the sounds of spectators in the regular televised broadcast appear as the result of an intervention and reproduction of the soundscape compared to their origin in the stands of the stadium setting. In attempting to specify the 'genealogy' of the sounds, it soon becomes clear how, generally, a distinction between the 'fake sounds' and the 'real sounds' is quite elusive.

From the perspective of transtextuality (introduced in Section 3.1), the sounds in the case match purportedly represent quotes. From this perspective, the broadcast includes copies in the form of excerpts of sounds of spectators that, on the face of it, appear to be identical to the reproductions of sounds from previous (and regular) televised broadcasts including the same teams. However, the specific broadcasts from which the sounds are copied are undisclosed and indeterminable based on the quality of the sounds – accordingly, although the previously cited producer seems to suggest otherwise, the sounds of spectators in the televised broadcast without spectators in situ appear highly generic. Moreover, because of being drawn from *FIFA*, the entire soundscape embodied by the sounds of spectators in the case match differs markedly when compared to previous televised matches. *FIFA* thus acts as an intermediary 'auditory membrane' or 'gatekeeper' as only some types of sounds are (allowed access to become) part of the soundscape, whereas others are 'filtered out'.

This '*FIFA*-ization' – including a filtering and 'sanitation' of the sounds of spectators – in turn implies that the soundscape of spectators in the match without spectators in the stadium setting bears obvious resemblance to the sounds of spectators emerging when playing a match in *FIFA*. For example, when playing with the home team of Tottenham, *Oh, When the Spurs Go Marchin' In* will accompany the game on several occasions, whereas other more match incident-motivated songs and chants are absent (Graakjær, 2020b). Also, as regards performer sounds, every stroke of the ball is accompanied by a thumping sound event. These examples illustrate how the game presents a simulation of the soundscape of the televised broadcast. Inversely, when recorded sounds of spectators are deployed in (matches such as) the case match, the video game seems to provide a model for the soundscape of spectators as it includes a clearer representation of ball strokes and reflects the reduced and sanitized collection of sound excerpts gathered by and deployed in *FIFA*. However, the soundscape of the case match falls short of demonstrating the meticulous synchronizations of what has been described as closely coupled sounds of spectators represented by the normal televised broadcasts – a dimension of the soundscape which the (algorithms of the) video game of FIFA generally reflects in more detail.

Incidentally, the practice of installing recorded sounds as exemplified by the case match – a practice which seem to have been largely accepted by television audiences (see, e.g. Hughes 2020; although see also examples of opposition in Homewood, 2020) – challenges what has previously been suggested regarding the significance of attending spectators: 'Television will notice our absence, one day. In the end, however much they mike up the crowd, they will be unable to create any atmosphere whatsoever, because there will be nobody there' (Hornby,

1992, p. 189) and, more recently, 'a crowd cannot, as yet, be simulated and then banished [because the] spectacle ... still needs a real crowd in a real stadium' (Goldblatt, 2020, p. 4). The practice seems to suggest that while spectators in the stadium setting are dispensable, when organizers, producers and broadcasters decide that the televised 'show must go on', the *sounds* of spectators play a pivotal role in meeting the audience's expectation of an 'internal audience' when watching football on television. Although the sprinkling of sanitized spectator sounds often lacks precise synchronization at decisive match incidents, the sounds apparently serve sufficiently to uphold a sense of normalcy, familiarity and tolerability, which trumps the appeal to 'authenticity' from the perspective of the television audience.

In a broader perspective, the intermediate productional influence on televised football by the game of FIFA illustrates how 'boundaries between the two media [televised sports and video game sports] blur' and that, obviously, 'the producers of videogames borrow and remediate the televisual, while producers of sports broadcasts keep an eye on sports videogames, looking for opportunities to reinvigorate their medium with a game-like aesthetic' (Stein, 2013, pp. 118, 134). In a similar vein, the interactions between the medias' (re)production of spectator sounds arguably exemplify how 'live performances now often incorporates mediatization to the degree that the live event itself is a product of media technologies' and that 'whereas mediatized performance derives its authority from its reference to the live or the real, the live now derives its authority from its reference to the mediatized, which derives its authority from its reference to the live, etc.' (Auslander, 1999, pp. 25, 39). Moreover, from the perspective of the 'authenticity' or 'realness' of the sounds, the interaction between the video game and the two versions of televised broadcasts might be considered as a case of hyperrealism in the sense that the soundscape embodies 'the generation by models of a real without origin or reality' (Baudrillard, 1981/1994, p. 1; see also Turner, 2013). Television viewers are offered copies (of copies) of sounds with no identifiable original; from this perspective, the soundscapes of the televised broadcasts embody a creation which represents something that do not actually exist.

# 5

# Conclusions

Motivated by a discrepancy between, on the one hand, a widely held belief *that* the sounds of spectators are important to the experience of football spectatorship and, on the other hand, a relative scarcity of scholarly explorations of that importance, this book has offered an introduction, synthetization and refinement of insights into the structure, distribution and significance of the sounds of spectators at football.

Initially, stimulated by suggestions of a lack of scholarly works on the subject matter, the book has offered the hitherto most comprehensive overview of existing contributions on the sounds of spectators at football. The overview shows that while it seems reasonable to suggest that, generally, there (still) exists a relative scarcity of scholarly works, a closer look at the available research reveals that a noteworthy number of contributions exist. As an indication of this – and perhaps unsurprisingly given the global appeal of football and a possible extraordinary significance of the sounds of spectators at the sport of football – there appears to be more contributions on the sounds of spectators at football than on this or any other type of sound at any other sports combined (for rare examples of examinations of the sounds of spectators at other sports, see Goldschmied et al., 2018; Granström, 2012; Heaton, 1992). Therefore, the suggestion of scarcity should be moderated and refined.

Firstly, the existing contributions are unevenly distributed in the sense that almost all existing contributions have focused on aspects of the sounds of spectators in the stadium setting. Whereas there exist at least fifty-one contributions including a substantial focus on aspects of the sounds of spectators in the stadium setting (see the table in the Appendix and Section 2.1), there are practically no contributions including a focused interest for the sounds in the televised broadcast. One of the consequences of this is that there exists very few systematic explorations of how the sounds of spectators in the stadium setting compare with the sounds of spectators in the televised broadcast. As a response to this situation, the book has offered a systematic exploration of the sounds of spectators in also the televised setting, and the exploration has specified how the televised sounds compare with the sounds as observed in the stadium setting. Secondly, the substantial number of contributions on the sounds of spectators in the stadium setting has been shown to be fragmented and focused upon only some aspects of the sounds while others have been largely overlooked. There is thus only little influence and reference between contributions – which has helped create the breeding ground for the somewhat misleading suggestions of a lack of scholarly works – even though most contributions have focused on potentially compatible aspects of the sounds. Predominantly, the existing contributions have focused on the symbolic meanings of the lyrics of chants and songs, whereas other aspects of significance as well as the structure and distribution of chant and songs – and other types of sounds – have been explored only sporadically. On this background, the book has drawn together, in a coherent form, insights from a variety of scholarly disciplines and publication outlets. Moreover, the book has offered steps towards an integration of the contributions by furthering the overcoming of the language barrier between contributions in the German and English languages. Hopefully, the book's overview of existing contributions can help inspire future research initiatives and prevent them from having to give the impression of addressing a topic of interest characterized by no or only little existing research. For example, it is neither necessary nor appropriate to suggest that chants and songs have been 'largely overlooked', and that songs have 'attracted little scholarly attention' (as explicitly suggested by previous contributions cited in the book's introduction).

A further contribution of the book is the selection of case materials and the adopted approach for exploring the case materials. Firstly, the book has devised a unique selection of case materials including observations of the sounds of spectators from three matches including the same home team in three different stadiums as well as the televised broadcasts of the same three matches – also put in perspective by the selection of an additional televised match played in a stadium without spectators. This selection of materials has facilitated an exploration of issues which have not been systematically examined in the existing contributions. For example, the selection of three matches including the same home team in three different stadiums has facilitated a focus on the implications of spatiality, and the exploration has highlighted the importance of declaring and examining the implications of one's POA as a participant-observer – an issue which has been largely neglected in previous contributions. Also, the selection of the televised broadcasts of the same matches has facilitated an exploration of how the structure, distribution and significance of the sounds in the stadium setting compare with the sounds of the televised broadcast – and the televised match with no spectators in the stadium setting has further inspired perspectives on the role of the sounds in the televised broadcast. Secondly, the book has devised a framework for a systematic qualitative textual analysis of the sounds of spectators at football both in the stadium setting and in the setting of the televised broadcast.

When assessed against the existing contributions, the book has offered supplementary and refined insights into the structure, distribution and significance of the sounds of spectators at football. As regards the stadium setting, insights offered by the book include the following:

- Structure:
  - A specification of other types of sounds than chants and song – for example, a presentation of typologies of sounds at football and sounds of spectators as well as a specification of various forms of segmented collective interjections.
  - An elaboration of other aspects of chants and songs than the symbolic, referential meaning of their lyrics – for example, an exploration of the distinction between different musical structures and types of transtextual relations.
- Distribution:
  - A specification of the sounds from the perspective of spatiality and temporality – for example, an exploration of the sounds from the perspective of 'a sense of place' and 'a sense of being placed' as well as a typology of couplings between sounds and match incidents.
- Significance:
  - A systematic differentiation of the communicative functions of the sounds beyond the symbolic, referential meaning of the lyrics.
  - An exploration of the possible non-communicative functions of the sounds.

One of the significant insights – which challenges a seemingly widely held belief – is that chants and songs should not necessarily be considered the only or even the most pertinent indicator of 'atmosphere' and engagement among spectators in the stadium setting. For example, the examination has shown that while chants and songs are usually merely moderately or loosely coupled with match incidents, segmented collective interjections embody a tightly temporally ordered and closely coupled communal expression (and experience) of highly focused intensity. Also, the examination has indicated that the issue of an 'optimal viewing position' – or 'the best seat' as referred to in Section 4.3 – is less relevant in a mediatized stadium environment in which jumbotrons offer all spectators approximately the same visual (mediated) access to match incidents. By contrast, as the PA system does not distribute sounds during the match (apart from the occasional announcements), the POA offers a unique, distinguishing experience in the stadium setting. Perhaps, an 'optimal listening position' (or an 'ideal POA') would be one from which both the away supporters and the home team supporters could be heard and deciphered. However, the large stadium environments – marked by great distances between groups of supporters – make it difficult to obtain such a position (the position is seemingly easier to obtain at smaller stadiums as indicated in Grøn & Graakjær, 2016). Also, a position 'in between' the most vocally engaged supporters would possibly deny the spectator the experience of being enveloped and overwhelmed by the sounds of spectators.

As regards the setting of the televised broadcast, the book has explored a widespread and important exemplar of televised sound which has not hitherto been subjected to extensive systematic examination. Insights offered by the book include the following:

- Structure:
    o A specification of types of sound – for example, a presentation of the typologies of 'football television sounds' and 'televised football sounds'.
- Distribution:
    o A specification of the sounds of spectators as representing a composite dimension of the televised soundscape – for example, the sounds seem to originate from a 'zone of audition' rather than from a specific 'point of audition' (except for the capture of the sounds by the commentators' microphones).
    o A specification of the relations between the (fluctuating) visuals and the (unwavering) sounds including the perspective of diegesis.
- Significance:
    o A systematic differentiation of the communicative functions of the sounds – for example, the sounds have been shown to be of crucial importance for the establishment of potential experiences of continuity and liveness.

o A specification of how the sounds appear similar to – yet differs from – other types of television sounds – for example, the sounds have been discussed in light of the 'laugh track' and 'background music', and the sound have been described as an 'auditory seismometer'.

The exploration of the sounds of spectators in the televised broadcast has inspired several modifications of specific suggestions offered in previous contributions. For example, the book's examination has demonstrated that actually you *can* follow along with your ears when watching football, continuity *is* indeed achieved also – and arguably first and foremost – by the sounds of spectators (which represent an ever-present and temporally unbroken part of the soundscape) and the sounds of spectators occasionally have the effect of creating a *tripled* moment in conveying what happens *now* while the visuals and the commentary might be occupied by a focus on what happened *just before* and summarizing what has happened *until now*.

The exploration has furthermore highlighted the important basic fact that the sounds of spectators in the televised broadcast differ markedly from the ('same') sounds as experienced in the stadium setting. Some of the differences appear almost paradoxical. For example, the performer sounds of ball strokes are available to the television spectators to a higher degree than to (most of) the spectators in the stadium setting. Also, due to the composite structure of the televised sounds, the possible delay effects of the sounds in the stadium setting are not transpiring in the televised broadcast which is marked by a higher degree of synchronicity. However, although the televised broadcast includes a wide range of (if not all) sound sources including spectators in all sections of the stadium, the sounds appear relatively indistinct. By comparison, in the stadium setting, the spectator can only (over)hear a small proportion of the sounds, but a selection of the sounds will usually appear highly distinctive.

There seems to be reason to emphasize these (among others) differences between the sounds in the stadium setting and the sounds in the televised broadcast. The sounds of the televised broadcast (or recordings from it through various curations of the sounds of spectators) have thus somewhat misguidedly been used as the empirical basis for examining the significance of the sounds in the stadium setting. Also, it is somewhat misleading to refer to the recorded sounds of spectators, deployed in televised broadcasts from empty stadiums, as 'fake', as the televised sounds of spectators have never appeared as 'real' when compared to their origin in the stadium setting. The use of recorded sounds of spectators has additionally illustrated the (increased) interaction between the television and video game industries. As the recoded sounds have been received relatively positively – or at least the sounds have been widely accepted – this could be seen as an indication of a current more welcoming environment for experimentation and use of recorded sounds of spectators in live football broadcasting.

As announced in the introductions to this book, the approach and insights of the book can hopefully be of use for students and researchers within sound studies, musicology, media and communication studies as well as sports studies. From the perspective of sound studies, the book draws attention to a substantial type of sound produced regularly and collectively by thousands of people observed by millions of people. The book offers several typologies of sounds, and it specifies how the sounds of spectators relate to other sounds as well as non-auditory incidents (in the stadium setting) and visual dimensions (in the televised broadcast). Moreover, as a reply to the suggestion once made that 'no one has applied communicational concepts to the field of sound before' (Truax, 2001, p. xvii), the book includes a systematic examination of the sounds from the perspective of their communicative functions.

From the perspective of musicology, the book draws attention to what is arguably the most widespread and significant form of collective musical practice in modern society – again, produced by the thousands and listened to by the millions. Although a (good) handful of specified musicological contributions exist, the musical performances and mediations of spectators have only been addressed sporadically in the context of musicology (see, e.g. Cohen, 2012, p. 597; Hesmondhalgh, 2013, p. 105; Middleton, 1990, pp. 17–18). Nevertheless, the musical performances of spectators – including extensive adaptions of pre-existing music – seem to epitomize that 'performance does not exist in order to present musical works, but rather, musical works exist in order to give performers something to perform' (Small, 1998, p. 8). Also, the musical performances in the setting of the stadium emphasize the relevance of asking not merely 'What is the nature or the meaning of this work of music?' but also (and perhaps more interestingly) 'What does it mean when this performance (of this work) takes place, in this place, with these participants' (Small, 1998, p. 10; italics in original).

From the perspective of media and communication studies, the book addresses a prime example of the continued relevance of live television broadcasting – in a television context otherwise characterized by streaming and viewing on demand. The book offers analytical perspectives on the role of the sounds in establishing, for example, continuity and 'liveness'. Specifically, the highly musicalized soundscape of the televised football match could be considered to represent a noteworthy case of 'music in television' – a topic which has hitherto not included a focus on the sounds of spectators at football (see, e.g. Deaville, 2011). Moreover, the book's examination of the sounds from broadcasts of matches with no spectators in the stadium setting amply illustrates the more general topic of mutual influences between (sports) television programming and (sports) video games.

From the perspective of sports studies, the book has emphasized the importance of sounds for sports spectatorship – a topic which has often been only marginally addressed in contributions on the aesthetics and experience of sports spectating (see, e.g. Gumbrecht, 2006, 2019; Guttman, 1986; Mumford, 2012). For example, the book indicates how the sounds of spectators play a crucial role in establishing the experience (in the stadium setting) and impression (in the televised broadcast) of 'atmosphere'. Also, the spectator is not only experiencing sounds but also (and most suggestively so in the stadium setting) potentially producing sounds; for example, in comparison with the modern theatre spectator, the book specifies the auditory dimension of how the sports spectator arguably 'assumes a playful freedom' (Kennedy, 2009, p. 278) by being able, among other things, to 'negotiate a relationship to other unknown spectators' and to 'condemn the performance's outcome and reject the manner of play' (Kennedy, 2009, p. 279). Furthermore, from the perspective of intersections of sports and music, the book supplements the otherwise predominant focus on recorded music available as self-contained products outside the setting of sports (see, e.g. Bateman & Bale, 2009; Laing & Linehan, 2013; McLeod, 2011; Paytress, 1996; Rowe, 1995).

From the broader perspective of 'sports sounds' the book has characterized the structure, distribution and significance of a particular type of sound within the broad category of what shall here be termed 'football sounds' – that is, sounds that somehow relate to football. As indicated in Table 5.1, the sounds of spectators have been examined as part of the 'sounds at football' which, on the one hand, include the 'sounds of football' – that is, the sounds of performers – and, on the other hand, are included in the broader category of the 'sounds for football', that is, the sounds that somehow relate to football – including sounds from 'outside' the progress of an actual football match over approximately ninety minutes as experienced in the stadium setting or through the televised broadcast.

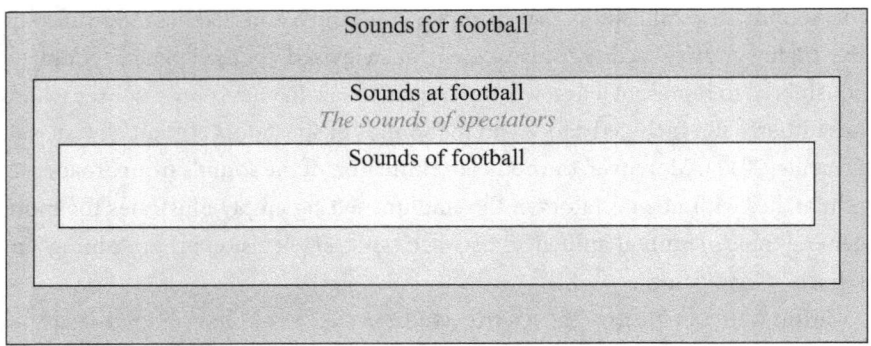

**Table 5.1** An Illustration of the Book's Topic Within the Context of Three Subtypes of 'Football Sounds'

Granting that the 'auditory is a crucial element of any sporting experience', and that the experience of watching sport 'is made up of a number of unique soundscapes' (Powis & Carter, 2019, p. 391), the book has provided insights into what might be considered a unique auditory dimension of the experience of football spectating. Whereas the book's textual examination has focused on a specific part of the 'sounds at football', Table 5.1 might then be proposed as a basic outline for the examination of the possible distinctiveness of the sounds of football compared to other sports including a wider variety of sounds.

As regards the possible distinctiveness of the 'sounds of football', it has been suggested that 'the sound of the boot on the ball is a sound mark' (Trail, 2013, p. 318). This seems reasonable when comparing the sound to, for example, 'the ping of the club on the golf ball' (Real, 2014, p. 20) or the sound of a ball stroke in tennis (see Section 4.3; for an examination of the sounds of skateboarding, see Maier, 2016). Also, the examination has indicated how the 'ball-on-boot' sound is regularly highlighted through the production of the televised broadcast. However, the 'ball-on-boot' sound is generally in the background to – if not entirely drowned out by – the continuous sounds of spectators especially in the stadium setting. This hints at the significance of the sounds of spectators in specifying the possible distinctiveness of the 'sounds at football' by comparison to, for example, the 'sounds at golf' and the 'sounds at tennis' where the performer sounds appear only intermittently and are generally more subdued.

As regards the 'sounds for football' (excluding the subtypes of 'sounds of' and 'sounds at' football) they might seem largely indistinctive when compared to the sounds for other sports regarding, for example, 'chat about the weekend's games on the train on Monday morning; sounds of media commentary, talkback radio calls' (Trail, 2010, p. 68) – although football talk could be considered to include a distinct variety of clichés (Hurrey, 2014) and to represent 'a paradigm for moral behavior and discussion' (Critchley, 2018, p. 104). When it comes to sounds in the immediate 'surroundings' of the progression (and broadcasting) of the football match, it might be the case that a distinctive type of 'music for football' has emerged. At least, such distinctiveness has been proposed in the context of other sports; for example, the National Association for Stock Car Auto Racing (NASCAR) has been said to relate particularly to 'blue-collar Southern white male country music', and the relation between music and National Basket Association (NBA) has been said to be 'most pronounced in the use of hip hop' (McLeod, 2011, pp. 79, 80). Also, specific tracks are regularly identified as particular 'footballish'; for example, Kasabian's *Club Foot* has been identified as 'perhaps the greatest football song of all-time' (Angeli, 2017) and as a track that 'still just screams football' (McCarthy, 2018; see also Graakjær, 2021a). However, based on the case materials and observations in existing contributions (see, e.g. Guschwan, 2016, p. 295; Jack, 2021, p. 31), it is doubtful whether there exists a distinctive relation between football and certain types of music – further research is needed to explore whether specific types of 'music for football' can be determined with respect to their function as, for example, entrance, goal and/or victory music (in the stadium setting) and/or title sequence music (in the televised broadcast).

A further example of 'sounds for football' is the singing performances of (former/future) spectators 'outside' the setting of football as several contributions have exemplified. For example, chants and songs have been observed to emerge outside the stadium right before and after the match (see, e.g. Jack, 2021; Kytö, 2011; Pearson, 2012), on the train (Woodward, 2011), on the phone (Davies, 1972, p. 182), at the airport (Crouch, 2018, p. 186), at musical concerts (where supporters' co-singing can produce so-called 'add-ins' to modify the meaning potentials of particular songs; see Millar, 2016), as part of television title sequences (Graakjær, 2021a) and as part of musical tracks (see, e.g. Bateman & Bale, 2009, p. 3; Lawn, 2020, p. 72; Paytress, 1996, p. 40; Redhead, 1987, p. 27). Whereas this book's examination has highlighted how spectators' singing at football is largely based on transtextual 'imports' of musical materials from outside the setting of football (mostly in the form of adaptions), these examples illustrate an 'export' of a musical practice which musicalizes and stands 'for football' in settings external to the football match.

When it comes to the 'sounds at football' and the role played by the sounds of spectators, the book's materials and approach can hopefully be applicable for future explorations of the sounds of spectators at football in the setting of the stadium and/or in the televised broadcast. Obvious examples of ways in which to broaden the scope of the present approach would be to explore in further detail some of the wider occurrences, conditions and consequences of the sounds of spectators. Whereas the book has predominantly focused on textuality, cotextuality and transtextuality, such a broadening would imply an examination of further aspects of contextuality. The examination could for example be widened to include the sounds of spectators at matches including other teams and other leagues and tournaments. Although the analytical framework is expectedly generalizable, the observed and exemplified sounds are necessarily influenced by the fact that the case material represents matches including Tottenham, the EPL and Danish television broadcasters. For example, the absence of a capo and musical instruments at the case matches could inspire an examination of spectators' instrument-based production of music as well as the influence of a capo. Also, the fact that the case matches are all played in relatively big and filled stadiums could inspire an examination of the sounds in small(er) stadiums. Additionally, this could include an examination of the sounds produced by television audiences (e.g. in homes, bars and at open-air airings), by football simulation video game players and their possible spectators.

Whereas the preceding examples have exemplified 'breadth'-oriented or synchronic broadenings of the scope of the analytical focus, a 'depth'-oriented or diachronic broadening could include an examination of how the sounds of spectators have developed over time. In addition to additional examinations of the historico-geographical origins (merely hinted at in Section 1.2), a pertinent issue is the widespread belief that spectators have grown quieter at football (including the EPL) in recent years. This purported development is arguably fuelled by a wide range of developments including the introduction of all-seater stadiums, kick-off times based on the needs of broadcasters and advertisers, the increased costs of attending, security and risk management and mediatized and consumption-oriented stadium environments (see, e.g. Bazell, 2011; Edensor, 2015; Gaffney & Bale, 2004; King, 2002; Numerato, 2015; Turner, 2013, 2017). Indeed, whereas the atmosphere at, for example, White Hart Lane in the early 1960s has been described as 'absolutely incredible, it was just like a wall of sound' and the crowd of the late 1970s and early 1980s 'seemed louder' (Cloake & Powley, 2013, pp. 29, 82; see also Cloake, 2013), from the mid-1990s observations have been made of a 'lack' and 'absence' of atmosphere (Cloake & Powley, 2013, p. 111). It is beyond the scope and case materials of this book to assess these assumptions. Firstly, the emergence of 'atmosphere' and spectators' production of sound is arguably contingent on numerous match-specific factors including (but expectedly not limited to) the opponent team and their supporters, previous matches and history between the involved teams, the attendance, the stadium structure, the current league standings, the importance of the match (in terms of, e.g., whether the teams are approaching relegation or winning the league), the progression of the match, the time of year, week and day as well as the weather conditions (see, e.g. Uhrich & Benkenstein, 2010). Secondly, the case materials do not allow for an examination of the validity of the assumptions that spectators were once louder and the atmosphere is now lacking. The overview of contributions has not included empirically based explorations of this issue, and while there might be some legitimacy to the assumption, it is based predominantly on anecdotes and might represent a 'football cliché that the atmosphere was better in the old days' (Cloake & Powley, 2013, p. 29). A thorough examination of the anecdotal experiences and assumptions is made difficult as 'there is barely any reliable sound archive against which to test the nostalgia-infused collective memory' (Goldblatt, 2014, p. 79).

While there are indeed several questions and issues to be further explored, it is hoped for that this book's contributions – that is, its research overviews, selection of case materials, proposed text analytical framework and specific insights into the structure, distribution and significance of the sounds of spectators at contemporary elite football – can serve to inspire.

# Appendix

As referred to and elaborated on in Section 2.1, the following table includes a list of fifty-one scholarly contributions characterized by a systematic and theoretically informed examination of (some aspect of) empirically specified sounds of spectators in the stadium setting. The contributions are listed in chronological order (from top to bottom) and profiled (see the columns) from a selection of perspectives relevant for the present purposes.

| Contribution | Field of Research | Empirical Method for Sourcing and Accessing the Sounds | Football | Spectators | Sounds | Main Finding(s) |
|---|---|---|---|---|---|---|
| Marsh et al. (1978) | Ethogenics | Participant observation supplemented by video recordings and interviews | An undisclosed selection of matches of Oxford United home matches in the season of 1974 | Supporters of Oxford United | Lyrics of chants and procedures of introduction of chanting | Specifies chant encouragements for the home team and chant insults directed at the opponents; discusses the role of the chant leader |
| Morris (1981) | Anthropology, zoology, sociobiology | Participant observation | Fifteen Oxford United home matches as well as an undisclosed selection of matches 'in England during the 1978/9 season' | Supporters of Oxford United | Chant lyrics; number of chants in matches and procedures of introduction of chanting | Offers a categorization of chant lyrics and counts of chants in matches |
| Holland (1997) | Sociology | Observation, interviews | An undisclosed selection of 'home' matches including Leeds United and Newcastle United during the 1989/90 and 1992/3 seasons | The 'home' supporters of Leeds United and Newcastle United | The lyrics of chants and shouts | Offers a categorization, examples and frequencies of racial abuse (including racial singing and 'monkey' chanting) and shows that black footballers have suffered disproportionate harassment |
| Bradley (1998) | Sociology | Participant observation is implied and supplemented by fanzines and surveys | A selection of matches including Glasgow Rangers and Celtic | Predominantly supporters of Glasgow Rangers and Celtic | The lyrics of chants | Identifies chants as indicative of social, political and religious identities and underlying features of (Scottish) society |

Appendix 131

| Contribution | Field of Research | Empirical Method for Sourcing and Accessing the Sounds | Football | Spectators | Sounds | Main Finding(s) |
|---|---|---|---|---|---|---|
| Kopiez and Brink (1999) | Musicology | Participant observation supplemented by recordings | The match between 1. FC Köln and Borussia Dortmund on 7 December 1996. Supplemented by a few other matches in Germany | The home and away team supporters of 1. FC Köln and Borussia Dortmund | The musical materials and lyrics of chants and songs | Offers a typology of different types of spectator sounds as well as a categorization of chant lyrics |
| Armstrong and Young (1999) | Anthropology, cultural analysis | Participant observation | An unspecified selection of matches from the 1960s to the 1980s, mostly at Bramall Lane (the home of Sheffield United) | The group of supporters of Sheffield United nicknamed 'The Blades' | The lyrics of chants (including sporadic identification of melodies) | A categorization based on the meaning of the chants' lyrics and a specification of the functions of the chants (relating to feelings and displays of cultural identification and social differentiation) |
| Robson (2000) | Ethnography | Participant observation supplemented by interviews | Sixty-five matches including Millwall from 1995 to1997 (a selection of matches is chosen for detailed examination) | Supporters of Millwall | Chants as rituals | Identifies how chants are not only significant for what they *say* but also for what they *do* in relation to commemorative ritualization |

| Contribution | Field of Research | Empirical Method for Sourcing and Accessing the Sounds | Football | Spectators | Sounds | Main Finding(s) |
|---|---|---|---|---|---|---|
| Back et al. (2001) | Sociology, ethnography | Participant observation supplemented by interviews and audio diaries | A selection of more than one hundred matches including one of the clubs Manchester City, Everton, Millwall and Crystal Palace as well as matches from the Euro 1996 and 2000 and 1998 World Cup internationals | Supporters of Manchester City, Everton, Millwall, Crystal Palace and the English national team | The lyrics of chants | Identifies how 'racialized' chants operate as a means for embodying and representing particular versions of local identity and history |
| Howard (2004) | Sound analysis | Selection of chants from recordings made at matches or from local radio stations | Unspecified selection of top-tier matches from the 2001/2 season in England | Supporters from each of the twenty top-tier clubs | The tuning accuracy and extent of tendency to go flat or sharp of twenty chants | Indicates a 'tunefulness league table' for the 2001/2 top-tier clubs from England |
| Boehm-Kreutzer (2006) | Musicology | Participant observation supplemented by sound recordings | An unspecified selection of home matches for FC Freiburg | Supporters of FC Freiburg | The musical structure of the spectators' chanting and the structure of chants | Indicates how the supporters are singing (using their voices) and specifies types of sounds and musical structures (based on the identification of thirty-four different chants) |

| Contribution | Field of Research | Empirical Method for Sourcing and Accessing the Sounds | Football | Spectators | Sounds | Main Finding(s) |
|---|---|---|---|---|---|---|
| Khodadadi and Gründel (2006) | Linguistics | Selection of (an unspecified selection of) chants obtained from Gumpp et al. (2005) | Unspecified | Supporters of various clubs from the German Bundesliga | The lyrics of chants | Offers a typology of chants based on the lyrics |
| Clark (2006) | Sociology, ethnographic | Participant observation | Twenty-three home games for Scunthorpe United at Glanford Park during 2002/3 | Home and away supporters | Identifies more than fifty different songs some of which are subjected to closer analysis with a focus on the lyrics | Indicates how chanting is an integral part of constructing and (re)negotiating collective identity |
| Luhrs (2007b) | Linguistics, cultural analysis | Participant observation | The League Division Two match between Notts County and Barnsley on 31 January 2004 | The chants from both home and away supporters | Identifies a total of thirty chants throughout the match | Indicates the use of divisive chants relying on (the twentieth anniversary of) the national miner's strike of 1984/5; offers a categorization of chants based on the lyrics |

| Contribution | Field of Research | Empirical Method for Sourcing and Accessing the Sounds | Football | Spectators | Sounds | Main Finding(s) |
|---|---|---|---|---|---|---|
| Jirat (2007) | Ethnography | Participant observation | The match between FC Schaffhausen and FC Aarau (in the Swiss Super League) on 4 May 2005 | The supporters of FC Schaffhausen | The auditory support in the form of songs, chants and cries | Identifies (and exemplifies a handful of) thirty-six different chants which are often initiated by a so-called Capo (song leader) |
| Schiering (2008) | Linguistics | Participant observation supplemented by audio recordings | An unspecified selection of matches (one chant is specified to have appeared on 13 May 2006) including Schalke 04 | The supporters of Schalke 04 | The lyrics of chants | Illustrates the expression and negotiation of regional identity through supporter's chants |
| Luhrs (2008) | Linguistics, cultural studies | Participant observation | A selection of English matches during the 2002/3 and 2003/4 seasons | Supporters at various English matches | The (various forms of) divisive lyrics of chants | Indicates how football chants can be seen as an example of the traditional linguistic genre *Blason Populaire* including local and regional stereotypes for displaying identities and rivalries |
| Brunner (2009) | Linguistics | Selection of chants obtained from www.fangesaenge.de | An undisclosed selection of matches from the German Bundesliga | Supporters at various matches in the German Bundesliga | The lyrics of chants including identification of melodies | Exemplifies and categorizes chants based on the lyrics |

| Contribution | Field of Research | Empirical Method for Sourcing and Accessing the Sounds | Football | Spectators | Sounds | Main Finding(s) |
|---|---|---|---|---|---|---|
| Hill (2009) | Music cultural history | Documents (e.g. historical recordings, newspaper articles) | FA Cup finals in the 1920s with a particular focus on the match in 1927 which was first to be broadcast by the BBC and to include the hymn *Abide with Me* | All spectators at the match(es) | The lyrics and practice of singing the hymn *Abide with Me* | Identifies how a hymn, as part of a well-known sporting ritual, plays a significant role in the formation of an English national identity through meanings relating to remembrance |
| Collinson (2009) | Sociology, ethnography | Participant observation is implied | An unspecified selection of matches including Sydney FC during 2006/7 | Supporters of Sydney FC | The lyrics of chants including identification of melodies | Indicates how the newly formed tradition of singing at football relies on a global song repertoire to create a local identity |
| Sandgren (2010) | Musicology | Observation of televised broadcasts | The live televised World Cup qualifying matches between Sweden and Denmark (6 June 2009), Malta and Sweden (9 September 2009), Denmark and Sweden (10 October 2009), Sweden and Albania (14 October 2009) | The supporters of the teams included | The melodic structure of the refrain from the track *Seven Nation Army* by The White Stripes | Examines the melodic structure of the refrain from the chant *Seven Nation Army* and compares it with a standardized formula of children's communicative songs |

| Contribution | Field of Research | Empirical Method for Sourcing and Accessing the Sounds | Football | Spectators | Sounds | Main Finding(s) |
|---|---|---|---|---|---|---|
| Schoonderwoerd (2011) | Musicology; cultural studies | Participant observation is implied | The match at Anfield between Liverpool and Unirea Urziceni on 18 February, 2010 | Supporters of Liverpool | The lyrics and melodies of chants | Exemplifies and discusses the appearance, origin and migration of chants |
| Kytö (2011) | Sound studies, ethnography | Participant observation supplemented by discussions with fans and mediated materials | A match at Inönü stadium between Besiktas and Genclerbirligi supplemented by observations in a pub and a park | Carsi, a supporter group of Besiktas | The lyrics of chants, other productions of sound and accompanying body movements | Indicates how Carsi's chants and singing practices construct group identity |
| Power (2011) | Cultural studies | Participant observation is implied | The match between Liverpool and Arsenal on 7 January 2007 | Home supporters of Liverpool | The specific chant of *Justice for the ninety-six* to the tune of *Go West* | Indicates how a spectator song can reconstruct the stadium as a political place and include aspects of identity and ideology beyond the specific match, local identities and the opponent |
| Vilter (2011) | Sociology | Sampling of chants from www.fangesaenge.de and the website of Hamburger Sport-Verein (HSV) | Unspecified | Supporters of HSV | The lyrics and melodies of chants | Offers a categorization (based on Morris, 1981) of HSV chants |

| Contribution | Field of Research | Empirical Method for Sourcing and Accessing the Sounds | Football | Spectators | Sounds | Main Finding(s) |
|---|---|---|---|---|---|---|
| Flint and Powell (2011) | Sociology, cultural studies | Unspecified | Unspecified (matches including Rangers FC and/or Celtic FC are implied) | The supporters of Rangers FC and Celtic FC | The lyrics of chants | Specifies how the informalized spaces of Scottish football should be understood as arenas where identities and values are expressed – through sectarian chants – and contested around hostilities established in non-football contexts |
| Pearson (2012) | Ethnography | Participant observation (before, during and after matches) | An unspecified selection of matches including Blackpool FC (1995–8), the English national team (1998–2006) and Manchester United (2001–11) | Supporters of the Blackpool FC, the English national and Manchester United | The lyrics of chants | Offers insights into the production of new chants and an overview of the most prevalent types of chants based on the contents of the lyrics |
| Luhrs (2014) | Linguistic, cultural studies | Participant observation is implied | An unspecified selection of matches from English football grounds during 2003 and 2004 | Supporters of various English clubs | The lyrics of chants | Indicates how chants express a celebration of the archetypal alpha male including divisive chants that rely on insults about women |

| Contribution | Field of Research | Empirical Method for Sourcing and Accessing the Sounds | Football | Spectators | Sounds | Main Finding(s) |
|---|---|---|---|---|---|---|
| Daiber (2015) | Linguistics | An unspecified selection of chants obtained (from 30 May to 6 June 2014) from www.fanchants.com | An unspecified selection of Zenit Sankt Peterburg's home matches | Supporters of Zenit Sankt Peterburg | The lyrics of the new signature chant for Zenit Sankt Peterburg | Discusses the intertextuality and familiarity of lyrics and their psychological implications from a Lacanian perspective |
| Beljutin (2015) | Linguistics | An unspecified selection of chants obtained from various print and web sources (including www.fangesaenge.de) | An unspecified selection of German and Russian club matches | Supporters of various Russian and German clubs | The lyrics of chants | Indicates similarities and differences between the symbolic meaning of the lyrics of Russian and German chants |
| Nannestad (2015) | Cultural studies, history | An unspecified selection of chants referred to in two football specials (*Sporting News* and *The Football Post*) | An unspecified selection of Swansea Town matches in the 1920s | Supporters of Swansea Town | The titles, placement and prevalence of chants | Specifies (types of) songs and discusses aspects of the significance of historic singing practice |
| Gron and Graakjær (2016) | Musicology | Participant observation | The match between AaB and Brøndby in the Danish Superliga on 1 September 2013 | Supporters of home and away supporters | The placement, lyrics and functions of chants in relation to the sounds distributed by the stadium's PA system | Indicates a typology of chants and their relation to other music in the stadium setting |

Appendix    139

| Contribution | Field of Research | Empirical Method for Sourcing and Accessing the Sounds | Football | Spectators | Sounds | Main Finding(s) |
|---|---|---|---|---|---|---|
| Guschwan (2016) | Ethnography | Participant observation is implied | An undisclosed selection of home matches of S.S. Lazio and A.S. Roma during the 2005–6 season | Supporters of A.S. Roma and S.S. Lazio | The lyrics of a selection of chants, songs and shouts | Catalogues the modes of expression employed by football fans at the (Italian) football stadium. Exemplifies how songs are used by fans to establish and display passion, partisanship and identity |
| Ricatti (2016) | Cultural studies | Unspecified | Numerous examples of chants and songs allegedly performed at matches including AS Roma | Supporters of AS Roma | The lyrics and melodic origin of the chants and songs | Provides a taxonomy of songs. Indicates how emotions about football are experienced, expressed and performed and how songs about football contributes to the development of emotional communities that are inherently political |
| Bonz (2016) | Ethnography | Participant observation is implied | An unspecific selection of matches including SV Werder Bremen | Supporters of Werder Bremen | The lyrics of chants | Indicates the sounds' affective impact and significance for identification |
| Fuller (2016) | Sound studies, ethnography | Participant observation | An Indonesian second-tier match between Persis Solo and PSGC Ciamis | Supporters of Persis Solo | The chants and other sounds as they emerge in the particular setting | Identifies and discusses features of chants and the sonic environment of a football match |

| Contribution | Field of Research | Empirical Method for Sourcing and Accessing the Sounds | Football | Spectators | Sounds | Main Finding(s) |
|---|---|---|---|---|---|---|
| Knijnik (2016) | Sociology, ethnography | Participant observation supplemented by interviews and online data | An unspecified selection of matches during the seasons of 2013/14 and 2014/15 in the A-league (Australian top tier) | Supporters of Western Sydney Wanderers | The lyrics of chants and examples of instrumental music (including trumpets and drums) | Indicates how the lyrics of the chants and the noisy carnival of the supporters express a multicultural identity and hopes for a non-conflictive community |
| Herrera (2018) | Ethnomusicology | Participant observation and interviews | An unspecified selection of matches in the autumn of 2016 at various football stadia in Buenos Aires | An unspecified selection of men belonging to middle- and lower-income brackets; mostly so-called 'core fans' | Chants and instrumental music (including brass instruments and various forms of drums) | An indication of how participatory 'moving-and-sounding-in-synchrony' creates a performative social space related to 'aguante' (suggesting a certain kind of masculinity) |
| Lee (2018) | Ethnography | Participant observation supplemented by interviews and attendance at supporter meetings outside the setting of the matches | A selection of mostly unspecified (and mostly home) matches involving New York City Football Club in the Major League soccer (USA) from March to October 2015 | A group of supporters called The Third Rail | The lyrics of chants and accompanying body movements | Explores the formation of a singing culture at the newly established New York City Football Club. Indicates how singing combines a shared focus on group symbols with bodily coordination and repetition to produce positive feelings |

| Contribution | Field of Research | Empirical Method for Sourcing and Accessing the Sounds | Football | Spectators | Sounds | Main Finding(s) |
|---|---|---|---|---|---|---|
| Lavric (2019) | Linguistic, pragmatics | Sampling of ninety chants obtained from the website www.fanchants.com | Undisclosed selection of matches including nine teams from Italy, Spain, and France (three teams from each country) | The supporters of the nine teams | The lyrics of chants | Proposes a categorization (including twenty subtypes) of the lyrics of chants from the perspective of participation frameworks and participant constellations |
| Marra and Trotta (2019) | Musicology, cultural analysis | Participant observation and field recordings from three pairs of stereo microphones in three different sections of the stadium synchronized with a radio broadcast | Twenty-one (most of which are unspecified) matches including the Brazilian football club Atlético Mineiro from 2011 to 2015 | The home supporters of Atlético Mineiro | Sounds as sonic techniques seen from the perspectives of intensity and rhythm, singing, and the chant *Eu Acredito* | Indicates how the techniques and qualities (beyond the meanings of the lyrics) of spectator sounds can be performed with the (spectator's) belief that the sounds can influence players' performance and the course of the match |
| Fantoni et al. (2020) | Linguistics | An unspecified sample of the lyrics of chants obtained from www.fanchants.com | An unspecified selection of matches including the 'big six' clubs in the EPL | Supporters of the 'big six' clubs in the EPL | The lyrics of mocking chants | Identifies aspects of interactions among participants (spectators, players, listeners) and the characteristics of mocking chants |

| Contribution | Field of Research | Empirical Method for Sourcing and Accessing the Sounds | Football | Spectators | Sounds | Main Finding(s) |
|---|---|---|---|---|---|---|
| Argan et al. (2020) | Linguistics | Selection of chants from YouTube | Unspecified | The supporters of thirteen clubs in the Turkish Super League | The metaphors of eighty-four chants | Identifies various types and incidences of metaphors in chants |
| O'Brien (2020) | Musicology; cultural analysis | Unspecified (various videos and written sources are implied) | The match between Argentine Boca Juniors and San Lorenzo (4 February 2018) | The supporters of San Lorenzo (and others) | The origin (and further distribution) of the melody and lyrics of the chant *Mauricio Macri, la puta que te parió* | Identifies the use and 'career' of a particular chant from an abusive contrafactum at stadiums, over a collective political statement at stadiums to mass-mediated popular music outside the stadium setting |
| Bell and Bell (2020) | Sociology | Participant observation and digital recordings supplemented by interviews | Ten matches of the national team of Northern Ireland during the 2014–15 qualifying games for EURO 2016 | The supporters of Northern Ireland | The lyrics, placement, introduction and popularity of fifty songs | Identifies what (almost exclusively non-sectarian) songs are introduced when (four conditions are specified) and how |
| Herd and Löfgren (2020) | Musicology; cultural analysis | Participant observation and interviews | An undisclosed selection of various Swedish matches between 2013 and 2018 (with an implied focus on matches including Gefle IF and AIK) | Supporters of Gefle IF and AIK | The lyrics, melodies and contexts of two songs | Identifies how specific chants can have mocking, and self-parodying implications |

| Contribution | Field of Research | Empirical Method for Sourcing and Accessing the Sounds | Football | Spectators | Sounds | Main Finding(s) |
|---|---|---|---|---|---|---|
| Irak (2021) | Sociology, sociopolitical analysis | Online search (the process is unspecified) | Unspecified selection of matches including Turkish clubs | Supporters of various Turkish teams | The use and lyrics of the particular chant Izmir March | Identifies and discusses how and why an old military song has become the symbol of dissidence and anti-regime protest |
| Tamir (2021) | Sociology, qualitative content analysis | Selection of chants obtained from an online forum and from an appeal to forum members to specify 'older chants' | An unspecified selection of matches including the Israeli club Maccabi Tel Aviv | The supporters of the Israeli club Maccabi Tel Aviv | The lyrics of ninety-eight chants over a period of five decades | Indicates both stable values (e.g. the home team is larger than life, the rival must be undermined) and changing trends (radicalization of hate and protesting commodification) |
| McKerrell (2021) | Social semiotics | Selection of chants (no information of selection process and criteria) | Unspecified selection of matches (matches including various British clubs are implied) | The supporters of various British clubs including Celtic FC, Rangers FC, Newcastle United and Manchester United | The metaphors of chants | Through an analysis of examples of chant lyrics' inclusion of (different types of) metaphors, the contribution shows how chants act as socially embedded and embodied communication |

| Contribution | Field of Research | Empirical Method for Sourcing and Accessing the Sounds | Football | Spectators | Sounds | Main Finding(s) |
|---|---|---|---|---|---|---|
| Marra (2021) | Sound studies, cultural analysis | Participant observation is implied supplemented by recordings | Unspecified selection of matches including Brazilian club Galo FA | The supporters of Galo FA | The insulting, swearing phrases of the lyrics of chants | Identifies how aggressive sounds of heteronormative insults in male fan performances strain, reinvent or re-enact gender biases in football arenas through sonic modulations of swearing |
| Zalis (2021) | Ethnomusicology | Participant observation | A (mostly unspecified) selection of matches including Ottawa Fury Football Club from 2014 to 2015 | The supporter group Stony Monday Riot | The functions and politics of chants and chanting and other forms of sound production | Discusses the functions and politics of the sound production of Stony Monday Riot as it emerges in a setting with other (conflicting) sounds produced by other spectators as well as the stadium organizers |
| Huddleston (2022) | Sociology, cultural analysis | Selection of chants obtained from various online sources | Unspecified (matches including the Argentine club River Plate is implied) | The supporters of the Argentine club River Plate | The lyrics of 'over 250' chants | Identifies a worldview in which engagement in violence is an effective method of improving social capital and a necessary demonstration of personal honour, *aguante* and masculine virtue |

# References

Allen, B. (2020). Meet the man who plays crowd noise sounds on a drum machine for Sky Sports Football. *GQ*. 10 July. Retrieved 19 June 2022, from https://www.gqmagazine.co.uk/sport/article/artificial-crowd-noises.

Allen, R. C., & Hill, A. (Eds) (2004). *The television studies reader*. Routledge.

Altman, R. (1986). Television/Sound. In T. Modleski (Ed.), *Studies in entertainment: Critical approaches to mass culture* (pp. 39–54). Indiana University Press.

Ameka, F. (1992). Interjections: The universal yet neglected part of speech. *Journal of Pragmatics*, *18*, 101–18.

Andrew, J. (2020). Who controls the fake crowd noise? How clubs are experimenting with match atmosphere in empty stadiums. *FourFourTwo*. 14 July. Retrieved 19 June 2022, from https://www.fourfourtwo.com/features/who-controls-the-fake-crowd-noise-how-clubs-are-experimenting-with-match-atmosphere-in-empty-stadiums.

Andrews, P. (2012). The sound of sport. What is real? *Acoustics Bulletin*, *37*(4), 30–3.

Angeli, E. (2017). Sky sports and the theme tunes: A successful relationship? *The Versed*. 22 November. Retrieved 19 June 2022, from https://www.theversed.com/84423/sky-sports-and-the-theme-tunes-a-successful-relationship/#.kNKdcvcDaU.

Argan, M., Özgen, C., Ilbars, B., Yetim, G., & Kaya, S. (2020). You'll never walk alone without metaphor: A study on the football chants. *Pamukkale Journal of Sport Sciences*, *11*(1), 7–22.

Armstrong, G., & Young, M. (1999). Fanatical football chants: Creating and controlling the carnival. *Culture, Sport, Society*, *2*(3), 173–211.

Armstrong, P. (2019). *Why are we always on last? Running Match of the Day and other adventures in TV and football*. Pitch.

Asakura, T., & Ishikawa, A. (2020). Field study on acoustic factors of onsite football spectating. *Acoustical Science and Technology*, *41*(6), 829–32.

Ashmore, P. (2017). Of other atmospheres: Football spectatorship beyond the terrace chant. *Sport & Society*, *18*(1), 30–46.

Augoyard, J.-F., & Torgue, H. (2005). *Sonic experience: A guide to everyday sounds*. McGill-Queens University Press.

Auslander, P. (1999). *Liveness: Performance in a mediatized culture*. Routledge.

Baccellieri, E. (2020). What's behind MLB's fake crowd noise? A conductor with an iPad. *Sports Illustrated*. 5 September. Retrieved 19 June 2022, from https://www.si.com/mlb/2020/09/05/baseball-fake-crowd-nosie.

Back, L. (2003). Sounds in the crowd. In M. Bull & L. Back (Eds), *The auditory culture reader* (pp. 311–27). Berg.

Back, L., Crabbe, T. & Solomos, J. (2001). *The changing face of football: Racism, identity and multiculture in the English game*. Berg.

Bale, J. (1993). *Sport, space and the city*. Routledge.

Bale, J. (2003a). *Sports geography* (2nd ed.). Routledge.

Bale, J. (2003b). A geographical theory of sport. In Verner Møller & John Nauright (Eds), *The essence of sport* (pp. 81–91). University Press of Southern Denmark.

Barnfield, A. (2013). Soccer, broadcasting, and narrative: On televising a live soccer match. *Communication & Sport, 1*(4), 326–41.

Barwick, B. (2013). *Watching the match: The inside story of football on television*. Carlton.

Bateman, A., & Bale, J. (Eds) (2009). *Sporting sounds: Relationships between sport and music*. Routledge.

Baudrillard, J. (1981/1994). *Simulacra and simulation*. University of Michigan Press.

Baumann, Z. (2004). *Identity*. Polity Press.

Bazell, M. (2011). *Theatre of silence: The lost soul of football*. Pegasus.

Bazell, M., & Andrews, M. (2019). *We've only got one song: Arsenal terrace songs and chants*. Legends.

Beljutin, R. (2015). Fankommunikation in Russland und in Deutschland: Gemeinsamkeiten und Unterschiede. In J. Born & T. Gloning (Eds), *Sport, Sprache, Kommunikation, Medien. Interdisziplinäre Perspektiven* (pp. 1–17). Giessener Elektronische Bibliotek.

Bell, J., & Bell, P. (2020). And this is what we sing – what do we sing? Exploring the football fan songs of the Northern Irish 'Green and white army'. *International Review for the Sociology of Sport, 56*(8), 1206–23.

Bensimon, M., & Bodner, E. (2011). Playing with fire: The impact of football game chanting on level of aggression. *Journal of Applied Social Psychology, 41*(10), 2421–33.

Bensy, B. R. (2020). *The story of you'll never walk alone: The history of Liverpool Football Club and its anthem*. Independently published.

Bignell, J. (2013). *An introduction to television studies* (3rd ed.). Routledge.

Billings, A. (Ed.) (2011). *Sports media: Transformation, integration, consumption*. Routledge.

Birdsall, C., & Enns A. (2012). Editorial: Rethinking theories of television sounds. *Journal of Sonic Studies, 3*(1), 1–8. Retrieved 19 June 2022, from https://pure.uva.nl/ws/files/1845067/121303.

Boehm-Kreutzer, A. (2006). 'Wenn wir auf der Nordtribüne stehn'. Die singenden fans der SC Freiburg. *Notenpapir. Magasin der Hochschule für Musik Freiburg, 1*, 5–11.

Böhme, G. (2017). *The aesthetics of atmospheres*. Routledge.

Bonnet, V., & Lochard, G. (2015). TV broadcasting: Toward a pluri- and inter-semiotic approach. In P. M. Pedersen (Ed.), *Routledge handbook of sport communication* (pp. 38–45). Routledge.

Bonetti, P. O., & Hunziker, P. (2006). Watching football on TV may potentially be life-threatening. *Swiss Medical Weekly*, *136*(228), 228.

Bonz, J., et al. (Eds) (2010). *Fans und Fans. Fussball-Fankultur in Bremen*. Edition Temmen.

Bonz, J. (2015). *Alltagsklänge – Einsätze einer Kulturanthropologie des Hörens*. Springer Verlag.

Bonz, J. (2016). Soccer stadium as Soundscape: Sound and subjectivity. In J. G. Papenburg & H. Schulze (Eds), *Sound as popular culture: A research companion* (pp. 149–57). MIT Press.

Boyle, R. (2014). Television sport in age of screens and content. *Television & New Media*, *15*(8), 746–51.

Boyle, R. (2019). Football and media matters. In J. Hughson, K. Moore, R. Spaaij & J. Maguire (Eds), *Routledge handbook of football studies* (pp. 179–88). Routledge.

Boyle, R., & Haynes, R. (2004). *Football in the new media age*. Routledge.

Bradley, J. (1998) 'We shall not be moved!' Mere sport, mere songs? A tale of Scottish football. In A. Brown (Ed.), *Fanatics! Power, identity and fandom in football* (pp. 203–18). Routledge.

Bremner, J. (2010). *Shit ground no fans. It's by far the greatest football songbook the world has ever seen* (2nd edn). Bantam Press.

Brown, A. (Ed.) (1998). *Fanatics! Power, identity & fandom in football*. London: Routledge.

Brown, P. (2017). *Savage enthusiasm: A history of football fans*. Goal Post.

Brunner, G. (2009). Fangesänge im Fussballstadion. In A. Burkhardt & Schlobinski (Eds), *Flickflack, Foul und Tsukahara: Der Sport und seine Sprache* (pp. 194–210). Duden.

Bryant, J., Comisky, P., & Zillmann, D. (1977). Drama in sports commentary. *Journal of Communication*, *27*(3), 140–9.

Bryman, A. (2016). *Social research methods* (5th edn). Oxford University Press.

Buchanan, D. A. (2002). Soccer, popular music and national consciousness in post-state-socialist Bulgaria, 1994–96. *British Journal of Ethnomusicology*, *11*(2), 1–27.

Buford, B. (1992). *Among the thugs: The experience, and the seduction, of crowd violence*. W. W. Norton.

Bull, M. (Ed.) (2019). *The Routledge companion to sound studies*. Routledge.

Bulmer, L., & Merrills, R. (1992). *Dicks out. The unique guide to British football songs*. Chatsby.

Burk, V. (2002). Dynamik und Ästhetik der beliebtesten TV-Programmsparte. Fußball als Fernsehereignis. In Herzog (Ed.), *Fußball als Kulturphänomen: Kunst – Kult – Kommerz* (pp. 233–50). Kohlhammer.

Buscombe, E. (1975). Cultural and televisual codes in two title sequences. In E. Buscombe (Ed.), *Football on television* (pp. 16–34). British Film Institute.

Butler, J. G. (2012). *Television: Critical methods and applications* (4th edn). Routledge.

Buxton. P. (2019). Spurs' stadium roof is on top of its game. *The Riba Journal*. 12 July. Retrieved 19 June 2022, from https://www.ribaj.com/buildings/spurs-fc-london-stadium-roof-tottenham-pip-july-august-2019.

Canter, D., Comber, M., & Uzzell, D. (1989). *Football in its place: An environmental psychology of football grounds*. Routledge.

Carrieri-Rocha, V. M., Duarte, M. H. L., & Vasconcellos, A. S. (2020). Acoustic stress in domestic dogs (Canis familiaris) living around football stadiums. *Journal of Veterinary behavior*, 37, 27–35.

Carter, B. (2020). Why the sports world needs fake crowd noise – and late-night comedy doesn't. *CNN*. 23 July. Retrieved 19 June 2022, from https://edition.cnn.com/2020/07/23/perspectives/sports-late-night-comedy-crowd-noise/index.html.

Catsis, J. R. (1996). *Sports broadcasting*. Nelson-Hall.

CBS News (2013). The rich history of 'When the Saints Go Marching In'. *CBS News*. 2 February. Retrieved 19 June 2022, from https://www.cbsnews.com/news/the-rich-history-of-when-the-saints-go-marching-in/.

Charleston, S. (2008). Determinants of home atmosphere in English football: A committed supporter perspective. *Journal of Sport Behavior*, 31(4), 312–28.

Chion, M. (1994). *Audio-vision: Sound on screen*. Columbia University Press.

Chion, M. (2009). *Film, a sound art*. Columbia University Press.

Chisari, F. (2006). When football went global: Televising the 1966 World Cup. *Historical Social Research*, 31(1), 42–54.

Clark, T. (2006). 'I'm Scunthorpe 'til I Die': Constructing and (re)negotiating identity through the terrace chant. *Soccer and Society*, 7(4), 494–507.

Cloake, M. (2013). *Sound of the crowd. Spurs fan culture and the fight for future football* (Ebook edn). Amazon.

Cloake, M., & Powley, A. (2013). *We are Tottenham: Voices from the White Hart Lane*. CreateSpace Independent Publishing Platform.

Cohen, S. (2012). Live music and urban landscape: Mapping the beat in Liverpool. *Social Semiotics*, 22(5), 587–603.

Collinson, I. (2009). 'Singing songs, making places, creating selves': Football songs & fan identity at Sydney FC. *Transforming Cultures eJournal*, 4(1), 15–27.

Comisky, P., Bryant, J., & Zillmann, D. (1977). Commentary as a substitute for action. *Journal of Communication*, 27(3), 150–3.

Connell, J. (2017). Groundhopping: Nostalgia, emotion and the small places of football. *Leisure Studies*, 36(4), 553–64.

Constable, N. (2014). *Match of the day: 50 years*. BBC Books.

Crisell, A. (2006). *A study of modern television: Thinking inside the box*. Palgrave Macmillan.

Critchley, S. (2018). *What we think about when we think about football*. Profile Books.
Crouch, P. (2018). *How to be a footballer*. Ebury Press.
Cummins, G. R., Berke, C. K., Moe, A., & Gong, Z. (2019). Sight versus sound: The differential impact of mediated spectator response in sport broadcasting. *Journal of Broadcasting and Electronic Media*, 61(1), 111–29.
Cummins, G. R., & Gong, Z. (2017). Mediated intra-audience effects in the appreciation of broadcast sports. *Communication and Sports*, 5(1), 27–48.
Curley, J., & Roeder, O. (2016). English soccer's mysterious worldwide popularity. *Contexts*, 15(1), 78–81.
Dahlén, P. (2008). *Sport och medier*. IJ-forlaget.
Daiber, T. (2015). Das Geschlecht des Spiels: Die symbolische Ordnung von Fangesängen. In J. Born & T. Gloning (Eds), *Sport, Sprache, Kommunikation, Medien. Interdisziplinäre Perspektiven* (pp. 133–53). Giessener Elektronische Bibliotek.
Danesi. M. (2020). *The quest for meaning: A guide to semiotic theory and practice* (2nd edn). University of Toronto Press.
Davies, H. (1972). *The glory game*. Mainstream.
Dean, R. (2021). Durrr-dur-dur-dur-dur-durrrr-durrrrrr: More than just White Stripes. *Sport in Society*, 24(1), 8–21.
Deaville, J. (2011). *Music in television: Channels of listening*. Routledge.
Deninger, D. (2012). *Sports on television*. Routledge.
Dingemanse, M. (2020). Between sound and speech: Liminal signs in interaction. *Research on Language and Social Interaction*, 53(1), 188–96.
Dörr, D. (2000). *Sport im Fernsehen: Die Funktionen des öffentlich-rechlischen Rundfunks bei der Sportsberichterstattung*. Peter Lang.
Duerden, J. (2020). Iniesta's Vissel Kobe ban singing, chanting due to coronavirus threat. *Soccer*. 22 February. Retrieved 19 June 2022, from https://www.espn.com/soccer/vissel-kobe/story/4057914/iniestas-vissel-kobe-ban-singing-chanting-due-to-coronavirus-threat.
Duggan, J. (2012). *The glory of Spurs*. Crimson.
Dunn, C. (2014). *Female football fans*. Palgrave.
Dunning, E., Murphy P., & Williams, J. (2014). *The roots of football hooliganism: A historical and sociological study*. Routledge.
Durkheim, E. (1912/2001). *The elementary forms of religious life*. Oxford University Press.
Durrant, P., & Kennedy, E. (2007). Sonic sport: Sound art in leisure research. *Leisure Sciences*, 29(2), 181–94.
Dutta, T. (2015). A brief history of football chants in England. *Goaldentimes*. 19 April. http://www.goaldentimes.org/a-brief-history-of-football-chants-in-england/.

EA Sports (2014). FIFA 15 – Barclays Premier League – stadiums. Retrieved 19 June 2022, from https://www.ea.com/en-gb/games/fifa/news/fifa-15-barclays-premier-league-stadiums-uk.

Edensor, T. (2015). Producing atmospheres at the match: Fan cultures, commercialization and mood management in English football. *Emotion, Space and Society*, *15*, 82–9.

Edwards, R. (2020). Sky Sports considers using CGI fans if Premier League returns behind-closed-doors. *Inews*. 30 April. Retrieved 19 June 2022, from https://inews.co.uk/sport/football/premier-league-project-restart-sky-bt-sport-tv-crowds-cgi-behind-closed-doors-2608326.

Edwardes, C. (1892). The new football mania. *The Nineteenth Century: A Monthly Review*, *32*(188), 622–31.

Elliott, R. (2017). Introduction. 25 years of the English Premier League. In R. Elliott (Ed.), *The English Premier League: A socio-cultural history* (pp. 4–12). Routledge.

Fantoni, N. R., Santosa, R. & Djatmika, D. (2020). The interpersonal meaning of mocking chant to football players by English Premier League supporters. *LiNGUA*, *15*(1), 23–35.

Finn, R. L. (1963). *Spurs go marching on: The European triumph 1963*. The Soccer Book Club.

Fitzgerald, B. M., & Trim, R. M. (1998). The 'Smartsound' noise adaptive public address control system. In P. D. Thompson, J. J. A. Tolloczko & J. N. Clarke (Eds), *Stadia, arenas and grandstands* (pp. 179–84). Routledge.

Flint, J., & Powell, R. (2011). 'They sing that song': Sectarianism and conduct in the informalized species of Scottish football. In D. Burdsey (Ed.), *Race, ethnicity and football: Persisting debates and emergent issues* (pp. 191–204). Routledge.

Flowers, B. S. (2017). *Sport and architecture*. Routledge.

Football Stadiums (2022). White Hart Lane: (Tottenham Hotspur). Retrieved 19 June 2022, from https://www.football-stadiums.co.uk/grounds/england/white-hart-lane/.

Francis, R. (1964). The Anfield Kop. *BBC Panorama*.

Fuller, A. (2016). Football soundscapes of Java. *Journal of Sonic Studies*, *12*. Retrieved 19 June 2022, from https://www.researchcatalogue.net/view/286556/286557.

Gaffney, C., & Bale, J. (2004). Sensing the stadium. In P. Vertinsky & J. Bale (Eds). *Sites of sport: Space, place, experience* (pp. 25–39). Routledge.

Gantz, W. (1981). An exploration of viewing motives and behaviours associated with television sports. *Journal of Broadcasting*, *25*(3), 263–76.

Gantz, W. (2014) Keeping score: Reflections and suggestions for scholarship in sports and media. In A. Billings (Ed.), *Sports media: Transformation, integration, consumption* (pp. 7–18). Routledge.

Gantz, W., & Lewis, N. (2017). Sport as audience studies. In A. C. Billings (Ed.), *Defining Sport Communication* (pp. 235–51). Routledge.

Gerhardt, C. (2014). *Appropriating live televised football through talk*. Brill.

Gilbert, J. (2004). Signifying nothing: 'Culture', 'discourse' and the affect. *Culture Machine*, 6, 1–14. Retrieved 19 June 2022, from https://culturemachine.net/deconstruction-is-in-cultural-studies/signifying-nothing/.

Giulianotti, R. (1999). *Football: A sociology of the global game*. Polity Press.

Giulianotti, R. (2002). Supporters, followers, fans, and flaneurs: A taxonomy of spectator identities in football. *Journal of Sport and Social Issues*, 26(1), 25–46.

Goffman, E. (1981a). Response cries. In E. Goffman (Ed.), *Forms of talk* (pp. 78–123). University of Pennsylvania Press.

Goffman, E. (1981b). Footing. In E. Goffman (Ed.), *Forms of talk* (pp. 124–59). University of Pennsylvania Press.

Goksøyr, M., & Hognestad, H. (1999). No longer worlds apart? British influences and Norwegian football. In G. Armstrong & R. Giulianotti (Eds), *Football cultures and identities* (pp. 201–10). Palgrave Macmillan.

Goldblatt, D. (2007). *The ball is round: A global history of football*. Penguin books.

Goldblatt, D. (2014). *The games of our lives: The meaning and making of English football*. Penguin Random House.

Goldblatt, D. (2020). *The age of football: The global game in the twenty-first century*. Picador.

Goldlust, J. (1987). *Sport, the media and society*. Melbourne: Longman Cheshire.

Goldschmied, N., Vira, D., Raphaeli, M., Bush, R. (2018). 'Air ball, Air ball!': A study of collective crowd chanting in collegiate basketball. *Group Dynamics: Theory, Research, and Practice*, 22(2), 63–75.

Goldsmith, B. (2013). 'Sportv'. The legacies and power of television. In B. Hutchins & D. Rowe (Eds), *Digital media sport: Technology, power and culture in the network society* (pp. 52–65). Routledge.

Graakjær, N. J. (2020a). Sounds of soccer on-screen: A critical re-evaluation of the role of spectator sounds. *Journal of Popular Television*, 8(2), 143–58.

Graakjær, N. J. (2020b). 'Listen to the atmosphere!': On spectator sounds and their potentially disruptive role in a football simulation video game. *The Soundtrack*, 11(1), 39–55.

Graakjær, N. J. (2021a). *Club Foot* for football – on the (re)construction of meanings of music and football through a television title sequence. *Sport in Society*, 24(1), 22–37.

Graakjær, N. J. (2021b). Analysing digital food sounds from a textual perspective: A case of champagne (?). In J. Leer & S. G. S. Krogager (Eds), *Research methods in digital food studies* (pp. 40–53). Routledge.

Granström, K. (2012). Cheering as an indicator of social identity and self-regulation in Swedish ice hockeysupporter groups. *International Review for the Sociology of Sport*, 47(2), 133–48.

Gray, D. (2016). *Saturday, 3pm*. Bloomsbury.

Griffiths, J. (1998). Sound, noise and acoustics in stadium design. In P. D. Thompson, J. J. A. Tolloczko & J. N. Clarke (Eds), *Stadia, arenas and grandstands* (pp. 173–8). Routledge.

Grosshans, G.-T. (1997). *Fussball im deutschen Fernsehen*. Peter Lang.

Gruneau, R., Whitson, D., & Cantelon, H. (1988). Methods and media: Studying the sports/television discourse. *Society & Leisure, 11*(2), 265–81.

Grøn, R., & Graakjær, N. J. (2016). Fodboldkampens musik: Om forekomsten af musik i forbindelse med en Superligakamp [The music of the match: On the appearances of music at a match in the Danish national football league]. In M. Krogh & H. Marstal (Eds), *Populærmusikkultur i Danmark siden 2000* (pp. 291–325). Syddansk Universitetsforlag.

Gumbrecht, H. U. (2004). *Production of presence*. Stanford University Press.

Gumbrecht, H. U. (2006). *In praise of athletic beauty*. Harvard University Press.

Gumbrecht, H. U. (2019). 'Allure' constrained by 'ethics'? How athletic events have engaged their spectators. In John Zilcosky & Marlo A. Burks (Eds), *The allure of sports in Western culture* (pp. 36–52). University of Toronto Press.

Gumbrecht, H. U. (2021). *The stadium as a ritual of intensity*. Stanford University Press.

Gumpp, S., Kohlhaas, N. & Kurth, S. (2005). *Lieder aus der Kurve. Gesangbuch für fussballfans*. Europa Verlag.

Gupta, M. (2020). A sound approach to delivering sports audio. *TV Technology*. 3 February. Retrieved 19 June 2022, from https://www.tvtechnology.com/opinions/a-sound-approach-to-delivering-sports-audio.

Guschwan, M. (2016). Performance in the stands. *Soccer & Society, 17*(3), 290–316.

Guttman, A. (1986). *Sports spectators*. Colombia University Press.

Hagood, M., & Vogan, T. (2016). The 12th man: Fan noise in the contemporary NFL. *Popular Communication, 14*(1), 30–8.

Hamilton, H. (2013). Ball (not) in play: Effective time in football. *Soccermetrics*. 26 June. Retrieved 19 June 2022, from https://www.soccermetrics.net/team-performance/effective-time-in-football.

Harris, R. J. (2004). *A cognitive psychology of mass communication*. Lawrence Erlbaum.

Haynes, R. (1995). *The football imagination: Rise of football fanzine culture*. Ashgate.

Haynes, R. (1998). A pageant of sound and vision: Football's relationship with television, 1936–1960. *International Journal of the History of Sport, 15*(1), 211–26.

Heaton, C. P. (1992). Air ball: Spontaneous large-group precision chanting. *Popular Music and Society, 16*(1), 81–3.

Herd, K., & Löfgren, J. (2020). Mocking others, parodying ourselves: Chants and songs used in Swedish football. *MUSICultures, 47*, 11–33.

Herrera, E. (2018). Masculinity, violence, and deindividuation in Argentine soccer chants: The sonic potentials of participatory of sounding-in-synchrony. *Etnomusicology, 62*(3), 470–99.

Hesling, W. (1986). The pictorial representation of sports on television. *International Review for the Sociology of Sport, 21*(2–3), 173–92.

Hesmondhalgh, D. (2013). *Why music matters*. Wiley-Blackwell.

Hey, S. (2006). Tales from the terraces: The chants of a lifetime. *The Independent*. 21 April. Retrieved 19 June 2022, from https://www.independent.co.uk/news/uk/this-britain/tales-terraces-chants-lifetime-5336050.html.

Hill, J. (2009). War, remembrance and sport: 'Abide With Me' and the FA Cup Final in the 1920s. In A. Bateman & J. Bale (Eds), *Sporting sounds: Relationships between sport and music* (pp. 164–78). Routledge.

Hilmes, M. (2008). Television sound: Why the silence? *Music, Sound, and the Moving Images*, 2(2), 153–61.

Hocking, J. (1982). Sports and spectators: Intra-audience effects. *Journal of Communication*, 32, 100–8.

Hognestad, H. K. (2006). Transnational passions: A statistical study of Norwegian football supporters. *Soccer & Society*, 7(4), 439–62.

Holland, B. L. (1997). Surviving leisure time racism: The burden of racial harassment on Britain's black footballers. *Leisure Studies*, 16(4), 261–77.

Holland, P. (2017). *The new television handbook* (5th edn). Routledge.

Holz-Bacha, C. (2006). *Fussball – Fernsehen – Politik*. Verlag för Sozialwissenschaften.

Homewood, B. (2020). Artificial crowd noise a rebuke to fans, supporters groups say. *IOL*. 17 June. Retrieved 19 June 2022, from https://www.iol.co.za/sport/soccer/premier-league/artificial-crowd-noise-a-rebuke-to-fans-supporters-groups-say-49491506.

Hopcraft, A. (1968). *The football man: People and passions in soccer*. Aurum Press.

Hornby, N. (1992). *Fever pitch: A fan's life*. Gollancz.

Howard, D. M. (2004). Measuring the tuning accuracy of thousands singing in unison: An English Premier Football League table of fans' singing tunefulness. *Logopedics Phoniatrics Vocology*, 29(2), 77–83.

Hoy, M. (1994). Joyful mayhem: Bakhtin, football songs, and the carnivalesque. *Text and Performance Quarterly*, 14(4), 289–304.

Huck, C. (2011). Football documentaries: Creativity v actuality/liveness. *Journal for the Study of British Cultures*, 18(1), 41–56.

Huddleston, W. (2022). Kicking off: Violence, honour, identity and masculinity in Argentinian football chants. *International Review for the Sociology of Sport*, 57(1), 34–53.

Hughes, M. (2020). Sky's fake crowd noise with chanting and celebrations from FIFA 20 video game wins the restart with 75 PER CENT of fans choosing to watch the Premier League with the new soundtrack. *Mail Online*. 18 June. Retrieved 19 June 2022, from https://www.dailymail.co.uk/sport/football/article-8436219/Three-quarters-fans-choose-watch-Premier-Leagues-return-fake-crowd-noise.html.

Hughson, J. (2014). Watching the football with Raymond Williams: A reconsideration of the global game as a 'wonderful game'. In J. Scherer & D. Rowe (Eds), *Sport, public broadcasting, and cultural citizenship: Signal lost?* (pp. 283–99). Routledge.

Hulmes, D. (1998). *The best book of football songs and chants ever!* Carlton Books Limited.

Hurrey, A. (2014). *Football clichés: A speculative effort, from distance, to translate the curious language of football.* Headline.

Høier, S. (2012). The relevance of point of audition in television sound: Rethinking a problematic term. *Journal of Sonic Studies, 3*(1), 1–12.

Inglis, S. (1996). *The grounds of Britain.* CollinsWillow.

Irak, D. (2021). Fight 'acceptable' with 'acceptable': Football, cultural battle in Turkey and the story of two 'doxas' over an old military song. *Sport in Society, 24*(1), 38–55.

Irwin, C. (2006). *Sing when you're winning: Football fans, terrace songs and a search for the soul of soccer.* André Deutch.

Jack, M. (2021). 'You call this democracy?' FC Saint Pauli supporters, football chants, and the police. In S. Miller et al. (Eds), *Football and popular culture* (pp. 25–38). Routledge.

Jakobson, R. (1960). Closing statement: Linguistics and poetics. In Th. Sebeok (Ed.), *Style and Language* (pp. 350–77). MIT Press.

Jakubowska, H., Antonowicz, D., & Kossakowski, R. (2020). *Female fans, gender relations and football fandom: Challenging the brotherhood culture.* Routledge.

Jethro, D. (2014). Vuvuzela magic: The production and consumption of 'African' cultural heritage during the FIFA 2010 World Cup. *African Diaspora, 7*, 177–204.

Jirat, J. (2007). Der zwölte Mann – die Schaffhauser Bierkurve. Ethnografie einer Fussball-Fankurve. *Schweizerisches Archiv für Volkskunder, 103*, 105–31.

Johnson, V. E. (2021). *Sports TV.* Routledge.

Kelner, M. (2012). *Sit down and cheer: A history of sport on TV.* Bloomsbury.

Kennedy, E. (2000). 'You talk a good game': Football and masculine style on British television. *Men & Masculinities, 3*(1), 57–84.

Kennedy, D. (2009). *The spectator and the spectacle: Audiences in modernity and postmodernity.* Cambridge University Press.

Kennedy, E., & Hills, L. (2009). *Sport, media and society.* Berg.

Keys, B. (2013). Senses and emotions in the history of sport. *Journal of Sport History, 40*(1), 21–38.

Khodadadi, F., & Gründel, A. (2006). Sprache und Fussball-fangesänge. *LINSE.* Retrieved 19 June 2022, from http://www.linse.uni-due.de/files/PDF_in_Katalog/publikationen/ESEL/Fussball_und_Sprache_2006.pdf.

King, A. (2002). *The end of the terraces: The transformation of English football in the 1990s* (2nd edn). Leicester University Press.

Knijnik, J. (2016). Imagining a multicultural community in an everyday football carnival: Chants, identity and social resistance on Western Sydney terraces. *International Review for the Sociology of Sports, 53*(4), 471–89.

Kopiez, R., & Brink, G. (1999). *Fussball-Fangesänge: eine Fanomenologie.* Königshausen und Neumann.

Kytö, M. (2011). We are rebellious voice of the terraces, we are Carsi: Constructing a football supporter group through sound. *Soccer & Society, 12*(1), 77–93.

Lacasse, S. (2000). Intertextuality and hypertextuality in recorded popular music. In M. Talbot (Ed.), *The musical work: Reality or invention?* (pp. 35–58). Liverpool University Press.

Laing, D., & Linehan, A. (2013). Soccer sounds. *Popular Music History*, 8(3), 307–25.

Lavric, E. (2019). Reale und fiktive Sender-Adressaten-Konstellationen in Fußball-Fangesängen – mit romanistischen Beispielen. *ATEM Archiv für Textmusikforschung*, 4(1), 1–31.

Lavric, E., Pisek, G., Skinner, A., & Stadler, W. (Eds) (2008). *The linguistics of football*. Gunter Narr Verlag.

Lawn, A. (2014). *Who are ya? Who are ya? Who are we? Why do we chant at football and what do those chants tell us about who we are as individuals and as a society?* Booktango.

Lawn, A. (2020). *We lose every week: The history of the football chanting*. Ockley Books.

Lee, M. (2018). Self and the city: Social identity and ritual at New York City Football Club. *Journal of Contemporary Ethnography*, 47(3), 367–95.

Lehmann, S., & Knibbeche, J. (2019). *Capo: Meine Stimme für Dynamo Dresden*. Burkhardt & Partner Verlag.

Lerner, A. (2020). Premier League broadcasts will have fake crowd noise. *The Short Fuse*. 21 June. Retrieved 19 June 2022, from https://theshortfuse.sbnation.com/2020/6/12/21289380/premier-league-project-restart-crowd-noise-empty-stadiums-arsenal-nbcsn-bt-sky-sports-broadcast.

Lichtenstein, D., & Nitsch, C. (2011). A European football family? German and British television broadcasts of the 2010 Football World Cup and the representation of Europe. *Global Media Journal*, 1(1), 1–20.

Locken, E., & Loughnane (2009). *The best Spurs football chants ever*. Interviewbooks.com.

Lotman, Y. M. (1990). *Universe of the mind: A semiotic theory of culture*. Indiana University Press.

Luhrs, J. (2007a). *Football chants and the continuity of the blazon Populaire tradition*. PhD thesis, University of Sheffield.

Luhrs, J. (2007b). Football chants: A living legacy of the 1984–85 miner's strike. *International Journal of Regional and Local Studies*, 3(1), 94–120.

Luhrs, J. (2008). Football chants and 'blason populaire': The construction of local and regional stereotypes. In E. Lavric, G. Pisek, A. Skinner & W. Stadler (Eds), *The linguistics of football* (pp. 233–44). Gunter Narr Verlag.

Luhrs, J. (2014). Blason populaire, football chants and the construction of masculinity. *Tradition Today*, 4, 46–59.

Lury, K. (2005). *Interpreting television*. Bloomsbury.

Maier, C. J. (2016). The sound of skateboarding: Aspects of a transcultural anthropology of sound. *The Senses and Society*, 11(1), 24–65.

Mann, M., Churnside, A., Bonney, A., & Melchior, F. (2013). Object-based audio applied to football broadcasts. *ImmersiveMe, 13*, 13–16.

Marland, D. (2020). Premier League returns with fake crowd noise and fans aren't sure about it. *Sport Bible*. 17 June. Retrieved 19 June 2022, from https://www.sportbible.com/football/football-news-reactions-premier-league-returns-with-fake-crowd-noise-20200617.

Marra, P. S. (2021). Sound, violence and gender performance in Brazilian football. In S. Miller et al. (Eds), *Football and popular culture* (pp. 39–50). Routledge.

Marra, P. S., & Trotta, F. (2019). Sound, music and magic in football stadiums. *Popular Music, 38*(1), 73–89.

Marriott, S. (1996). Time and time again: 'Live' television commentary and the construction of replay talk. *Media, Culture & Society, 18*, 69–86.

Marsh, P., Rosser, E., & Harré, R. (1978). *The rules of disorder*. Routledge.

Marshall, T. (2014). *'Dirty northern b\*st\*ards!' And other tales from the terraces: The story of Britain's football chants*. Elliott and Thompson Limited.

Mason, T. (1981). *Association football and English society 1863–1915*. Harvester Press.

Mathieson, J. (2009). We muted the sound of Celtic fans' chanting during minute's silence, admit Sky. *Daily Record*. 9 November. Retrieved 19 June 2022, from https://www.dailyrecord.co.uk/news/scottish-news/we-muted-sound-of-celtic-fans-chanting-1041599.

McCarthy, M. (2018). The greatest sports theme tune bracket – round 1. *Balls.ie*. 15 January. Retrieved 19 June 2022, from https://www.balls.ie/culture/round-1-balls-o-vision-song-contest-determining-greatest-sports-theme-tune-ever-381049.

McGowan, L. (2019). *Football in fiction: A history*. Routledge.

McKerrell, S. (2015). Social distance and the multimodal construction of the Other in sectarian song. *Social Semiotics, 25*(5), 614–32.

McKerrell, S. (2021). Kicking metaphors of the body around in the mediation of self and other: Conceptual metaphor in the *multimodal* construction of football songs and chants. In S. Miller et al. (Eds), *Football and popular culture* (pp. 13–24). Routledge.

McLeod, K. (2011). *We are the champions: The politics of sports and popular music*. Ashgate.

McNeill, W. (1995). *Keeping together in time: Dance and drill in human history*. Harvard University Press.

McParland, R. P. (2009). The sounds of the audience. *Mosaic: An Interdisciplinary Critical Journal, 42*(1), 117–32.

Merriam-Webster (2022). Significance. Retrieved 19 June 2022, from https://www.merriam-webster.com/dictionary/significance.

Merrills, R. (1997). *Dicks out 2: You're not singing any more?* Red Crad.

Mey, J. (1993). *Pragmatics – an introduction*. Blackwell.

Middleton, R. (1990). *Studying popular music*. Open University Press.

Millar, S. (2016). Let the people sing? Irish rebel songs, sectarianism, and Scotland's Offensive Behaviour Act. *Popular Music*, *35*(3), 297–319.

Miller, T. (2010). *Television studies: The basics*. Routledge.

Milne, M. (2016). *The Transformation of television sport: New methods, new rules*. Palgrave Macmillan.

Morris, D. (1981). *The soccer tribe*. Jonathan Cape.

Morse, M. (1983). Sport on television: Replay and display. In I E. A. Kaplan (Ed.), *Regarding television: Critical approaches – an anthology* (pp. 44–66). The American Film Institute.

Mullen, L. J., & Mazzocco, D. W. (2000). Coaches, drama, and technology: Mediation of Super Bowl broadcasts from 1969 to 1997. *Critical Studies in Media Communication*, *17*(3), 347–63.

Müller, E. (2008). *Fussball, Fernsehen, Unterhaltung. Zur ästhetischen Erfahrung des Fusssball im Stadion und am Bildschirm*. Retrieved 19 June 2022, from https://mediarep.org/bitstream/handle/doc/875/montage_AV_17_1_2008_151-172_Mueller_Fussball_Fernsehen_Unterhaltung_.pdf?sequence=7.

Mumford, S. (2012). *Watching sport: Aesthetics, ethics and emotion*. Routledge.

Mumford, S. (2019). The aesthetics of football. The beautiful game? In J. Hughson, K. Moore, R. Spaaij & J. Maguire (Eds), *Routledge handbook of football studies* (pp. 236–244). Routledge.

Nannestad, I. (2015). 'Bubbles', 'Abe my boy' and 'the Fowler war cry': Singing at the Vetch Field in the 1920s. In A. Bateman (Ed.), *Sport, music, identities* (pp. 28–37). Routledge.

Navvab, M., Heilmann, G., & Sulisz, D. W. (2009). Crowd noise measurements and simulation in large stadium using beamforming. *Eleventh International IBPSA Conference*, Glasgow, 2154–61.

Neal-Lunsford, J. (1992). Sport in the land of television: The use of sports in network prime-time schedules 1946–50. *Journal of Sport History*, *19*(1), 56–76.

Newman, M. (2020). Basketball was filmed before a live studio audience. *LARB*. 18 August. Retrieved 19 June 2022, from https://lareviewofbooks.org/article/basketball-filmed-live-studio-audience/.

Nishio, T., Larke, R., Heerde, H., & Melnyk, V. (2016). Analysing the motivations of Japanese international sports-fan tourists. *European Sport Management Quarterly*, *16*(4), 487–501.

Numerato, D. (2015). Who says 'no to modern football?' Italian supporters, reflexivity, and neo-liberalism. *Journal of Sport and Social Issues*, *39*(2), 120–38.

Oberschelp, M. (2013). *Die Hymne des Fussballs: 'You'll never walk alone'. Eine Kulturgeschichte*. Verlag die Werkstatt.

O'Brien, M. S. (2020). From soccer chant to sonic meme: Sound politics and parody in Argentina's 'Hit of the Summer'. *MUSICultures*, *47*, 116–38.

O'Connell, D., & Kowal, S. (2008). *Communicating with one another: Toward a psychology of spontaneous spoken discourse*. Springer.

OhneSchiri (2000). *Ohne Schiri habt ihr keine Chance. Die besten Fangesänge für den 1. FC Köln*. Belchen Verlag.

Oldfield, R., Shirley, B., & Spille, J. (2015). Object-based audio for interactive football broadcast. *Multimedia Tools & Applications, 74*, 2717–41.

Oriard, M. (1981). Professional football as cultural myth. *Journal of American Culture, 4*(3), 27–41.

Otte, F. W., Millar, S.-K., & Klatt, S. (2020). What do you hear? The effect of stadium noise on football player's passing performances. *European Journal of Sports Science, 21*(7), 1035–44.

Owens, J. (2021). *Television sports production* (6th edn). Focal Press.

Paramio, J. L., Buraimo, B., & Campos, C. (2008). From modern to postmodern: The development of football stadia in Europe. *Sport in Society, 11*(5), 517–34.

Parker, C. (2009). *One ginger Pelé! Football's funniest songs and chants*. New Holland.

Paytress, M. (June 1996). Football crazy! *The Record Collector: A Quarterly Journal of Recorded Vocal Art, 202*, 32–43.

Pearson, G. (2012). *An ethnography of English football fans: Cans, cops and carnivals*. Manchester University Press.

Pendleton, D. (2018). *Kick-off: The start of spectator sports*. Naked Eye.

Penz, O. (1990). Sport and speed. *International Review for Sociology of Sport, 25*(2), 157–67.

Petticrew, M., & Roberts, H. (2006). *Systematic reviews in the social sciences: A practical guide*. Blackwell.

Philipson, A. (2020). *All or nothing: Tottenham Hotspur*. Amazon Video.

Pinch, T., & Bijsterveld, K. (Eds) (2012). *The Oxford handbook of sound studies*. Oxford University Press.

Piskurek, C. (2018). *Fictional representations of English football and fan cultures: Slum sport, slum people?* Palgrave Macmillan.

Plenderleith, I. (2018). *The quiet fan*. Unbound.

Portnoi, G. (2011). *Who are ya? Football's best ever chants*. Simon & Schuster.

Poulton, E., & Durell, O. (2016). Uses and meanings of 'Yid' in English football fandom: A case study of Tottenham Hotspur club. *International Review for the Sociology of Sport, 51*(6), 715–34.

Power, B. (2011). *Justice for the ninety-six*: Liverpool FC fans and uncommon use of football song. *Soccer & Society, 12*(1), 96–112.

Powis, B., & Carter, T. F. (2019). Sporting sounds. In M. Bull (Ed.), *The Routledge companion to sound studies* (pp. 391–9). Routledge.

Powley, A., & Cloake, M. (2016). *The Lane: The official history of the world famous home of the Spurs*. Vision Sports.

Pugh, W. (2020). For fake sake. Sky Sports and BT Sport will continue using fake crowd noise even after return of fans. *The Sun*. 3 December. Retrieved 19 June 2022, from https://www.thesun.co.uk/sport/football/13375449/sky-sports-bt-sport-fake-crowd-noise/.

Quinn, K. (2020). The sound of no hands clapping: How AFL, NRL and EPL 'fill' empty stadiums. *The Age*. 1 July. Retrieved 19 June 2022, from https://www.theage.com.au/culture/tv-and-radio/sound-of-the-crowd-tv-sport-keeps-it-real-with-the-faux-human-league-20200625-p556bk.html.

Raney, A. A., & Bryant, J. (Eds), *Handbook of sports and media*. Routledge.

Raunsbjerg, P. (2001). TV sport and aesthetics: The mediated event. In G. Agger & J. F. Jensen (Eds), *The aesthetics of television* (pp. 193–228). Aalborg University Press.

Real, M. (2005). Television and sport. In J. Wasko (Ed.), *A companion to television* (pp. 337–60). Blackwell.

Real, M. (2014). Theorizing the sports-television dream marriage: Why sports fit television so well. In A. Billings (Ed.), *Sports media: Transformation, integration, consumption* (pp. 19–39). Routledge.

Reber, E., & Couper-Kuhlen, E. (2020). On 'whistle' sound objects in English everyday conversation. *Research on Language and Social Interaction*, 53(1), 164–87.

Redhead, S. (1987). *Sing when you're winning: 'Football final' – the last football book*. Pluto Press.

Redhead, S. (1997). *Post-fandom and the millennial blues*. Routledge.

Reisigl, M., & Wodak, R. (2015). The discourse-historical approach. In R. Wodak & M. Meyer (Eds), *Methods of critical discourse studies* (pp. 23–61). Sage.

Repp, B. H. (1987). The sound of two hands clapping: An exploratory study. *Journal of the Acoustical Society of America*, 81(4), 1100–9.

Ricatti, F. (2016). 'Unico grande amore': AS Roma supporters football songs. *Italian Culture*, 34(1), 34–48.

Rich, M. (2020). Sitting in silence with 5,000 fans: The new sound of Japanese sports. *New York Times*. 9 September. Retrieved 19 June 2022, from https://www.nytimes.com/2020/09/09/world/asia/japan-coronavirus-jleague-soccer.html.

Robinson, J., & Clegg, J. (2019). *The club: How the Premier League became the richest most disruptive business in sport*. John Murray.

Robson, G. (2000). *'No one likes us, we don't care': The myth and reality of Millwall fandom*. Berg.

Rodaway, P. (1994). *Sensuous geographies: Body, sense and place*. Routledge.

Roehl, A. (2021). Superbowl artificial crowd noise. *Acentech*. 4 February. Retrieved 19 June 2022, from https://www.acentech.com/blog/superbowl-artificial-crowd-noise/.

Rose, A., & Friedman, J. (1997). Television sports as mas(s)culine cult of distraction. In A. Baker & T. Boyd (Eds), *Out of bounds: Sports, media, and the politics of identity* (pp. 1–15). Indiana University Press.

Rosser, J. (2017). Tottenham star Harry Kane reveals 'one-season wonder' chant continues to spur him on as records tumble. *Evening Standard*. Retrieved 19 June 2022, from https://www.standard.co.uk/sport/football/tottenham-star-harry-kane-reveals-oneseason-wonder-chant-continues-to-spur-him-on-as-records-tumble-a3727446.html.

Rowe, D. (1995). *Popular cultures: Rock music, sport and the politics of pleasure*. Sage.

Rowe, D. (2011). *Global media sport: Flows, forms and futures*. Bloomsbury.

Rowe, D. (2020). And the winner is ... TELEVISION! Spectacle and sport in a pandemic. *Forumbloggen*. 23 September. Retrieved 19 June 2022, from https://idrotts forum.org/forumbloggen/and-the-winner-is-television-spectacle-and-sport-in-a-pandemic/.

Rowe, D., & Baker, S. A. (2012). 'Truly a fan experience'? The cultural politics of the live site. In R. Krøvel & T. Roksvold (Eds), *We love to hate each other* (pp. 301–17). Nordicom.

Russell, D. (1997). *Popular music in England 1840–1914: A social history* (2nd edn). Manchester University Press.

Russell, D. (2008). Abiding memories: The community singing movement and the English social life in the 1920s. *Popular Music*, *27*(1), 117–33.

Sandgren, P. (2010). Seven Nation Army: Med ett riff som sjungs till fotboll. *RIG – Kulturhistorisk Tidsskrift*, *93*(3), 129–46.

Sandvoss, C. (2003). *A game of two halves: Football fandom, television and globalisation*. Routledge.

Scally, J. (2009). *A load of balls: Footballs funny side*. Mainstream.

Scannell, P. (1996). *Radio, television and modern life*. Blackwell.

Scannell, P. (2014). *Television and the meaning of 'live'*. Polity Press.

Scannell, P. (2019). *Why do people sing? On voice*. Polity Press.

Schafer, M. (1977). *The soundscape: Our sonic environment and the tuning of the world*. Destiny Books.

Schiering, R. (2008). Regional identity in Schalke football chant. In E. Lavric, G. Pisek, A. Skinner & W. Stadler (Eds), *The linguistics of football* (pp. 221–31). Gunter Narr Verlag.

Schirato, T. (2007). *Understanding sports culture*. Sage.

Schmidt, J. (1981). Et stadion i stuen? Om fodbold i fjernsynet. In F. Mortensen, J. Poulsen & P. Sepstrup (Eds), *Underholdning i tv* (pp. 110–27). Nyt Nordisk Forlag.

Schoonderwoerd, P. (2011). 'Shall we sing a song for you?': Mediation, migration and identity in football chants and fandom. *Soccer & Society*, *12*(1), 120–41.

Schultz, B. (2002). *Sports broadcasting*. Focal Press.

Schultz, B., & Arke, E. (2016). *Sports media: Reporting, producing and planning*. Focal Press.

Schwab, J. T. (2006). *Fussball im Film: Lexikon des Fussballfilms*. Belleville.

Seddon, P. J. (1999). *A football compendium: An expert guide to the books, films and music of association football* (2nd edn). The British Library.

Serrano-Durá, J., Serrano-Durá, A., & Martínez-Bello, V. (2019). Youth perceptions of violence against women through a sexist chant in the football stadium: An exploratory study. *Soccer & Society, 20*(2), 232–70.

Shadle, C. (1983). Experiments on the acoustics of whistling. *The Physics Teacher, 21*(3), 148–54.

Shaw, A. (2011). *Shall we sing a song for you? The good, the bad and the downright offensive – Britain's favourite football chants*. John Blake.

Siegel, G. (2007). Double vision: Large-screen video display and live sports spectacle. In H. Newcomb (Ed.), *Television: The critical view* (7th edn) (pp. 185–206). Oxford University Press.

Sky Sports (2020). Crowd noise available for Sky Sports Premier League games: How it works. 18 June. Retrieved 19 June 2022, from https://www.skysports.com/football/news/11661/12004035/crowd-noise-available-for-sky-sports-premier-league-games-how-it-works.

Small, C. (1998). *Musicking: The meanings of performing and listening*. Wesleyan University Press.

Smith, G. (2006). BBC commentary ends up taking a sound beating. *The Times*. 9 February. Retrieved 19 June 2022, from https://www.thetimes.co.uk/article/bbc-commentary-ends-up-taking-a-sound-beating-ffp757rv6n9.

Smith, J. (2008). *Vocal tracks: Performance and sound media*. University of California Press.

Snape, D., & Spencer, L. (2003). The foundations of qualitative research. In J. Ritchie & J. Lewis (Eds), *Qualitative research practice: A guide for social science students and researchers* (pp. 1–23). Sage.

Solvoll, M. K. (2016). Football on television: How has coverage of the Cup Finals in Norway changed from 1961 to 1995? *Media, Culture, and Society, 38*(2), 141–58.

Sors, F., Grassi, M., Agostini. T., & Murigia, M. (2021). The sound of silence in association football: Home advantage and referee bias decrease in matches played without spectators. *European Journal of Sports Science, 21*(12): 1597–1605.

Statista (2022). Top-20 European football clubs breakdown of revenues 2018/2019 season. https://www.statista.com/statistics/271636/revenue-distribution-of-top-20-european-soccer-clubs/.

Steen, R. (2014). *Floodlights and touchlines: A history of spectator sport*. Bloomsbury.

Stein, A. (2013). Playing the game on television. In M. Consalvo, K. Mitgutsch & A. Stein (Eds), *Sports Videogames* (pp. 115–37). Routledge.

Stein, J., & Ruge, L. (2018). *Fankurve: Die Fangesänge auserwählter Fussballbundesligisten aus der Saison 2017/2018*. CreateSpace.

Sterkenburg, J., & Spaaij, R. (2016). *Mediated football: Representations and audience receptions of race/ethnicity, nation and gender*. Routledge.

Stewart, B., Smith, A., & Nicholson, M. (2003). Sport consumer typologies: A critical review. *Sport Marketing Quarterly*, *12*(4), 206–16.

Stieler, M., Weismann, F., & Germelmann, C. (2014). Co-destruction of value by spectators: The case of the silent protest. *European Sport Management Quarterly*, *14*(1), 72–86.

Storer, T. (2019). Tottenham chants: Lyrics & videos to the most popular Spurs songs. *Goal.com*. 12 October. Retrieved 19 June 2022, from https://www.goal.com/en-us/news/tottenham-chants-lyrics-videos-to-the-most-popular spurs/1ah8hkjbh863a1rgwbdmz6fug7#the-spurs.

Sumpter, D. J. (2010). *Collective animal behavior*. Princeton University Press.

Swanepoel, D. W., & Hall, J. W. (2010). Football match spectator sound exposure and effect on hearing: A pretest-post-test study. *South African Medical Journal*, *100*(4), 239–42.

Tagg, P. (2013). *Music's meaning: A modern musicology for non-musos*. MMMSP.

Tagg, P. (2014). *Everyday tonality II: Towards a tonal theory of what most people hear*. MMMSP.

Tamir, I. (2021). 'I am grateful that god hates the reds': Persistent values and changing trends in Israel football chants. *Sport in Society*, *24*(2), 222–34.

Thrills, A. (1998). *You're not singing anymore! A riotous celebration of football chants and the culture that spawned them*. Ebury Press.

Toffoletti, K. (2017). *Women sport fans: Identification, participation, representation*. Routledge.

Tota, A. L. (2001). 'When Orff meets Guinness': Music in advertising as a form of cultural hybrid. *Poetics*, *29*, 109–23.

Trail, M. (2010). How to swarm: Researching sounds of football's play. *Creative Approaches to Research*, *3*(1), 67–81.

Trail, M. (2013). 'And she flies! Beautiful': The dislocating geography of football sound. *Coolabah*, *11*, 315–22.

Transfermarkt (2022). Attendances 2019/20. Retrieved 19 June 2022, from https://www.transfermarkt.com/bundesliga/besucherzahlen/wettbewerb/L1/saison_id/2019/plus/1.

Truax, B. (2001). *Acoustic communication* (2nd edn). Ablex.

Turner, M. (2013). Modern 'live' football: Moving from the panoptican gaze to the performative, virtual and carnivalesque. *Sport in Society*, *16*(1), 85–93.

Turner, M. (2017). Modern English football fandom and hyperreal, 'safe', 'all-seater' stadia: Examining the contemporary football stage. *Soccer & Society*, *18*(1), 121–31.

Uersfeld, S. (2018). Bundesliga fans announce silent protest over ticket prices, kickoff times. *ESPN*. 25 September. Retrieved 19 June 2022, from https://www.espn.com/soccer/german-bundesliga/story/3646168/bundesliga-fans-announce-silent-protest-over-ticket-prices-kickoff-times.

Uhrich, S., & Benkenstein, M. (2010). Sport stadium atmosphere: Formative and reflective indicators for operationalizing the construct. *Journal of Sport Management*, 24(2), 211–37.

Unkelbach, C., & Memmert, D. (2010). Crowd noise as a cue in referee decisions contributes to the home advantage. *Journal of Sport & Exercise Psychology*, 32, 483–98.

van Leeuwen (1999). *Speech, music, sound*. Palgrave Macmillan.

Vilter, K. (2011). *Fußballfangesänge-nur etwas für Männer? Eine empirisch-phänomenologische Untersuchung*. Verlag Dr. Muller.

Waddington, I., Malcolm, D., & Horak, R. (1998). The social composition of football crowds in Western Europe. *International Review for the Sociology of Sport*, 33(2), 155–69.

Warner, S. (2011). 'You only sing when you're winning': football factions and rock rivalries in Manchester and Liverpool. *Soccer & Society*, 12(1), 58-73.

Webbie (2020). The oldest football song. *Football and Music*. 3 June. Retrieved 19 June 2022, from https://www.footballandmusic.co.uk/the-oldest-football-song/.

Weed, M. (2007). The pub as a virtual football fandom venue: An alternative to 'being there'? *Football and Society*, 8(2–3), 399–414.

Weed, M. (2010). Sport fans and travel – is 'being there' always important? *Journal of Sport & Tourism*, 15(2), 103–9.

Welch, J. (2013). *The biography of Tottenham Hotspur*. Vision Sports.

Wembley (2022). Rules and regulations. Retrieved 19 June 2022, from https://www.wembleystadium.com/plan-your-visit/stadium-guide/rules-and-regulations.

Wenner, L. A. (1998). Playing the mediasport game. In L. A. Wenner (Ed.), *MediaSport* (pp. 3–13). Routledge.

Whannel, G. (2009). Television and the transformation of sport. *Annals of the American Academy of Political and Social Science*, 625, 205–18.

Whannel, G. (2014). The paradoxical character of live television sport in the twenty-first century. *Television & New Media*, 15(8), 769–76.

Williams, B. R. (1977). The structure of televised football. *Journal of Communication*, 27(3), 133–9.

Williams, R. (1968/1989). As we see others. In A. O'Connor (Ed.), *Raymond Williams on television: Selected writings* (pp. 33–6). Routledge.

Willoughby, G. (1989). From turnstile to tube: Sport and the aesthetics of television in South Africa. *Theoria: A Journal of Social and Political Theory*, 74, 69–78.

Wilson, J. (2018). *Inventing the pyramid – the history of soccer tactics*. Nation Books.

Winner, D. (2010). *Brilliant orange: The neurotic genius of Dutch football*. Bloomsbury.

Wittek, H. (2013). Microphone usage for sports broadcasting. *Live Production*. 26 May. Retrieved 19 June 2022, from http://www.live-production.tv/case-studies/production-facilities/microphone-usage-sports-broadcasting.html.

Woodward, K. (2011). Sounds out of place. *Soccer & Society*, 12(1), 76.

Woodward, K., & Goldblatt, D. (2011). Introduction. *Soccer & Society*, *12*(1), 1–8.

Woolridge, J. (2008). These sporting lives: Football autobiographies 1945–1980. *Sport in History*, *28*(4), 620–40.

Worrall, M., & Otton, W. (2017). *Carefree! Chelsea chants and terrace culture*. Gate 17.

Wren-Lewis, J., & Clarke, A. (1983). The World Cup – a political football. *Theory, Culture and Society*, *1*(3), 123–32.

Yin, R. K. (2014). *Case study research: Design and methods* (5th edn). Sage.

Yusha, A. (2020). How 'crowd noise' works in Premier League. *Business Standard*. 18 July. Retrieved 19 June 2022, from https://www.tbsnews.net/splash/how-crowd-noise-works-premier-league-107857.

Zalis, J. (2021). Capital culture, political performance: Listening to football in Ottawa 2014–2015. In S. Miller et al. (Eds), *Football and popular culture* (pp. 51–68). Routledge.

Zborowski, J. (2016). Television aesthetics, media and cultural studies and the contested realm of the social. *Critical Studies in Television*, *11*(7), 7–22.

# Index

Note: Page numbers in bold font refer to tables.

add-in' 125
adoption *see also* rearticulations,
      adoptions
   description 51
   of the song 51–2
African Nations Cup in 2006 88
Alex Oxlade-Chamberlain 43
Armstrong, G. 20
Armstrong, L. 49
Arsenal 25–7, 43, 67, 69, 71, 73, 108
asynchronous clapping 41–2
atmosphere of stadium 2, 27–8, 55, 62,
      74, 76, 78, 103–4, 109, 114, 119,
      123, 126–7
auditory lacunae 62, 100
auditory signature 69
aural close-up shots 90
authenticity, sense of 104
autocommunication 77–8

Back, L. 20, 76
background music or constant
      musicalization 107, 113
'ball-on-boot' sound 124
*The Battle of the Republic*, American Civil
      War song 38
Beljutin, R. 23
Bell, J. 66
Bell, P. 66
breadth-oriented or synchronic
      broadenings 126
Brink, G. 19–20, 27, 28, 39, 41, 46, 49, 65
broadcast practices 10
Bryant, J. 32
Bryman, A. 10
Buford, B. 27
build environment 13–14, 56–7
Bulmer, L. 25
Buscombe, E. 31

*capo* or chant leader 27, 47–8, 64–5, 65,
      126, 130
case materials 4, 11, 13–16, 16, 24, 40–1,
      61, 118, 125–7
   English setting of 40
   multiple 23
   selection of 118–19, 127
   single 22–3
   trends of the selection 23
chants and songs
   acts of communication 77
   away supporters 90
   categorizations of 70–1, 90
   chant, characteristics 46
   coined chant curations 25–6
   compared to interjection and
      clapping 50–3
   coupled with match incidents
      119–20
   couplings 66–7
   divisive 71
   examination 19
   grouping of Arsenal chants 26
   integrative 71
   lyrics of chants and songs (*see* lyrics)
   melodic structures 46
   musical works reworked for 50–3
   non-communicational functions 76
   in Romance languages 22
   song, characteristics 46–7
   specific chants 27–8
   subject of historical interest 26
   symbolic meanings 118–19
   two-note chant 98
Chion, M. 106–7
clapping 40–1
   asynchronous 41–2
   collective, arhythmical 79
   and interjections 64, 79

synchronous clapping or 'synchro-clapping 41
Clarke, A. 32
close couplings 66–7
*Club Foot,* Kasabian's 125
collective effervescence, concept of 79
collective interjections 43, 67, 70, 78, 98–9, 102, 119–20
  segmented **44**, 44–5
  stand-alone 43
collective nonmusical sounds 67
collective singing 77
*Come on You Spurs* 42, 46–8, 71
Comisky, P. 32
commentary, role of 107
conative function
  stadium setting 71–2
    chants and songs 71
    divisive chants and songs 71
    non-musical acts 72
    overlap of addresser and addressee 72
  televised broadcast setting 101–3
    imaginary dialogue between viewer and programme 103
    internal audience sounds 101
    spectators sound and laugh tracks, difference 102
    sports coverage 103
    use of laugh tracks 102
constitutive factors, act of communication 68
continuous musicalization 63
contributions, influence and reference between 118
co-production of players 93
copsais (customisation of popular songs as sung in stadia) 51
couplings 65–7
  close couplings 67
  loose coupling 66
  moderate coupling 66
  with specific match-related incidents 65–6
  types **67**
Covid-19 63, 94, 108–10
creation of television production team 84
creators and types of sounds **36**
Crisell, A. 30

Darude 38, 39
Davies, H. 48, 61, 125
decontextualizations 51
depth-oriented or diachronic broadening 126
diataxis 62–3
differences in televised broadcast and stadium setting 121–2
distance
  between fans 56–7
  between pitch and surrounding seats 57
distinctive sounds, identification 15
divisive chants and songs 71, 133–4
Durkheim, É. 79

EA Sports 109–10
*EA SPORTS FIFA* 109
Edensor, T. 56
editorial manipulation 94
editorial media outlets 25
effective playing time 38, 97
emotive function
  stadium setting 68–71
    actualization of 70
    neutralisation 69
    rhythmic shouting 69
    singing 68–9
    stigma exploitation 69
    value reversal 69
  televised broadcast setting 100–1
    enhancement of programme 101
    quasi-cinematic dramatization of events 101
    sonic signals and commentators sound 100
English Premier League (EPL) 11, 13, 25, 63, 89, 100, 109, 126
enhancement of programme 101
*Entourage* 110
ethos of realism 104
exhalation and groaning 37, 43
existing contributions, distribution of 117–18
extra-diegetic sounds of spectators 94–5, 102, 111, 113

fake soundtrack 113
fans 6

distance between 56–7
external acting out of identification 103
*FIFA-* ization 114
Finn, R.L. 38
Friedman, J. 32

German club chants collection 25
*Glory, Glory, Tottenham Hotspur* 38, 52
Goffman, E. 70, 72
Graakjær, N.J. 41, 48
Grøn, R. 41, 48
Grundel, A. 26
Gumbrcht, H.U. 77
Guttman, A. 6

home player supporters 106
Hopcraft, A. 28
Hornby, N. 27
Hulmes, D. 26

I-I direction of communication 72
imaginary dialogue between viewer and programme 103
insights on
  distribution 119
  significance 119–20
  structure 119
  televised broadcast 120–1
interjections and clapping 64
internal audience sounds 101
internal display energy 65
international broadcasts
  commentators in stadium 83, 88
  EPL matches 13
  live broadcasts from English First Division 12
  public service station Danmarks Radio 12
  televised matches in Scandinavia 13
  Tottenham Hotspur 13
international sound 81
intraaudience effects 76
intra-stadium space 54
intra-urban space 54
*An Introduction to Television Studies* (Bignell) 29
Irak, D. 65
iterative force of music 51

Jakobson, R. 68, 72, 75
Johnson, V. E. 32

Kennedy, E. 32
Khodadadi, F. 26
Kopiez, R. 19–20, 28, 39, 41, 46, 49, 65

laugh tracks 101–2, 113, 121
  and spectators sound, difference 102
'lavaliere' microphone 90
Lawn, A. 26, 96
Lee, M. 46
Lichtenstein, D. 32
'listening-in-search' 106
live and the non-live, fusion of 96
live commentary broadcasts 12
locations in open-air grandstands 58
loose coupling 66–7
loose synchronization 99
Lovren, Dejan 43
lyrics
  of chants and songs 23–4
  linguistics 23
  and tribal chants, examination and categorization 19

Mann, M. 82
Marra, P.S. 20–2
Marriott, S. 32, 97
Marsh, P. 28
Marshall, T. 26
matches with no spectators in stadium setting 108–15
  absence of masking sounds 110
  background music or musicalization 113
  delays in observed match 112–3
  deployment of multiple, operating microphones 111
  editorial manipulations 113
  fake soundtrack 113
  *FIFA-* ization 114
  filtering and sanitation 114
  flat crowd noise and special sounds 109–10
  lack of synchronization 115
  mishaps and temporal mismatches 112
  mismatch, spectator reaction and match incidents 111

potentially controversial sounds 110
practice of adding spectators sounds 113
pre-recorded spectator sounds 109
signature songs 110
switch off and on, added recorded sounds 110
transtextuality 114
match incidents, information on progression 73
match-monitoring 'auditory seismometer' 105
*Match of the Day* programme 12
*McNamara's Band* 38
media and communication studies, perspective of 122–3
mediated curations of sounds 21
melodic tonal sequences 45–6
melodies 36, 45–7, 50, 57, 110, 131, 135–6, 142
Memmert, D. 7
Merrils, R. 25
metalanguage, speaking of language 75
metalingual function 74–5 *see also* poetic and metalingual functions
microphones, types 89
middle grounded sounds 90
mid-1960s football
 assertive singing and chanting, English spectators 11–12
 community singing movement 12
 performance of hymns 12
Miller, T. 30
minimally participating observer 10–11
mishaps (occasional) 111
moderate coupling 66–7
monophony 47
Morris, D. 12, 19–20, 40–1, 66, 72, 74, 76
multimicrophone recording 21
music 36, 45–8
 *capo* or chant leader 47
 chants and songs 46
 folk-music 50
 instrument, use of 47, 64
 iterative force of music 51
 lyricisation 51
 melodic tonal sequences 45–6
 melodies 47
 pre-existing 15, 48–51, 53

song, characteristics 46–7
syllabic singing 45
types and genres 50
musical instrument, use of 64
musicalization 107
musicology, perspective of 122
mystical bodies 77

National Association for Stock Car Auto Racing (NASCAR) 94, 113, 125
National Basket Association (NBA) 125
*neutralisation* 69
*New Television Handbook, The* 29
New York City Football Club 56, 140
Nitsch, C. 32
non-musical acts 72
non-verbal utterance 42

object language, speaking of objects 75
object sounds 36, 40–2
 asynchronous clapping 42
 clapping 40–1
 synchronous clapping or 'synchro-clapping 41
*Oh, When the Saints Go Marchin' In* 49, 52–3
*Oh, When the Spurs Go Marchin' In* 15, 27, 45–7, 52, 63–72, 77, 88, 90, 110, 114
Oldfield, R. 82
*One Season Wonder* 53–4, 66, 72, 110
opposing supporters 60, 75
optimal listening position 120
Oxlade-Chamberlain, Alex 43

Parker, C. 26
participant observation 10–11, 20
Pearson, G. 28
personal memoirs, Hornby's 27
personal mobile technology 85
phatic function
 stadium setting 75–9
  autocommunication 77–8
  collective, arhythmical clapping and interjections 79
  collective effervescence, concept of 79
  intraaudience effects 76
  non-communicational functions 76

physical channel and psychological connection 75
rhythms, collectively produced 77
singing and other forms of musical sounds 78
televised broadcast setting 107–8
  background music or musicalization' of the broadcast 107
  zone of liveness 107
place, sense of 56–7
  being placed 57–62
  build environment 56–7
  differentiation of spectators 61–2
  distance between fans 56–7
  distances between pitch and surrounding seats 57
  location of POA 58–9
  locations in open-air grandstands 58
  opposing supporters 60
  significance of build environment 56
  visual appearance of 'away supporters' 59–60
  vocally supporting spectators 61
Players' vocal sounds 36–7
poetic and metalingual functions
  stadium setting 73–5
    metalanguage, speaking of language 75
    metalingual function 74–5
    object language, speaking of objects 75
    selection and combination, modes of arrangement 73
  televised broadcast setting 107–8
    background music or musicalization of broadcast 107
    zone of liveness 107
point of audition (POA) 21, 87
  differentiation of 87
  location 58–9
  observational and active 89
pre-Covid-19 matches 109
pre-existing music 15, 48–51, 50, 53
Premier League Licensees 82
Premier League Production (PLP) 82
pre-prepared programming, sounds of 81
previous (dissimilar) adaption 53
prime camera 92

production team's influence on sounds 95
public announcement (PA) system 35–9, 43, 54, 56, 84, 120, 138
  -distributed sounds 39

quality of the sounds 36
quasi-cinematic dramatization of events 101
Queens Park Rangers 110

racial abuse 15
Real, M. 30
rearticulations, adoptions 51–4
  adaption of song 51–2
  adoption, description 51
  comparison between styles of performance 53
  copsais 51
  iterative force of music 51
  loss of original meaning 53–4
  previous (dissimilar) adaption 53
  relyricisation 51
recontextualizations 51
referential function
  stadium setting 72–3
    information on match incidents 73
    referent, orientation toward the context 72–3
  televised broadcast setting 103–7
    commentary, role of 107
    ethos of realism 104
    external acting out of fan identification 103
    home player supporters 106
    indication of atmosphere of stadium 103
    listening-in-search 106
    match-monitoring 'auditory seismometer' 105
    sense of authenticity 104
    vicarious evaluations 105
relyricisation 51
response cries or exclamatory interjections 43
rhythmic shouting 69
Robson, G. 20, 76
Rose, A. 32

Ruge, L. 25
Rule Britannia 51

*Sandstorm* (1999) 39
Scannell, P. 78, 97, 102, 108
Schafer, R. M. 9
scholarly work
 contributions **130–44**
 lack of 117
Scottish league on Remembrance Day 95
segmented collective interjections **44**, 44–5
selection of shots from the live televised broadcast of Tottenham-Leicester Match **86**
semiotic perspectives on sound and music 9–10
Seven Nation Army 51
Shaw, A. 26
shotgun microphones 89
Siegel, G. 32
silence, short periods 63
singing 68–9, 78
 performances of spectators 120
slow-motion replay 84, 96, 97
'small-smile' whistle 42
Soccer-Rhythmus (the football rhythm) 41
social media 25
social situation 68
song, characteristics 46–7
sonic signals and commentators sound 100
Sors, F. 7
sounds
 of performers and organizers 35–9
  exhalation and groaning 37
  organizer sounds through stadiums' PA system 37–8
  players' vocal sounds 36–7
  verbal announcements 38–9
  vocal and object sounds 36
  vocal sounds and interaction with physical objects 36
 role of 126
 of spectators 35, 39–40
  illustration 5–6
  indication of excitement 3
  influence on referee decisions 7
  influence on revenue 1
  observations, televised broadcast 3

 perspective of spectatorship 7
 in stadium setting (*see* stadium setting, sounds of the spectators)
 suggestions 2
 televised broadcast, observations 3 (*see also* televised broadcast, sounds of spectators)
 text analytical perspective 8–9
 from the televised broadcast of football **83**
 types of sounds of spectators **40**
 typology 39
 variety of 35
 and visuals, chosen relations **92**
soundscape analysis 8–9
soundscape of the stadiums 57
sound sourcing, televised broadcast setting 88–91
 aural close up shots 90
 'lavaliere' microphone 90
 middle grounded' sounds 90
 observational POA and active POA 89
 shotgun microphones 89
 superimposed, foregrounded sounds 90
 two-note chant 91
 types of microphones 89
 zone of audition 89
sound studies, perspective of 122
Southampton club anthem 52
space-time continuum of the scene on screen 93, 95
spectator
 description 6
 differentiation of 61–2
sports and music, perspective of intersections of 123
sports coverage 103
sports sounds, perspective of 123
sports spectatorship, examination of 5–6
sports TV's formal grammar 32
stadium
 intra-urban space 54
 unusual features and marked differences 55
Stadium Kanjuruhan of Malang in East Java 56
stadium setting, sounds of the spectators 5–6, 10, 18–29

awareness of the sounds 18–19
case materials (*see* case materials)
chant (*see* chants and songs)
distance effects 21
distribution and significance 22
fields of research 20
films and novels 27
home supporters 22–3
location of the sounds 21
lyrics (*see* lyrics)
multimicrophone recordings 21–2
non-scholarly contributions and resources 24–5
omni-listening 21
physical setting 14
point of audition (POA) 21
recordings, 20
semi-fictitious representations 27–8
sociobiological approach 19–20
sourcing and accessing the sounds 20–1
specified sounds, examination of 18
time of publication 18
stand-alone collective interjection 43
Stein, J. 25–6
stigma exploitation 69
St John, Ian 49
subtypes
  commentary 84
  football sounds 124
superimposed, foregrounded sounds 90
superimposed sonic signals 87
supporters, description 6
sweetening, practices of 94
syllabic singing 45
synch points 99
synchronized sound 98–9
synchronous clapping or synchro-clapping 41
syncrisis, perspective of 62–3, 96

Tagg, P. 47
Tamir, I. 23
televised broadcast, sounds of spectators 6, 29–33
  anecdotal contributions 30
  media, impact of 30
  sports programming 29–30
  textual significance 30–1
  verbal and visual dimensions 31–2
temporal perspectives, televised broadcast setting 95–9
  fusion of live and the non-live 96
  implications of the sounds 96
  loose synchronization 99
  production team's influence on sounds 95
  slow-motion replay 96–7
  synch points 99
  synchronized sound 98–9
  tripled moment 98
  visual and verbal accompaniment 96
  visuals and the commentary 98
Tottenham Hotspur stadium 14, 55–7
Tottenham Hotspur *versus* Chelsea at Tottenham Hotspur Stadium (22 December 2019) 14, 59
Tottenham Hotspur *versus* Leicester City at White Hart Lane (29 October 2016) 14, 37–8, 58–9, 62, 67, 82, 85–6, 91, 97, 104
Tottenham Hotspur *versus* Liverpool at Tottenham Hotspur Stadium (28 January 2021), 14, 109–14
Tottenham Hotspur *versus* Liverpool at Wembley Stadium (22 October 2017) 14, 38, 42–3, 52–3, 56, 65–7, 71, 73, 77, 88, 96, 108
transformation 9, 48
transtextuality 48–50
  pre-existence of a chant or song 48–9
  rework on pre-existing source 50
  transformation 48
tripled moment 98
Trotta, F. 20–2
two-note chant 91
types of sounds and creators 35, **36**

Unkelbach, C. 7

value reversal 69
verbal
  accompaniment 96
  announcements 38–9
vicarious evaluations 105
video cameras 93

visual accompaniment, televised broadcast setting 91–5
  chosen relations between sounds and visuals **92**
  co-production of both players 93
  editorial manipulation 94
  extra-diegetic sounds of spectators 94
  practices of sweetening 94
  prime camera 92
  space-time continuum of the scene on screen 93, 95
  video cameras 93
  zone of audition 93
visual appearance of the away supporters 59–60
visuals and the commentary 98
vocal and object sounds 36
vocally supporting spectators 61
vocal sounds
  massed callings 43
  non-verbal utterances 42–5
  response cries or 'exclamatory interjections 43
  'small-smile' whistle 42
  stand-alone collective interjection 43
  subcategory of talk 42
  variants of segmented collective interjections **44**, 44–5
vocal sounds and physical objects, interaction 36

Wembley Stadium 40, 41
Williams, R. 31
Wren-Lewis, J. 32
www. fanchants.com 25–6, 110
www.45football.com 50

Yankee Stadium 56
*You'll Never Walk Alone* 26, 49, 51
Young, M. 20

zone of audition 89, 93
zone of liveness 107

www.ingramcontent.com/pod-product-compliance
Lightning Source LLC
Chambersburg PA
CBHW061837300426
44115CB00013B/2424